Jennifer Hayashi Danns, 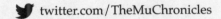 Scouse writer who spe............................. teaching English, raising her very genki children and finding time to explore active volcanoes and iridescent caves. She is an alumna of Faber Academy online and has published short stories and poems in various anthologies.

Jennifer loves Siamese cats, pistachio ice cream and David Bowie's goblin king in *Labyrinth*.

jenniferhayashidanns.com

BENEATH THE BURNING WAVE

The Mu Chronicles: Book One

JENNIFER HAYASHI DANNS

One More Chapter
a division of HarperCollins*Publishers*
1 London Bridge Street
London SE1 9GF
www.harpercollins.co.uk
HarperCollins*Publishers*
1st Floor, Watermarque Building, Ringsend Road
Dublin 4, Ireland

This paperback edition 2022
2
First published in Great Britain
by HarperCollins*Publishers* 2022
Copyright © Jennifer Hayashi Danns 2022
Jennifer Hayashi Danns asserts the moral right to
be identified as the author of this work

A catalogue record of this book is available from the British Library

ISBN: 978-0-00-849118-5

Printed and bound in the UK using 100% Renewable Electricity
by CPI Group (UK) Ltd

For Midori River and Airi Sky.

I love you.

May you always see yourselves in literature.

Author's Note

Beneath the Burning Wave explores the origin of gender and the story begins with neopronouns.

Pronouns can be used to identify a person instead of using their name. He/him/his are masculine pronouns. She/her/her are feminine pronouns. Many people also now use the singular "they".

On the ancient island of Mu, where gender is as fluid as the waves that crash on the shore, the Maymuan people use mu/mem/mir.

New (neo) pronouns can be used instead of traditionally gendered pronouns or the singular "they".

For example:

She waved at her friend.
They waved at their friend.
Mu waved at mir friend.

Author's Note

I invite you to sail with me to the ancient island of Mu where we will find forbidden twins Kaori [KAA–ow–Ri] and Kairi [KAA–i–Ri].

I hope you will embrace all you find there.

Content Notice

Dear Reader,

Beneath the Burning Wave explores various themes, including violence. I hope this book can be a place to safely explore difficult topics.

The fictional characters commit acts of violence against themselves, each other, children and animals. There is dialogue that includes fatphobic language and there are references to a character experiencing sexual assault.

The terrible effects of violence are also, importantly, explored in this book and, in witnessing the catastrophic consequences, I hope we can reflect then choose to reject violence in all its forms and choose love, light and hope.

If at any time you feel overwhelmed please take a step back, and if you want to discuss your feelings about violence I strongly urge you to use the resources listed below.

Love,
Jennifer

Childline (UK)

0800 1111
childline.org.uk
Support for children and young people in the UK, including a free helpline and one-to-one online chats with counsellors.

Samaritans (UK)

116 123 (freephone)
jo@samaritans.org
Chris, Freepost RSRB-KKBY-CYJK
PO Box 90 90
Stirling FK8 2SA
samaritans.org
Samaritans are open 24/7 for anyone who needs to talk. You can visit some Samaritans branches in person.

Prologue

Four Hundred Orbits Ago

"Namu May Mu. Thank you, merciful Mu, for one," the rearer said, wrapping the screeching maymu tight, its flailing arms bound to conform before its first breath was exhaled. The carrier lay exhausted but ecstatic. Sweat drenched mir bare body. The size of mir belly had given the island nightmares. "Surely not another with two?" they had whispered into the cool night. They had only just tried to forget the last sacrifice.

It is never easy to murder a little one, even for the greater good.

The carrier moaned as mir womb trembled again. The rearer sighed and turned away. Later, alone in mir hut, mu would sob, but not now. Now mu must fulfil mir island duty.

The rearer pulled the second maymu from the carrier, careful to avoid further tears.

"I'm so sorry," the rearer whispered to the soul in mir arms but the words did not match the dusk falling in mir eyes.

The rearer placed them side by side on the grass. The first maymu began to wail again, unable to escape the tight shroud. The second the rearer hadn't bothered to wrap. It was silent but its head swivelled, instinct confirming its fate. It was as though it was trying to absorb everything. The kiss of humidity on its skin, the trace of salt on its lip.

It swallowed one of the stars blinking above.

The island elder, an Experienced, was summoned. Mir island duty was to destroy the twins and ensure neither ever walked on the island of Mu. The prophet made sure to witness the slaughter.

Together they lay. Two shattered shells. Their carrier had been dragged deep into the forest where mir screams could not disturb the others.

The prophet gazed down on the two tiny corpses and shuddered. Not for their loss, but with fear of what could have been if they had been allowed to survive.

Maymuans are perfect. Balanced. May, the sun. Eternal fire. The instinct to burn and consume. Mu, the moon. Eternal water. The wisdom to calm and always flow forwards. But split into two? Fire would destroy without mercy. Water would drown without purpose.

The prophet took a stabilising breath and tried to calm mir racing heart. Mu had done all mu could. For most of mir life cycle the prophet had meticulously etched glyphs into the wall, documenting every scene that woke mem each rise drowning in mir own cold terror.

The prophecy had been etched for all to see.

There could never be twins alive on Mu.

Scroll One

Chapter One

KAORI

W hy now, in the final preparations for the hunt, do my hands shake? My stupid obi won't form the symbol of an ankh. Again, I wrap the long strip of black cloth around my waist, tying it in a knot by making a circle loop at the top and leaving the end to hang down. I can finally breathe. I won't survive tonight without creating the symbol of life for protection.

My silver dagger is secure on my hip. I swivel from side to side, gazing down at myself in admiration. I love how the blade shines against my dark ceremonial robe.

"Kaori, we must go."

Naho is standing in the opening. I hope mu didn't see my display of vanity. Naho looks so dignified in our wide-sleeved wrap robe. The delicate fabric hangs well on mir broad shoulders skimming mir flat stomach and narrow hips. Mu has tied mir long braids back with twine. Like the fine silver thread running through the cloth, Naho's hair is streaked with time. My robe refuses to stop gaping over my curves and smoothing out the places where the fabric clings to my belly doesn't help much either. Within two steps to match Naho's tall stride the humid night air has stuck my tunic to my thick thighs.

We make our full-moon walk to the beach, winding our way down the red dirt path separating the gamgam huts. The moon has cast a silver shadow over the woven benme roofs, turning the black night deep blue. Curious eyes peek out of openings. On some of the huts, carefully knotted ankhs hang.

Is tonight the night I don't return?

Normally I find their stares bolster my courage, but tonight I depend on Naho to bow and acknowledge their unease. Naho always waits for me so we can walk together. To be honest, I would prefer to make the short journey alone like the rest of the hunters, but tonight in the creepy blue light my fingers fumble until they rest in Naho's warm hand. We pass the final row of huts and trample across an exposed tangle of benme roots until we reach a grassy clearing. The air tastes salty and waves crash in my ears as we approach a soaring stone pyramid.

Reaching the temple of the Experienced is a horrible reminder I have to face the eldest Experienced Takanori tonight.

How much longer can I keep my secret from mem?

I squeeze Naho's hand tight despite the temple being the sign for Naho to run ahead and arrive alone. When I release Naho's hand mu doesn't leave, even though we can see the shadows of the hunters on the beach; the others have already formed a circle.

Naho guides me into the moonlight reflecting off the temple's unique feature: gold doors. No other structure on the island has doors. Only the Experienced are allowed privacy.

A golden glare rests on Naho's high cheekbones, making mir brown eyes glow. I don't like looking into Naho's eyes; their intensity reminds me of my twin, Kairi, and I always feel like Naho can see more than I want to reveal.

"Tonight will be difficult for you but it is very important you remain both strong and calm. Do you remember our eternal training?"

I nod in response, not trusting my voice to conceal my apprehension. How will I ever forget?

It was only four orbits ago, just after my thirteenth orbit began. I had my new name and a hut with an opening. It was horrible. I missed the other unnameds and the sharp corners and doors of the temple. My head ached from tight braids restraining my curls; my hut had too much fresh space and not enough noisy unnameds squabbling and perpetual burning hunmir wood.

At first the other newly released would visit. I couldn't get rid of Saki – mu would come every rise, chattering about how excited mu was to be out of the temple. Saki was so pretty even then but mu was also always such a shell-kisser and now mu had even more opportunities to be perfect. But eventually even Saki didn't visit as much because there was so much to learn about our new home, Mu.

I hated being alone. Kairi and Kentaro had disappeared off together but at least I could depend on Aito who was also still in shock. We would squeeze ourselves into an imaginary corner of my round hut and pretend we were in the unnameds' chamber, many bodies squashed together instead of only us two.

Aito came one rise to say mu had been allocated jungle hunter duties in the same hunter pack as my twin. If two as different as overcautious Aito and reckless Kairi could be allocated the same duty, then how did the Experienced decide? I wanted to be a rural. Kentaro was a rural and we already had the other island duty so I assumed we would be together.

I was allocated water hunter. I'd thought only Kairi and Kentaro knew about my connection with water. I suppose there are no secrets when there are no doors. Kairi and I are the only twins on Mu. Everyone says it is a gift from and for the island. I don't know what they expect from me or Kairi. How are we a gift?

I try and live the same life as any other Maymuan, unlike Kairi who enjoys sticking out like the fin of a dolphin. No one can remember a time when there have ever been twins. Not even the Experienced, and they have lived the longest.

With all eyes on us maybe it was stupid to believe we

could hide our powers. I can control water. From the sky or ground. Wherever there is water I can push, pull, and draw it. I have never heard any Maymuan say they can do the same. The only other one who can is Kairi, who can manipulate fire. From a spark mu can burst a flame. From a flame mu could torch a temple.

"Hello," said a beautiful Maymuan standing at my opening. Mu was holding a dark folded robe. "I am Ayana."

I glanced at Aito huddled against the wall.

Ayana smiled. "Is this your pairing, Kentaro?"

No, Kentaro was probably in a tree somewhere sucking the face off my twin. I shook my head.

Ayana frowned. "You need to go."

Aito sprinted out without hesitation – the first of many times mu would abandon me without a backward glance.

Ayana handed me the robe.

"Thank you," I said, stroking the streaks of silver thread. Ayana was staring at me. I had learned to accept those kinds of stares. Kairi and I are as rare as a blue buha but Ayana had a different energy to the other gawping Maymuans. "I'm scared," I admitted, surprising myself.

Ayana knelt down. "It's okay. You will be fine." I didn't believe mu and it must have shown on my face because mu continued, "I was a water hunter."

"Was?" I asked. Allocated duties are eternal.

"Yes, until I"—Ayana hesitated—"fulfilled my other duty."

"Oh. Sorry," I said, not wanting to meet mir gaze

anymore. I wrapped my arms around my legs and rolled up like a coco.

Ayana squeezed my knee and looked cautiously over mir shoulder to check the opening was empty. "I heard you are gifted with water." Mu shook mir head to stop me interrupting and said, in a rush, "Focus on the eternal in the ocean, not the sensation on your shell."

Ayana quickly scrawled an ankh with mir finger in the dust of the floor and scuttled out.

What the ratty hell did mu mean?

The memory rushes over me.

I arrive at the shore. Waiting there is Experienced Takako and Experienced Takafumi. Takako's long grey dreadlocks shimmer gorgeously in the rise's sun but there is nothing lovely in mir cold stare. Takafumi watches me closely as I approach.

All of the Experienced are intimidating but there is something about Takafumi which makes my skin flinch. Mu reminds me of a nabgar. The cold black eyes. How the nabgar prey on others' suffering. They wait for a smaller creature to fail and then swoop in, scoop them up in their hooked beaks and take them away to devour. Takafumi always seems to be waiting for something and I am afraid for when mu finds it.

Standing in a line with their backs to me are the other

initiated water hunters. My robe matches theirs but none of their legs are trembling.

"On your back," Takako barks. "Face the sun."

I lie on the hot sand and the hunters pounce. They begin burying me until only my nose and mouth are above ground. I can still hear the waves crashing, the slap of fleeing hunter feet and then the unmistakeable sound of water splashing into a conch shell.

I will have to drink salt water. It will be disgusting but I can do it.

"Kaori, do you vow to prey on water for all eternity?"

"Yes," I reply.

"Do you vow to take only what we need?"

"Yes."

"Without disturbance."

"Yes."

"Or fear."

"Yes," I say.

"Prove it," Takafumi hisses.

Feet stomp the sand around my prostrate body.

"Do not disturb the sand."

What?

A strip of fabric – it feels rough, like gobu – is pulled tight over my nose and mouth. My scream is unheard. Instinct makes me thrash my legs in the sand. I try to calm but the water is poured. Salt burns my nose and shreds my throat. Water becomes fire. I choke on the burning wave.

I wake on my hands and knees retching into my burst grave. There is a gaping hole where I once lay.

I squint up at Takako and Takafumi, who are watching me. Takafumi remains impassive and calmly pours the last of the water from the conch into the sand. "Again, next rise."

It would take me twelve rises to pass the initiation.

I can't bathe in my memories any longer. Naho's face is scrunched up with the urgency of mir instruction.

"Good. You will need your eternal training tonight. You must control your fear. What we hunt is not your only threat. Do you understand?"

I nod.

Naho grips my shoulders tight. "I need to hear you say it."

I swallow and clear my throat. "Yes, I understand."

Naho strokes the top of my head, moving mir hand gently over my braids. "Don't wait too long to follow me." Unable to linger any longer, Naho leaves.

I watch Naho descend the hill to the beach. Naho always seems to know what is happening on Mu. For our hunt we each have a torchbearer. Mine is Kentaro. I only found out from Kentaro this rise that Naho's torchbearer, Kanta, is sick. I can't believe who Takanori has chosen to replace poor Kanta! But how does Naho know? That is surely who mu is referring to with all mir warnings?

I shudder as a squeaky black bat swoops over my head, flapping warm air on the exposed scalp between my croprows. The heavy night presses down on my chest, urging me to turn back and go home. I can't. I have to fulfil my island duty.

I run down the low grassy hill and join the hunter circle on the beach between Naho and Saki, completing the circle of twelve. I bow my head when a steady fist pounds the stretched snakeskin membrane of the nunum. The heavy beat reverberates across the shore, penetrating my bones.

The sand throbs as the painted Experienced approach, flanked by our twelve hooded torchbearers. Together their feet stomp across the beach in rhythm with the nunum.

Without lifting my gaze I can see the craggy faces of the Experienced encrusted with flaky white chalk chipped from the cliff towering over our ceremony. A scarlet streak of clay dyed with morgon petals masks their eyes. Grey dreadlocks sit knotted on the tops of their heads like girnum's nests spun with silver branches. Immaculate ankle-length red robes shroud curved spines.

I can feel Takanori's hairy, sinewy hands beating the nunum with all of mir might. At Takanori's side is my twin, Kairi, raising mir knees high and forcing mir feet through the sand's delicate skin. Kairi has thrust mir flaming torch above mir head, piercing the night sky, antagonising the moon. Flickering flames dance in the deep wooden cracks of Takanori's powdered face and skim across the polished sheen of Kairi's tight, dark skin.

Takanori and the Experienced have chosen Kairi to participate for the first time in our hunting ceremony because Naho's torchbearer is sick.

There was no way Kairi could be humble. When mu was chosen mu ran to my hut to brag. If the Experienced knew what Kairi could do with fire they would never have allowed mem to join. Yet again, Takanori proves that being the longest living person on the island is no guarantee of wisdom. It is a shame it is forbidden to kill tortoises.

None of this matters now because I have a greater problem at hand. The Experienced and the torchbearers have surrounded us. I crouch down and rock onto my knees, applying as little pressure as I can to the sand, and I lower my forehead to the ground. I listen. Gradually the breathing of the others and the crunch of sand fades away until all I can hear is the sound of the waves lapping the shore.

The water relentlessly ebbs and flows but I can still only hear the waves individually. Each wave breaking then splashing, reduced to foam, one after another.

If I don't hurry up, Saki is going to stand up before I do. Tonight I have to be the first person to enter the cave. I glance to my right at Naho and mu is staring at me. Naho can already hear. Naho is giving me the chance to stand first. I can't pretend to hear what I don't, it is too dangerous.

Why is it taking me so long tonight?

I can't focus.

Saki stands up. Tears cloud my vision and again I look to Naho and mu shakes mir head. Naho is right; the only thing worse than not being first is if I cry in front of them. Others stand and make their way towards the cave. I know Kairi is laughing at me. And Takanori is laughing too.

No. This is the one place where I am free. They cannot have it. I take a deep breath of the moist air, and salt sprays through my nose to my mouth. The taste plunges me head first into the ocean where the waves are no longer crashing alone; they are one. I crash and roll but I am not afraid. I stand up.

I run towards the cliff face. Jagged rocks around the small cave entrance bite my bare feet and my robe hitches up as I crawl on my hands and knees through the tight tunnel leading into the cave. Inside is pitch black. The moon has yet to appear over the crack in the ceiling. In the darkness, I feel a succession of gentle hands squeezing mine.

Naho is the final hunter to enter, moments before molten pearl seeps across the cave walls. We lift our faces to greet the moon and bathe in its light as we chant "Namu May Mu".

Our chanting vibrates the stalactites and loosens the rocks at our feet. The torchbearers have left their torches outside with the Experienced and have crawled into the cave with our nets. I reach out to accept mine from Kentaro but mu walks past me and gives the net to Naho.

Kairi is in front of me with mir hood pulled low, framing mir smirk. Is there nothing Kentaro won't do for Kairi?

I had thought Kentaro liked being my torchbearer. I grab the net in Kairi's hand but mu keeps tight hold of it, forcing me to hiss at mem. Kairi smiles as my anger echoes. Everyone is looking at us, clearly thinking the twins are drawing attention to themselves as usual. The sooner this part of my ceremony is over the better.

Mymig you, Kentaro.

I perform a deep bow to Kairi in gratitude for the net but mu only stares back at me. I kick mem and mu nods mir head then takes mir place guarding the entrance with the other torchbearers. I take my place at the edge of the pool. The light recedes, casting shadows. Outside, the Experienced pound the nunum.

One.

I take a step forwards. The last of the moon gives the water an oily sheen, like squid ink.

Two.

Darkness returns.

Three.

I step into the water.

The hairs on my legs sway like seaweed. I can feel what is not water. Disturbances. I find the space between the movement. Past the undulating body. There it is. There is the still. I plunge my hand into the water and clench my fist beneath the snake's head.

With a crash the snake comes thrashing out of the water. Air whistles through the snake's fangs and rattles around its throat as it opens its mouth wide in attack. The tail cracks like a whip. The tip lashes the hilt of my blade tucked in my obi. The hectic rhythm whacked out by the captured snake matches my frantic heart.

I must not cower even though I fear the piercing of my skin. Every snake hunter is terrorised by the threat of fang breaking skin: the wave of nausea as poison penetrates my capillary; the betrayal of my veins distributing venom; my arteries swelling until my insides are outside.

Ignoring the sweat dripping from my forehead I uncurl the body coiled around my arm and toss the snake into my net. I give thanks by tapping the ankh on my belt. Again and again I snatch writhing snakes from the water. Each one I know will provide food for the island. Each one will impress Kairi. Each one could kill me. But this is the role I was given.

This is my island duty, and when my net is full I will enjoy the euphoria of fulfilling my role.

I hand my catch to Kairi and we crawl out of the cave to complete my ceremony. The Experienced are standing facing the cliff, their palms, arms, and legs spread wide on the chalky surface with their lips whispering "Namu May Mu" into the porous wall.

Kairi retrieves mir torch from a bracket between Experienced Takafumi and Experienced Takako and almost trips over in mir haste to bring me the snakes. I stifle a laugh when I see mir face in the flame. Kairi's eyes are wide and mir mouth is hanging open. Mir chest is heaving with anticipation.

I pull one snake by its tail from the bag. It coils and hisses in mid-air. Kairi makes no move to help me. Mu is staring dumbfounded, hypnotised by the snake's suspended dance. I am not going to bother asking mem to do what Kentaro usually would. Kairi has been useless as my torchbearer; maybe mu will finally understand humility. I will finish the ceremony by myself.

I lower the snake. It slithers on the sand and tries to escape but I hold its tail tight. While its eyes search for freedom, I lodge my bare foot below the back of its head and kneel down. Replacing my foot with my hand, I flip it over.

The snake makes a final strike for survival. The jaw has swung down. A forked black tongue flickers in a white mouth. Two sharp fangs quiver with fury. I draw my dagger from my obi. Chanting "Namu May Mu", I thrust my blade into the cavity and pierce the venom gland. I ignore the tail thrashing in the sand and place the tip of my knife on my tongue and feel the numbness spread to the back of my throat.

Kairi is leaning so far over me mu has almost set fire to my hair. I turn the blade over and place the tip on Kairi's tongue, resisting the urge to shove it straight down mir throat after mir antics in the cave.

"More," Kairi slurs with a numb tongue.

I sever the snake's head then plunge the blade deep into the sand so Kairi can't try and lick more venom. I dip my fore and index fingers into the snake's blood and smear two lines diagonally from the left of my forehead across my eye, nose, and lips down to the right side of my chin and I smear blood from right to left on Kairi.

A strong hand grips my shoulder.

"Well done, Kaori, You may feel pride for your achievements tonight."

There is no mistaking mir voice, deep and unwavering, from orbits of loyal Maymuan obedience. The last of my pleasure evaporates as I look into Takanori's cold black eyes.

"Thank you," I mumble.

Takanori turns to Kairi. "Perhaps your half is a greater hunter than you."

"No. It's easy to catch snakes." Kairi crackles with indignation. "Mu couldn't catch a boar. Could you, Kaori?"

Yes, I probably could but Kairi has that look about mem which makes me want to drop my chin and protect my throat.

"I don't know... I have never tried."

"Because you couldn't. I could catch as many snakes as you, even more."

"Perhaps one day we will give you the opportunity," Takanori says with a tight-lipped smile. "Excuse me, I must congratulate the other hunters."

Good, mu is leaving. In my periphery I am surprised to see Kairi bowing to Takanori. I bow too, hoping Takanori didn't notice my delay. When I straighten up Takanori pinches my chin between mir thumb and clenched fingers.

"I hope you will fulfil your other role with as much enthusiasm as you performed tonight's task."

Don't break mir gaze or mu will know.

"Kaori!" Kentaro runs over and jumps on me. "You did so well tonight. I can't believe how many you caught!"

Takanori clears mir throat.

Kentaro flinches and says, "Sorry, Experienced... but wasn't Kaori brave tonight?"

"Indeed, and you served Naho well. Perhaps we should make this arrangement permanent?" Takanori smiles as Kentaro's face falls. "How charming. Your loyalty to your maymu carrier is admirable."

Kentaro, Kairi, and I stand in silence as Takanori leads the rest of the Experienced back to the temple. I hate Takanori so much. Even though I am annoyed at Kentaro for earlier, I can't bear to see mir sweet owl face crumble under the pressure Takanori inflicts on us all.

Saki passes and tries to catch my eye to give me a smile. Even though my heart skips a beat at the sight of mem, I pretend not to see. I know Kairi is going to punish me for Kentaro's praise and Takanori's provocation.

"Oh Kaori, you are so great," sings Kairi, "I love you, I want to kiss your ugly face every day and make disgusting maymus."

Kentaro blushes. "Kaori did fulfil mir role."

Kairi dives on Kentaro, tripping mem up and pushing mir face into the sand.

"Leave mem alone," I shout, "stop being so jealous."

"Jealous? Of you?" Kairi scrubs mir face with the palm of mir hand, smearing the snake blood.

"Go and get the bag, Kairi. We're the only ones left. We need to take the snakes to the smokehouse." I turn to help Kentaro up from the floor. Kentaro pushes me away as I try and brush the sand stuck to mir coarse brown robe.

I can't wait for this night to be over.

"Where's Kairi?" Kentaro says, looking from the bag of snakes nestled in the sand to me.

A fresh set of footprints reveal Kairi's return to the cave.

"You should have stopped mem!" I say.

"Me? Why didn't you?" Kentaro snaps.

"I was trying to help you off the floor! Let mem go. I hope mu drowns in there. Kairi has been nothing but useless the entire hunt anyway."

"We can't leave mem. You know what Takanori said will have hurt Kairi," Kentaro whines like a maymu.

What? That I am a better hunter?

I am.

I am so sick of Kairi's jealousy and mood swings. How small do I have to pretend to be to make Kairi value mir own life?

Chapter Two

KAIRI

Stupid cockroach Kaori. As if mu is the only one who can catch a snake. *Bahm.* I try not to gag as the smell of singed hair fills the narrow tunnel. It's ratty hard to crawl through this tunnel with my torch. My knees are stinging and I have burnt all the hairs on my arm. I should have made Kentaro come with me and carry the torch.

I'm in. Bits of cave are stuck in the graze on my knee.

Dirty Kaori making me come in here. They all think the sun rises out of mem. *Kaori is so pretty, Kaori is so brave.* Kaori is a jellyfish blob, oozing on the shore with a rock smashed in its head. I am glad we don't look like each other anymore. As mu got wider I am taller, leaner, sharper.

Where do I go now?

Where's that pond?

Urgh.

Bahm! I curse again. Water is plopping from the ceiling onto my face, dripping the snake blood into my mouth.

Maybe I should go back. I haven't brought a net to put the snake in anyway.

A droplet falls on the tip of the torch.

The hiss of extinguished flame taunts, *your half is greater than you.*

The words echo, becoming louder as they swirl around the cavern. I punch my ears, trying to stop the words from piercing my eardrum. I pull down hard on my earlobes.

Please stop. Please.

I lurch forwards and close my eyes as the earth trembles.

Please stop. I didn't mean it.

Keep your eyes closed. Focus on the torch. You worthless piece of bahm.

I focus on the ground and not on Takanori's voice in my head. My chest is heaving but at last the ground is still. I open one eye and steal a look at my damage. The torch flame is burning bright. A hysterical giggle echoes around the cavern.

Thank you.

Apart from some fallen bits of rock nothing seems changed. At least I haven't buried myself alive or impaled myself falling on a stalagmite.

Move forwards, you freak, and stop talking to yourself.

I can make out the edge of the pond but I can barely see anything else. Why am I carrying this stupid torch like a dirty carrier? I only need a flicker of its flame to make my own fire. Heat flows in my veins and spreads across my shoulders and neck. I shove the smouldering torch into a damp corner and with a flick of my finger burst the flame up the side of the glistening wet wall, setting the hollow alight.

Thick black smoke smothers the stalactites. Firelight scorches the surface of the oily water, blazing a violent orange across the cave. Shadows perform a grotesque dance, grimacing and contorting in the unnatural heat.

Can't I just lean over, stick my hand in, and get a snake? Peering over the edge I don't think it is deep enough here. Maybe a bit further into the cave.

Looking around the lit cave I can see the water here is much more than a pond. It goes so far back I can't see a rear wall.

Earlier, when the moonlight was shining through the crack in the ceiling, I thought I was in a small cavern but ratty hell, this space is even bigger than the inside of the Experienced temple. The water looks thicker and darker the further back it goes.

Discovering the space is bigger than I thought makes me feel more confined. I wish I was outside with Kentaro rather than stuck in here choking on seared mould. I have to catch a snake. Quick.

There is a small ledge protruding from the cave wall. It hangs over a dark part of the water much deeper than where cockroach waded in. I bet there are bigger snakes there than mu has ever caught.

My hand slips on the wall and my bare foot can't grip the slick rockface. The ridiculous robe I was made to wear for the snake hunt ceremony is not helping either. I hate this rough wraparound thing. It's too long. I hate anything that constricts my movement. I direct a blast of fire at the wall. Steam hits my face, firing a musky blast of ripe blood up my nose. It tastes like one of my rusty arrow heads is lodged in my throat.

I hate myself for retching.

Pathetic.

Resting my head against the wall the warm stone is a comfort. It is also now dry.

Get a grip of yourself and get a snake, you ratty coward.

I clutch the rockface and drag my body across to the ledge, shuffling slowly on my stomach towards the edge. My hand reaches down but can't quite touch the surface. I have to pull myself further along until my torso is hanging over.

My fingertips break the water. I can see something.

Lowering my face for a closer look I find two dark eyes staring back at me. I gasp and the creature opens its mouth wide.

I fall into its open trap.

I crash into the water, spinning and rolling until the thick water clutches my ankles and drags me down into its murky depths. Above me, the tip of the ledge is illuminated by the blazing orange ceiling. I try to kick my legs and rise to the surface but my robe is too heavy. Instead I am sucked deeper. The orange is disrupted by savage slashes of black. Long slender bodies paint black stripes in the water.

Oh bahm. The snakes are here.

I scream.

Oil floods my lungs and I sink further.

A terrible roar resounds around me. Rushing water is battering the walls, shaking the cave. I am lying in a dry basin surrounded by snakes who seem as disoriented as I am. They are coiled up tight, mirroring my own body position.

I don't know what has happened. I can only see what is near me. It is as black as a crow in the rest of the cave again. My body feels like it has been trampled by a sounder of boars. There is a rancid puddle of vomit frothing next to me.

"Get up."

Standing above me is a magnificent golden soul set against a backdrop of churning water held back by an invisible wall. "A fat golden soul," I murmur.

"I'm not fat! Get up, bonehead."

Kaori drags me to my feet then slaps me hard across my face.

"What was that for?"

Kaori looks at me with narrowed eyes.

"I almost died!" I say.

"Yes, I know. I just saved you!"

"No, you didn't. I was about to swim back up before you came."

"Is that right? I'll put this water back where I found it then, shall I?" Kaori says.

"No, no! Don't do that."

Kaori has a hideous smug smile on mir face.

"Is that my torch?"

"Yes, here you are. We have to get out of here. Go on, Kairi, you lead the way. We have to go. Now." Mu follows me across the basin adding, "Kentaro must be so worried about us."

I stop and Kaori slams into my back.

"What are you doing? I can't hold the water like this forever. If we don't hurry up the cave will collapse."

"I have to get a snake."

"Kairi, what is wrong with you? Leave them."

"I *have* to get a snake."

"Why?"

"Go and get me one."

Kaori laughs at me. "Why would I do that?"

"If you don't, I will tell Takanori you and Kentaro haven't been trying to create a new maymu."

The sheet of water starts to leak at the top, creating a waterfall.

"What are you talking about?"

Too late, Kaori.

I know that when cockroach and Kentaro go to the creation hut they don't do anything. Kaori hid mir bleeding for over three orbits but it was pointless. The Experienced know everything. They indulged mem for a while probably because mu is so popular with the rest of the deluded on this island. But even perfect Kaori is not above island law. A seventeen orbit carrier without a maymu is a freak.

We are both already freaks because we are the first twins born in this awful place. Our carrier should have killed

Kaori when mu slid out second. I am not a half. A before. Kaori is an after.

The water is rising above my toes. The snakes begin to stir.

"Get me a snake, Kaori."

"You would never tell Takanori. You don't want me to create with Kentaro anymore than I do."

True. The thought of Kentaro and Kaori together makes me feel light-headed. If mu made a maymu with Kentaro I would kick it out of mem.

Kentaro belongs to me. Mu has been mine ever since the thirteenth orbit ceremony where each Maymuan is paired with their other for the sole purpose of creating maymus to populate the island. The way it should work is that, after the ceremony, when the one who can carry first bleeds the pair enter a lottery and if drawn they have to go to the creation hut.

As the first ever twins, the Experienced decided Kaori and I are two halves of a whole Maymuan. I am may. Kaori is mu. Kaori is the light. I am the dark. So say the Experienced. Everyone thinks Kaori is the finer half but mu isn't. I am stronger and faster. I am not held back by feelings and pitiful tears like mu is. I am better than Kaori and I am superior to all of the balanced Maymuans.

At our ceremony we were *both* paired with Kentaro. It was a decision which shocked the island because there has never been a three-soul pairing. I can't bleed, and it is too disgusting to even think I would create with cockroach, so Kaori and Kentaro have the island duty of creating maymus. I don't have to go to the creation hut at all with a dirty carrier.

I don't like carriers. I think they are pathetic for letting a maymu take their purpose. After a carrier has a maymu they no longer have other island duties like water or jungle hunting. They don't seem to live as long as Maymuans and even if they did they are never allowed to become Experienced.

"I don't care what you and Kentaro do," I say.

Kaori is wavering. Mu has bitten down so hard on mir bottom lip it is bleeding.

"Get me a snake." Water is splashing against my ankles, soaking the hem of my robe. "And push this water back up."

The waterfall stops.

"No one will believe you caught it on your own."

"Yes, they will."

"Kentaro won't."

I lurch at Kaori and snatch mir dagger from mir obi. I point the tip at mir right eye.

"Do it. And we don't have time for all the usual chanting bahm," I say, tucking the blade behind the simple knot in my twine obi.

Kaori slowly crouches down over the shallow water. Mu glances at me then springs up, clutching a snake, and hurls it at my face. Predictable Kaori. I direct a blast of fire from my torch, roasting the snake alive. The ash sprinkles over my robe.

"No, Kairi!" mu shouts.

"This is your fault," I say.

"We killed with no reason," Kaori says, clearly upset.

I don't have the patience for this.

"*You* killed it." My words have the desired effect.

"No. Namu May Mu," Kaori chants.

Come on, you stupid cockroach, now hurry up and get me a ratty snake!

"May the island be merciful," I say, feigning solemnity.

Kaori wails, "Namu May Mu," but returns to the water and draws out a long black snake. Mu offers it to me.

"You hold it until we get to the tunnel. We have to leave. Now."

I am worried about the water. Kaori's turmoil has pushed the water back even further in the cave, increasing the pressure on the walls. It looks like the thumping water has already carved a big hole on the left wall.

Wait... What is that?

"Kaori, *look*."

"Haven't you had enough for one rise? Please."

Mu wobbles across the basin towards the exit tunnel.

"Wait!"

I chase mem to the exit. As soon as my foot leaves the basin Kaori releases the water. With a crash it returns to its natural place.

"You won't believe what I just saw!"

"I don't care."

"It was—"

"I don't care!"

"It was like this," I say, clutching at the knot in mir obi.

That gets mir attention.

"What?"

"It was an ankh. Above an opening."

"Don't be ridiculous."

"It was. Do it again. Push the water back."

Mu looks at me with disgust, snatches the torch from my hand, and thrusts the snarling snake in my face. "Don't destroy this snake. Take it to the smokehouse so it can be slaughtered as food for the island."

The snake and Kaori are identical. Their black eyes are ablaze with frenzied hatred. Their mouths are dripping malice. With a shudder I realise they both want to annihilate me. I have to be careful.

"Okay. I will take the snake to the smokehouse. Thanks, Kaori."

Kaori stares without blinking but mu does carefully pass me the snake to hold. I smile at mem. Mir eyes become wrath again.

"Thanks? You're disgusting. I hate you. Don't speak to me again."

"Don't be like that."

I reach out for mem but mu has gone.

Chapter Three

KAORI

"Mu held your hunting dagger to your eye?"

"Yes."

"Oh Kaori... I'm sorry."

"What are you apologising for? It wasn't you, was it? It was mem."

Kentaro and I are in the creation hut. I am lying on the floor. The leaves from the benme trees caress the roof, establishing a gentle rhythm. My back arches as the sunlight penetrates the fissure in the wood. With a sigh I open my eyes and see Kentaro's face is all scrunched up like mu is chewing a mouthful of ants.

We are not creating. We are talking about Kairi. As usual.

"Kentaro, please say what you want to say."

"You know I can't."

I often envy the Maymuans. I envy their balance and calm. I long for their feeling of wholeness. Now is not one of those times. Observing Kentaro's battle to avoid saying anything controversial about Kairi is pitiful. It is like watching someone retch through sewn-up lips. I don't think keeping your opinions to yourself is a Maymuan thing. I think it is a fear-of-the-Experienced thing. I don't believe saying nothing is always for the greater good.

"This is about as private as it gets." I say gesturing around the creation hut.

The hut doesn't have a door but it does have several long strips of megg woven with white seashells hanging from the top of the opening. A morgon-scented breeze chimes the shells. I don't know why Kentaro is worrying about being overheard. The creation huts are in the mountains, each hut on its own cloud-piercing peak. The peaks are high enough to ensure you should need help to reach the top.

I suppose the shared experience of scaling the mountain at dawn plus the gorgeous location is supposed to aid creating. It doesn't make a difference to me. No seashell serenade or magnificent sunrise will make me want to be a carrier.

"Just say it, Kentaro."

Kentaro steals a furtive glance at the opening then whispers, "Kairi is getting worse, isn't mu?"

I try not to laugh because Kentaro is speaking in earnest. But after all that build-up, is that all mu has to say? Do boars roll in dirt? I mean, come on. You would think mu had confessed to drinking tortoise blood or wanting to sacrifice one of the Experienced.

I follow the dragonflies that hover above us, enjoying the warm air in the hut. Translucent wings flutter, keeping their thin gold bodies afloat. I consider their simple existence and I imagine plucking their wings mid-flight and watching those shards of gold crash, scatter, and roll across the benme floor. As if privy to my wickedness, the dragonflies jerk and twitch, navigating unseen obstacles, eluding my cruel thoughts.

"Yes. Kairi is getting worse."

"What is wrong with mem?" Kentaro whispers, making me feel obliged to lean in and whisper back.

"I think it is us in here that really gets to mem."

"But mu knows this is a duty not a choice."

"I don't think Kairi *does* understand that."

Kentaro brushes away a fly. "But I swapped places with mem during the snake ceremony. Kairi knows I prefer mem to you."

How very charming.

I am not attracted to Kentaro at all but it still hurts.

"Now you mention it, what the hell were you thinking?" I am pleased to see shame smear across Kentaro's round face. "You do know Kairi poisoned Kanta, don't you?"

"What? No mu didn't."

"Mu did! Kanta has been plopping out mignu berries ever since. I don't know if mu will be well enough by the next full moon to be Naho's torchbearer."

"That's awful."

"I know."

Kentaro scratches mir toes against the woven floor and mumbles, "Mu said bad things about Naho too."

"What did mu say?"

Kentaro's eyes widen as my voice cracks.

"Nothing. It doesn't matter."

"What? Tell me."

"I'm sorry. I shouldn't have brought it up. I know how close you and Naho are."

Do you?

Does everyone know?

I execute my haughtiest Kairi impersonation.

"Tell. Me. Now."

"Kairi was wondering why Naho still hunts when mu is old enough to be… erm… an Experienced."

Kentaro says the last part fast, as if that will slow my reaction.

"No mu isn't! Mu can't be older than forty orbits. The Experienced have to be at least sixty orbits to enter the temple. Think about it. Takanori must be over seventy orbits! Mu was already in the temple when we lived there!"

"I know, Kaori. I told mem."

"Did you?

"Well, I tried to."

"Oh ratty hell! Why do you let mem get away with so much? This is why mu treats you like jungle sludge, you know."

"And what do you do? Slope off to the other side of the island on your own to confide in fish?"

I feel like Kentaro has slapped me in the face with a ratty

38

fish. I can't believe mu can be so unkind. I suppose it is impossible to be so close to Kairi without some of mir callousness rubbing off. It is so sad.

The shrill rattling song of cicadas allays the weary silence between us.

"What are we going to do, Kaori?"

The sound of a twig snapping outside at the back of the hut makes us spring apart.

'What was that?" Kentaro says.

"I don't know but can we please stop whispering? No one can hear us anyway."

"Maybe we should stop speaking."

"And sit here in silence?"

"Well... we could do what we are supposed to do up here."

I wish I could take Kentaro's willingness to create with me as a compliment, but mu has made it clear that for mem, creating with me is akin to milking a goat. A functional rather than pleasurable experience.

I don't know how Kentaro can be so detached. I love to touch and be touched. Perhaps too much, because Naho noticed. Mu came to my hut with a nimi root for me to chew afterwards which stops an accidental creation. Naho told me not to tell anyone, but whenever I go and collect more there is always someone else there with their hands covered in soil and a little smile on their face.

It would make life easier if I was like Kairi and I fell for someone who it was impossible to create with. I did have something with Saki but... I don't know. I think I prefer my opposite rather than my same. I have been chewing a lot of root with Aito recently.

I know I could also use the root with Kentaro but why should I?

"You know I have no intention of ever creating with you."

"Listen, Kaori, it's not about you. It is for the island."

It never fails to amaze me how Kentaro finds mir tongue when it comes to our situation. It's not about me? No, it is only my body transformed for almost an orbit. A new maymu growing inside me. Becoming me. Then I would have to give it to the island to be raised by all. But mu would be mine. I don't know how any carrier can give away a maymu but especially ours!

How could our carrier give Kairi and me up? Mu must have known how difficult it would be for us to live on this island, which values conformity, as abnormal twins. Two halves which don't fit together. I wish there were other twins. How can Kairi and I have just appeared? It would be like a barmuna with two beaks or a buha with two tails. They can't develop from nothing, can they?

Most of all I wish I knew who our carrier was.

Do I?

I'm not sure. Maybe. I don't know.

What would I say to mem? At least it is not only Kairi and me who don't know for certain who our carrier is. No one knows. All new maymus born within the same orbit are taken by the Experienced and handed to the rearers over on the other side of the island.

After five orbits they are returned to the Experienced to live in the temple until the end of their twelfth orbit when they are given names and allocated island duties. Kairi and I were assigned hunting duty. I hunt snake; mu hunts boar.

But Kairi doesn't have the extra duty of trying to be a carrier.

I know it is wrong and selfish to think this way but I feel so unlucky. Four orbits ago there was an infestation of locusts in the crop fields. It was terrible. Many Maymuans died of starvation. Since then Takanori has been obsessed with replacing the lost population.

If it was a normal time, Kentaro and I would have faced the half-orbit creation lottery which decides who must create. Instead, now *all* pairings must try to create.

Knowing my misfortune, my carrier probably died during the infestation.

Kairi solidified my fear of becoming a carrier when mu took me with mem during one of mir many prowls around the island.

Mu came for me at night. Mu wouldn't say where we were going, mu only whispered I had to be quiet and stay close to mem. I hoped we were going to get some honeycomb. We hadn't scaled the trees together for so long my heart hummed a little as I tried to emulate mir light-footed stealth.

We crept past the sleeping huts and entered the forest in

the opposite direction to my familiar path to the beach. I slowed to appreciate a half moon between the splayed leaves.

"What are you doing? I told you to stay close," Kairi hissed.

"Look at the moon. It's beautiful."

"Kaori, come on. Who cares about the ratty moon? Without the sun it would be nothing. Just a crusty piece of rock floating about with no purpose."

Kairi tapped the base of the benme tree I was leaning on then climbed like a little monkey up the curved trunk. Mu returned with a bright-green coco. Mu smashed it against a rock and handed me the smaller half. The warm, sweet milk dripped down my chin and I scraped my teeth against the meaty white pulp.

"I haven't got time to watch you stuff your face. Why can't you just drink the milk?"

I blushed. I don't care about my size but when Kairi mentions it, with mir high cheekbones and sharp hip bones, I do feel a sliver of shame.

"I have only drunk the milk. I was only licking the last bit," I lied, throwing the rest of the coco into the trees. "I'm ready. Let's go."

Soon, heavy habim leaves swung overhead, obscuring the stars, and thick, gnarly vines tripped my feet. The forest had become the jungle where Kairi hunts wild boar. And still we tramped on, deeper and deeper into the labyrinthine undergrowth until a wretched scream hacked through the wilderness.

Kairi spun, bearing mir teeth at me in a terrible grin. Mu beckoned me further and in an unnatural clearing littered with the stumps of decapitated trees, I saw mem.

It was a carrier screaming, sweating, and grunting like the wild boars Kairi hunts. Kairi laughed at mem the same way mu does before impaling a boar. Mu bled like the slaughtered – raw redness dripping down mir exposed legs. Anointing the maymu. Staining the hands of the Experienced.

I shudder. I can't bear the memory.

The Experienced. Takanori. The zealot. I hate mem.

"Why should Takanori be able to tell me when and who I create with?" I say.

"This is your halfness talking, Kaori. You are making it too personal."

This must be what Kairi feels all the time. Rage. I could stab Kentaro in the eye now. I despise when mu or anyone else brings up my so-called halfness. I can talk about being a half but no one else can. What they mean is I am too emotional. I *am* emotional. I think this is something to be emotional about. I don't understand Kentaro.

"I thought you loved Kairi."

Kentaro's head flicks back like mu is avoiding my blade at mir face.

"What does that have to do with anything?"

"What does that have to do with anything! What is

wrong with you? How could you create with me knowing how demented it would make Kairi?"

"It is not about you, me, Kairi, or even Takanori. It is for the island."

Poor Kentaro.

I have tried to make you understand how bad it would be if you and I create.

You have left me with no choice.

I hang my head in defeat.

"Are you okay, Kaori?"

I shake my head in what I hope resembles despair.

"What are you thinking?"

I lock eyes with Kentaro.

"I think you are right," I whisper.

"What?"

"I think you're right, Kentaro." I raise my voice, "We must create. For the island."

"Are you—?"

Kentaro's words are cut off by the sound of crashing in the bushes behind the hut and the dull thud of something striking the back wall. Kentaro looks at me in horror and runs out of the opening. I follow behind mem. I watch Kentaro as mu tries to scramble through the dense undergrowth. Branches scratch and rip mir skin as mu screams, "Kairi! Kairi! Come back!"

I pull my silver dagger out of the back of the hut.

∼

"Kaori, wake up. You must come quick."

I was enjoying a nap after all the drama of the rise. I hope whoever has entered my hut uninvited has a good reason for disturbing me.

Please don't be Kentaro.

I can't endure any more of mir self-pity. Mu should know my twin's cruelty by now.

"Kaori? Can you hear me?"

I want to ignore Saki's voice but the sharp urgency in mir words forces me to sit up.

"What is it?"

"It's Kairi."

I groan and make to lie back down but Saki drags me by my wrist.

"I'm sorry but I can't take anymore of Kairi, Saki. Please leave me alone," I say, swatting mir hand away.

"You don't understand. Something happened during the boar hunt."

I know Kairi had a hunt this afternoon. I had wondered if mir creeping around and eavesdropping might have put mem off going.

"What has mu done now?" I can't stop myself from asking.

"Kaori, you have to come now. The Experienced are going to execute Kairi tonight."

Chapter Four

KAIRI

Kentaro gasps at my appearance. I am dressed for a hunt in only my megg loin cloth, a sight Kentaro has seen many times. Mu stares because I am soaked in fresh blood.

"It's not mine," I mumble. "How did you get here?"

"Shun told me they had taken you." Kentaro is still gawping at my blood-soaked torso.

"And they let you in here?" I ask.

Kentaro nods.

The Experienced really are going to kill me if they have let Kentaro enter their temple. I rest my head against the stone wall. There is no door, only an opening. I could run. But to where? I am imprisoned by water. How can I escape the shore? I take a deep breath, soot from the burning torch on the wall scratches my throat. I slowly exhale. Tears sting my eyes.

Kentaro peers into a bucket of stream water the Experienced have left in my cell.

"I am not thirsty," I say.

"I wasn't thinking of drinking it," Kentaro says and tears a strip of cloth from mir robe sleeve. Mu dips it into the bucket.

"Come here," Kentaro whispers with a tenderness which threatens to make my tears fall.

I approach mem and mu begins to gently wipe the blood from my body.

Chapter Five

KAORI

I have no memory of getting to the temple of the Experienced. All I know is Saki's words propelling my limbs forwards and obscuring my vision.

The Experienced are going to execute Kairi tonight.

I push my way through the heavy gold temple doors into a dimly lit cavernous hall. Twelve tall stone pillars surround it. At the base of each pillar is a small pit of fire which provides neither warmth nor comfort. Instead, the orange glow casts an eerie flicker on the faces of the twelve Experienced figures that are carved into each pillar. It makes the open mouths look like they are reciting the glyphs depicted above them.

Namu Experienced.

The pillars bear the grisly burden of a skull-encrusted ceiling. The fleshless face of every dead Maymuan bores down on me with hollow eye sockets. Soon, Kairi's skull will be embedded up there.

A chill cools my sweat-soaked forehead. The change of temperature brings with it the realisation that I have no idea where I am going. I haven't been inside this building since my naming ceremony. I only know this floor. It is where Kairi and I lived for seven orbits. This is the home of the unnamed.

On my right are two openings. I know the one furthest from me, between Experienced Takako's pillar and Experienced Takafumi's pillar, leads to the sleeping quarters. A room full of woven mats, red ants, and restless nights.

The closer opening leads to where we used to eat. Before each meal, the Experienced would lead us in a chant of gratitude for the food. While we ate, Experienced Takafumi would tell us how one day we would provide food for the island, but it never seemed real to me. I couldn't picture a Maymuan growing our vegetables, fruit, or grain. Or catching snakes, boars, or crickets.

I was incapable of imagining what I had never seen.

I would look around the room and try to envisage the Experienced hunting but I knew they were not strong enough. The same for us unnameds; we were too weak.

The other unnameds would often fantasise about what role they would fulfil outside. But not me; I was willingly oblivious to the rest of the island. I never wanted to leave the temple. Kairi, however, couldn't wait to get out and start providing. That's how the Experienced interpreted mir enthusiasm. Eager to provide. More like eager to kill.

"Kairi."

Mir name ricochets around the empty hall. Where is mu? They wouldn't hold mem in the storeroom to the left or down the dark tunnel that leads outside to the waste holes. Even Takanori is not that cruel. I shudder at the thought of the waste holes, where rats the size of tortoises guard the latrines.

There is only one other room on this floor to consider: the activity room. I hurry towards the opening at the far end of the hall.

One step into the passageway tells me Kairi will not be here because I can hear the unnameds practising joy: the sweet plucking of a bugir; a taut goat intestine vibrating against hollow bamboo; the pound of a nunum; a hand slapping a stretched snakeskin membrane; and a voice like a girnum soaring across the sky seeking its mate hums in my ear.

I should head back to the hall but the sound draws me towards the forbidden. I rub my thumb over the thin raised bugir scars on my fingers. Even trying to save Kairi from execution is no excuse for what I am about to do. The unnameds have not seen anyone other than each other, the rearers, and the Experienced. They will be terrified if they catch me watching them.

I crouch down just before the passageway ends and peer around the opening into the room.

Experienced Takako has mir back to me. Takako's long grey dreadlocks cascade over mir shoulders, pouring down to mir waist. Facing Takako are the unnameds, each lost in their own joy, eyes closed or absent in the pleasure of the melody they are creating. The expansive room is crackling with the pure energy of the unnameds. Dragonflies carved and inlaid with gold twinkle on the walls amongst shimmering iridescent pearls shucked from oysters harvested at low tide.

Despite the overwhelming scene, I identify the one voice which has distracted me from my quest to find Kairi.

I watch the unnamed with the voice. Mu is swaying from side to side with mir mouth open wide, melody gushing from mir soul. Mu, like all of the unnameds, has mir hair untied. Mir face is framed by a fluffy little black cloud. In the light flickering from the numerous torches, mir dark skin glows like sunlit amber.

The room begins to sway from more than just the rhythm. I feel a peculiar fear for this unnamed. I want to run into the room and snatch mem and protect mem from all I know.

I know practising joy in the temple is sowing a memory seed which will blossom and bear a bitter fruit. I know mu will never again feel how mu does in this room.

Thoughts of Kairi, Kentaro, and creating make me clutch my own tight braids, feeling deep envy of the unnamed's freedom in captivity. I have to clap my hand over my mouth to stifle my sob. The unnamed's eyes click open and find me helpless on the floor.

Mu keeps singing but mu smiles even wider and I can see mir first set of teeth sparkling in pink gums. I should go but I can't break our connection. The unnamed offers mir hand to me then soars higher. I try and follow mem but the burden of Kairi impedes my flight. The unnamed closes mir eyes, leaving me alone in the musty passageway.

I return to the main hall to find Naho pacing the floor.

"Where have you been? I was so worried."

What is mu doing here? Naho must have eyes and ears sprouting out of every cave and crevice on this island.

"What happened to you? Your face... legs... are you okay?"

Dirt has stuck to the sweat on my legs. A little bit of blood is dripping from my knee. I must have tripped on the way here from my hut. I can feel the sting of branch scratches on my face. My eyes must be bloodshot after seeing the unnameds. And I am wearing my sleeping tunic.

"I am fine, Naho."

Mu clearly doesn't believe me.

"Do you know where Kairi is?" I ask, even though I am certain mu knows. Naho seems to know everything.

Mu points up at the skull ceiling. For a horrible moment I think mu means Kairi is already dead but I realise Naho would not tell me in such a cruel way.

"How do we get up there?"

I say "we" because as far as I am concerned Naho now has to help me find Kairi.

"I don't think it is a good idea for you to go up there, Kaori."

"Wh—"

"Not in your current state." Naho surveys me from head to toe.

I respect Naho. I really do. But I don't appreciate the

strange Maymuan priority mu is placing on my appearance right now.

"They are going to kill mem! Help me."

Naho makes a futile attempt to knock some of the dirt from my legs.

"Naho, we have to go now!"

I chase Naho out through the gold doors. The sky surrounding the moon is bruised. Yellow and green bleeds from the glowing orb, making the black night purple. Naho hesitates on the steep stone staircase that runs up the entire height of the temple.

From the bottom step it looks like the stairs end at an opening for level one. However, from the edge of the forest I have seen that the staircase runs through two further openings on a second and third level. The stairs don't end until they reach a large flat platform on level four. There are two large stone tortoise statues flanking the staircase at the summit.

I have never been up these stairs. Actually, that is not entirely true. A game we once played in the orbit after our naming ceremony was to challenge each other to climb these steps. Kentaro would go no higher than four or five steps. That took mem as much courage as it took Kairi and me to go up about halfway. Kairi said mu had been up all the way to the opening but Kentaro and I never saw mem. If Naho is correct, Kairi has finally achieved mir goal.

Naho seems stuck on the first step but a sharp poke in the back sends mem flying up the stairs. The hall on level two is much smaller than the hall on the ground floor. This hall has been sliced in half by a large room straight ahead. Above the opening of the room is a carving of a tortoise inlaid with gold. To my left and right are identical silent passageways. Muffled voices and the fragrant perfume of burning hunmir wood emanate from the opening straight ahead.

"Wait." Naho blocks me from moving forwards. "Kairi is down there." Mu points to the passageway on the right.

"How can you be sure?"

Naho ignores me and mu heads towards what must be the Experienced chamber.

"What are you doing?" I can't believe mu is going to stroll in there. Mu must have lost mir mind. "Come with me to find Kairi."

"Then what? We have to try and stop this."

I know Naho is fearless in the cave when we hunt but mir behaviour is unbelievable. Stop this? I haven't thought any of this through. I only wanted to get to Kairi. I don't know what I was planning to do after finding mem. Stop the execution? Is it even possible? I feel the girnum sing again.

I fly at Naho and wrap my arms around mem. At first mu is as stiff as a smoked snake but mu relaxes and coils around me, squeezing tight.

When we part I feel embarrassed about my physical emotion but Naho doesn't seem to mind. Mu heads through the tortoise opening and I turn right.

The passageway is dark but full of smoke. There must be a torch lit somewhere. I follow the sooty scent until I hear a gentle murmur. I recognise the voice but the tender tone is unfamiliar. It is Kentaro.

For the second time tonight I find myself creeping around an opening, on the prowl like Kairi. What I see when I peek around this opening makes my lungs contract.

Kentaro is sitting in the corner of the small bare room with Kairi's head in mir lap. Kairi, despite the heat from the torch on the wall, is shivering. And crying. Kentaro's soothing noises as mu strokes Kairi's head trigger a memory that turns the passageway floor to water.

It was the orbit before we left the rearers to live here in this temple and the last I remember of love.

"Please help me."

Kairi looks from my swollen little finger to the scorpion scuttling away across the sand. Kairi flees, leaving me writhing with fear.

Please come back. Don't leave me here on my own.

My finger swells to the knuckle.

Heavy feet slap the sand. It is a rearer. Mu makes me sit up then grabs my hand.

"Is mu okay?" Kairi begs, tugging at the hem of the rearer's tunic.

"Quick, go and get some guma leaves. As many as you can."

"I want to stay."

"Go now!"

Kairi tramples into the undergrowth. The rearer pulls the twine holding back mir hair and ties it tight around the bottom of my little finger. I am relieved. This is not so bad. I see a flash of metal.

A strange chill brings numbness. I look for my little finger but it is no longer there. Heat seeps from my knuckle. I sway as silver bees swarm. I lean into them but they nudge me onto my back.

"No!" Kairi screams, diving into the sand and lifting my upper body so mu can slide mir lower body underneath. Mu gently rocks me from side to side and I feel Kairi's tears run down my cheeks.

I can hear the rearer's jaw click as mu chews the guma leaves. My knuckle stump stings as mu applies the moist compress.

"Do me," Kairi says. I can see mem waving mir little finger at the rearer. "Please do me."

The rearer ignores mem and keeps chewing and applying guma leaves. Kairi murmurs and sobs for the loss of my little finger and our symmetry.

The rearer pauses from chewing to say, "At least we will be able to tell you apart now."

Chapter Six

KAIRI

The dull thump of heavy footsteps echoes down the passageway. *Bahm.* They are coming for me. I stand and wipe dust from my robe to avoid Kentaro's burning stare. I can't give mem what mu wants. A loving, passionate final moment. What would be the point? I will be dead by sunrise and Kentaro will have Kaori. I don't care what Kentaro says; I know what I overheard in the creation hut.

"Kairi, I lov—"

"It's okay. We don't have to... you know." I can't look at mem.

Outside, the footsteps have been replaced by raised voices.

My desire to ignore Kentaro is surpassed by my need to know who is shouting outside. What the ratty hell is going on out there? Kentaro peers out of the opening.

"I can't see properly," Kentaro whispers. "It looks like a

couple of Experienced. Someone else is there too. It sounds like they are arguing with whoever it is."

I pace around the bare room. I can't allow these so-called Experienced to pass judgement on me. Who cares about a few extra slaughtered boars? These ratty Maymuans, they don't understand me; they never will. I am more than they will ever be.

The torch hanging in the bracket on the wall winks at me. Should I do it? Could I do it? Burn the whole temple down and take every last one of these miserable parasites with me?

I push the flame and it begins to spread across the wall. Kentaro squeals in terror.

"Kairi! No! What are you doing? You haven't heard what the Experienced have to say yet. It might be okay. Please, Kairi."

Thick suffocating smoke billows against the ceiling.

Kentaro seizes the front of my robes. "Please don't do this. Please."

I stop the spread of the fire but the flames continue to scorch the back wall. Kentaro has panic in mir eyes and mu is right to be afraid. I can tell mu is scrambling in mir mind, desperate to find what will stop my inferno.

The answer is nothing. Nothing is going to stop me. Because I know exactly what is going to happen to me. It happened to the farmers who were responsible for allowing the locusts to destroy the crops four orbits ago.

I wasn't supposed to be there. Only those who had lived

at least fifteen orbits were invited to gather around the Experienced temple before dawn.

I wanted to know what all the excitement was about. They tried to suppress it, the filthy Maymuans, but from every hut came the eager chirp of crickets as they muttered to each other. I should have known to stay away by the toxic mix of fear and glee in their voices.

The Experienced marched the farmers up the outside staircase of the temple all the way to the top level, past those horrible reptilian statues. The way the farmers walked was strange. I remember feeling funny inside as I watched them. It was like they were floating or maybe gliding? I don't know, but it was creepy. Everyone around me started swaying and chanting "Namu May Mu". The farmers lined up on the raised platform. As the sun rose behind them it was like they were glowing. The sun illuminated their immaculate white robes.

The Experienced each threw a handful of ground hunmir wood into a large urn full of fire. Long, heady tendrils of smoke scuttled and scurried across the platform. Then, with all the ceremony of a torch being snuffed out, everyone stopped chanting.

Across the platform I saw a light flash then the front of the first farmer's robe became red and mu fell to mir knees. The second time the light flashed I made sure to watch closely. I wish I hadn't.

The farmer screamed "Namu May Mu!" and stabbed memself in the stomach with a long silver knife then mu pulled it down and mir intestines slid to the ground before mu did. I didn't watch the rest of the farmers but after each scream of "Namu May Mu" I was convinced I could hear the tearing of skin. The slithering of intestines. The crack of knee bone against stone. Finally, the screams stopped and I looked up. Takanori was halfway down the line of farmers, slicing each head clean off their shoulders.

I am not going to let them do that to me. I would rather burn to death in this poky room than perform some sick penance ritual for these Maymuans. My flames crackle with renewed vigour.

"What about the unnameds?"

Shut up, Kentaro.

"They are here, you know, like we were, living downstairs."

Stop. Stop now.

"Are you prepared to roast them alive too?"

No, no, NO!

"What have they done? Kairi! Answer me! What have the unnameds done to deserve this?" Kentaro pleads.

"So what if the unnameds die?" I yell. "What right have they to live?" I can't control my pain any longer. My hand curls into a fist.

"Kairi! Stop hitting yourself!" Kentaro shouts. "Please, Kairi, I don't know what to do. I don't know how to help you."

Kentaro has locked my wrists with mir thin fingers. "Get off me." I snap Kentaro's hold like a twig. Mu stumbles to the floor.

Leave me alone. You make me weak.

But I can't. I can't hurt them. I don't want to hurt Kentaro.

What am I doing? Help me.

I didn't mean for any of this to happen.

I can't breathe.

I don't know what I am doing. I slide to the floor and curl up like a coco. The fire recedes.

Kentaro cautiously approaches and gently wraps mir body around mine.

I begin to breathe again.

"Kairi!"

Kentaro and I break apart.

I don't understand. Kaori is here but mu looks like a wild animal. Mu is dirty and I think mu is wearing mir night tunic. Before I can get any words out, Takafumi and Takako run into the room.

This is it. They are here for me. But they grab Kaori instead. Mu is screaming through Takako's slim fingers. Takafumi seizes Kaori's kicking legs and they lift and carry mem across the room.

Kentaro looks how I feel – mir mouth is moving without words as Kaori is hoisted through the opening, thrashing and rolling like a captured crocodile. Or a hippo.

Kentaro reaches for my hand. "Don't you see, Kairi? We do love you, you know. Why won't you accept that?"

I was thinking something similar but I hate how literal and Maymuan Kentaro is being. Nobody gets any benefit from expressing memself, and why does everything have to be so sickly honeycomb all the time?

"Kaori shouldn't be involved with this. Mu shouldn't have come."

"At least we agree on something, Kairi," a deep voice booms.

How long has Takanori been standing in the opening? I drop Kentaro's hand. Takanori aims a pointed glance at my lonely palm then smiles as mu surveys the charred walls.

"Now, if you have finished with your little bonfire we would appreciate your presence in our chamber."

I scowl at Kentaro. Why does mu always have to make me look so weak? I want to explain, to say something defiant to Takanori, but mu has already swept back down the passageway leaving the Experienced Takumi to escort me to my fate.

Chapter Seven

KAORI

My bones shudder on the stone wall Takako has tossed me against. As if depositing a sack of grain, Takako and Takafumi stroll away without a backward glance. I try and get my bearings after my unceremonious exit from Kairi's cage.

I was expecting to feel the warm embrace of the humid night, but the chill on my skin means I am still in the temple. Cloying incense stings my eyes and animated whispers fizz in my ears. I hear a gasp as I lift the hem of my night tunic to wipe the tears from my eyes. Some more oversensitive Experienced are in whatever this place is, then.

"If you insist on invading our temple can you at least present yourself with some dignity?"

Urgh. Takanori.

"Where is Kairi?" I ask, hastily dropping my hem.

"Patience, your half is near." Takanori smirks. "And I expect you to stand when addressing me in my chamber."

Oh bahm.

My legs are still wobbly after Takafumi's intrusive grip but I am able to stand.

I am in the Experienced chamber.

Underfoot is a delicate woven mat. My feet know they are not on simple benme leaves. I think this is made from ganba, the sour shrubs which grow by the cove. The design is like something Kentaro makes outside of mir island rural duty.

I have a woven megg water bag Kentaro made only for me resting against the wall in my hut. It is extraordinary; it can hold a day's water from the stream without leaking a drop.

Do the rurals make special things for the Experienced? Did Kentaro design this floor for the Experienced? Do the Experienced have private relationships and arrangements with some of the Maymuans?

I am getting all twisted up. This situation is scrambling my mind. I need to focus and concentrate on what is happening now.

Although there are only two fire pits at the back of the room, the dried golden ganba leaves glow and illuminate the many horrible things in this room aside from Takanori.

In a semi-circle, eleven of the twelve Experienced sit on thrones that grow out of the floor. The ganba have been seamlessly woven into chairs raising the dead leaves to an eerie afterlife. The high backs have spread their wings like the plumage of a magnificent barmuna. At the crest is the source of the eye-watering incense. Hanging above the head of each Experienced is a dead tortoise. It must be dead because it has no head and its shell has been hollowed out as a receptacle for burning hunmir wood.

Takanori catches my disgust and performs a weird rhythmic tap on the right armrest of mir chair. There is the tortoise head. Poking out of the chair arm as in life it would have poked out of its shell. I can't drag my eyes from it: the sinewy flaccid neck straining in inquiry; the bemused, docile smile under swollen, bulbous eyelids.

I don't know why the Experienced have embraced the tortoise as their symbol. There is nothing compliant or submissive about any of them. Each sits erect on their unnatural perch, shrouded in long red robes. Lustrous grey dreadlocks frame shrewd black eyes. I scan each chair and fall deeper into hell until a soft pair of eyes locks onto mine.

Naho.

I had completely forgotten about mem.

Mu stands behind Takanori's chair. I feel better knowing mu is here but *why* is mu allowed to be in here?

A scuffle at the opening announces Kairi's arrival. Kairi has shaken off Takumi's tight grip and mu strides into the chamber with mir chin pointing at the roof. I don't think defiance is the way to go in here. Kairi's proud entrance has clearly ruffled the executioners' feathers. The Experienced shift in their chairs in an attempt to increase their stature and intimidate my twin.

A perverse thrill shivers through my body. I am excited.

It is exhilarating to watch Kairi face these terrors. I admire mem for not crawling into the Experienced chamber on mir hands and knees.

Then Kentaro ruins the effect somewhat by racing into the room and giving Kairi an awkward embrace from behind. Kairi almost topples forwards but mu regains mir composure and shrugs Kentaro off like a soiled rabbit pelt.

"Are there any others you wish to invite to my chamber?" sneers Takanori.

Kairi ignores mem but I notice a pulsation under mir skin as mu grinds mir teeth. I beckon Kentaro over to my corner and Takumi fills the vacant throne.

Twelve self-righteous Experienced stare at Kairi.

"You may kneel," says Takanori, but again Kairi ignores mem and remains standing.

The other Experienced tut and shake their heads, unable to comprehend Kairi's insolence, but Takanori appears to be enjoying memself. Mu is absently fingering the tortoise head and a smile plays around mir lips.

"My fellow Experienced, I urge you to endure this affront because the half before us knows no better. Mu cannot be held accountable for mir actions in the same way as a Maymuan."

The Experienced sigh and nod, enjoying feeling pity for "the half". The twitch in Kairi's jaw now looks like a tooth trying to kick its way out of the side of mir face. At the word *half*, Kentaro holds my hand and I am wringing mir *whole* blood out of it. How dare Takanori speak about me and Kairi like that.

"Do I have to extinguish the fire pits?" Takanori asks.

What?

"No," Kairi answers, making my head spin. What is happening? It is like there are two levels in this chamber. One I am aware of – the trial of my twin – and another level where a different battle is being fought, but I don't know what the rules are nor do I know what is at stake.

I mean, look at Naho. Mu is swallowing so much mir throat resembles Kairi's jaw but mir eyes are unblinking. Since Kairi strutted in, Naho has not glanced at me once. Not even to check if I am okay after Takanori's horrible words about being only a half. Also why is mu over there with the Experienced instead of standing by me?

"Let us begin," commands Takanori. "Namu May Mu."

"Namu May Mu," echo the Experienced.

"Namu Experienced."

"Namu Experienced."

Their self-indulgent affirmation fills the smoky chamber.

"Kairi, earlier you fulfilled your island duty and embarked on a boar hunt."

Takanori takes Kairi's slow eye blink as confirmation of truth.

"The quota for your entire pack was five boars. You alone killed ten." Takanori pauses to allow the gravity of mir words to sink in. Ten boars instead of five.

Kentaro and I both slump against the stone wall. How is Kairi going to receive forgiveness for this? And those poor boars. *Namu May Mu.*

"Not only did you kill over the pack quota but you did

not slaughter correctly. In fact, you rendered the majority of the boars unfit for Maymuan consumption."

Kentaro drops my clammy hand and I try to catch the tears pouring from my eyes.

Unfit for Maymuan consumption?

Kairi, what have you done?

A horrible memory pounds my head.

The rat squeals as Kairi scoops it up from the corner of the unnamed chamber. We have only been in the Experienced temple for one orbit.

"Look!" Kairi says, holding the rat out to me.

I look nervously at the opening. All the other unnameds have left to practise joy.

"We should go," I say.

"Come here. Touch it." The rat has coiled its tail around Kairi's arm.

I don't want to. I watch Kairi from the door. Mu is squeezing the rat and closely watching its face. How its eyes dart and its teeth shiver in panic.

The rat's squeals become more and more shrill.

"What are you doing?" I hiss.

Kairi laughs.

The squeals become unbearable. I rush over to Kairi and try to knock the rat from mir fist.

"It's okay," Kairi says, swatting me away. "It's all soft anyway."

"You're hurting it," I sob. "Stop it!"

Kairi squeezes again and there is a sickening crunch. The tail unravels and hangs limp.

"I..." Kairi stammers, shock on mir face, but there is also a thrilled gleam in mir eye.

It is Kairi's first kill.

Chapter Eight

KAIRI

They are only ratty boars. Get over it.

The reptiles are all swooning and freaking out on their stupid thrones. Every movement they make results in a grating creak of dry ganba. I wish I had a hatchet to hack at their exposed roots. They are judging me for killing a few boars but it is absolutely fine for them to use a head as an armrest.

Filthy rats.

And I wish Kaori's wrinkled, saggy lover would stop giving me the mournful-eye treatment. Mu always tries to talk to me, but I am not cockroach Kaori. I don't need some creep watching over me all the time. Cockroach is heaving and gasping behind me. Mu would rather resurrect a few hairy boars than spare my life.

Takanori is lecturing on, squeezing every last drop out of mir swollen morality teat.

Dirty traitor.

I was never supposed to appear in front of the Experienced for anything I do.

We had an understanding.

I don't want to live anymore anyway. I am already dead. You all buried me. I am free. I am your fear. I am the air. The sky. The dying. The dead. You are all living in my tomb. I am outside breathing while you suffocate in my stench. Look at you. Your sanctimony. You feast on willing, weak minds to elevate your own sick soul. I *am* you. You are me. I am half of nothing. You are nothing. Truth is not in this chamber. No one in this chamber seeks truth. You are not judging me. You are judging yourself. You would do what I do if you had the guts. Instead, you are submerged in stagnant red pools. You pretend to be horrified but I see your pleasure. It drips down your legs. Lick it up. It is as close to escape as you will get. I am the horizon. The point of no return. You can finish me but I will begin again.

Yes, I killed the boars.

It is the role you gave me. You ask me to be a killer then condemn me when I kill.

I did everything you asked. I tied my megg loin cloth, polished my rusty arrow heads, and sharpened my short, hollow gamgam spear.

I was made to kill.

I didn't want what happened to happen but it did and it doesn't matter how I feel about it. Nothing can change the past. I don't know if Kentaro and the creation hut were on my mind or not. Even if they were, so what? What happened, happened. And was probably always going to happen.

I met the four other hunters in the clearing where the forest becomes a jungle. They were twittering away like little girnums, pushing and shoving each other. I was pleased they stopped playing when I approached. I checked their weaponry then the final preparation was to tie the tusks.

As the most important hunter, I am always the last to receive my necklace and therefore I am first to bestow. The other Maymuans with hunting duties don't have a leader. We are supposed to be equals but, sorry, there is no way these weasels are as gifted as I am.

As usual, I gave Aito mir necklace.

I could give Tetsu, Shun, or Ikki their necklace first but I like Aito to know mir place. Far beneath me. Aito likes to visit my twin's hut in the dead of night so I make sure to tie mir boar tusk necklace extra tight against mir throat every time.

After Shun finished the ceremony by tying my necklace, we forced our way through the thick habim trees and began stalking our prey.

Everyone thinks cockroach is so great because a snake fang could pop mir body but I would choose poison over death by boar. Boars are vicious. A boar at full charge can shatter my ribcage then chomp through my tendons just like how Kaori guzzles coco.

In the jungle, day becomes night; sound and smell replace sight. The jungle pulses with predators. From cruel monkeys who attack from on high with lips taut over razor-tooth-filled black gums to the tics and parasites purring over rancid pools of green bile water, desperate to burrow beneath my skin. The best I can do is rub my body with the flesh of a ganba fruit and believe I will survive.

We prowled through the dense undergrowth communicating by hand and head motions. I led. I clenched my hand into a fist and thrust my arm in the air when pungent faeces filled my nose. The specks of excrement caught in the coarse boar bristles had exposed its position. I crouched low over the vines and filtered out the rasp of wind rustling the dense habim leaves.

I ignored the squawk of a gaudy buha and fought my innate instinct to fear the screech of a nabgar. I sought the snort of humid air sucked up wide flared nostrils and the squelch of prickly haired trotters on jungle sludge.

I gestured to my pack to split and flank the beast in a four-corner pyramid base formation. I waited, rocking on the balls of my feet as they assumed position. I whistled, pushing air through my pursed lips into the shadows and swiftly four whistles returned. I whistled again but this time sucking in air, making a shriller sound, the cue for my pack to draw in the corners towards the victim in the centre.

I sprinted towards the boar and laughed when I saw the

usual disorientation on its ugly face. It couldn't escape. My pack had it surrounded. I drew an arrow from my quiver and placed it in my bow.

Staring down the shaft, I watched the beast grunt and squeal in futility, chasing its own tail in anguish. I released my arrow and it embedded perfectly in the fleshy neck below the boar's ear.

It toppled over with a thud and undignified splash of soggy leaves.

Pathetic.

Its torso heaved frantically in pitiful desperation to survive. Its glassy black eye conveyed a baleful glare. I wrenched my arrow out of its neck and plunged my sharpened gamgam into the gaping hole. I knelt down and sucked on my hollow spear until my mouth was full of warm, thick blood. I drank deeply then removed my gamgam and stepped back as the rest of my pack drank from the boar.

After Tetsu had quenched mir thirst, we sat around the beast and Aito began the chant of "Namu May Mu". I don't have any desire whatsoever for this aspect of the hunt, but tolerating this mumbo jumbo appeases my pack so I muttered the words until the last drop of blood was drained.

When hunting boar, killing the first one is easy. It is the second, third, fourth, and fifth that are difficult because we have to drag the smelly carcasses with us. I have to become more alert as time passes, not more exhausted. I drink greater quantities of blood after each kill so by the time of the fifth hunt I feel feral.

~

"We can't slaughter this one. It has no tusks."

I don't know why Aito thought mu had the right to tell me what to do. I pulled tighter on my bow and shouted, "Hold formation."

This was only the fourth boar. We had to fill our quota but these maggots were loosening the trap.

You are not supposed to kill tuskless boar but it is not forbidden like tortoise.

"I don't think we should do this," Aito bleated.

We? It was my decision. I aimed my arrow at mir face and mu shut up. I focused again on the boar. It was not afraid of me. It was not trying to escape. Instead, it gazed at me with curious eyes.

My pack had held their position but Aito looked as if mu was trying to wring water from mir own neck and the others didn't have their hands on their weapons either.

None of those parasites had the stomach to do what was needed to be done. But I had no doubt when we returned they would be more than willing to bask in the praise of a successful hunt and they would accept their quota of meat from the preparers.

Hypocrites.

But I hadn't released my arrow. Something in the anxiety of my pack and the calm of the boar disturbed me. The boar surveyed me with its soft black eyes then turned to shuffle away.

Shoot it. Now.

My arrow pierced its neck, unleashing a terrifying squeal. It swayed then wilted onto the ground like morgon petals plucked by an unnatural wind. I couldn't quite catch my breath to order my pack to approach. They seemed as rooted to the jungle floor as I was. I licked the sweat from my upper lip and found my voice again.

"Approach."

No one moved.

"Approach, you ratty cowards!"

We crowded around the boar, which continued to squeal in a way that churned my stomach.

Pull the arrow out of its neck.

I couldn't.

Pull the arrow out of its neck or they will all laugh at you.

Hoping the pack hadn't noticed how my hand trembled, I gripped my arrow head. The squeal became shriller as I closed my eyes and slowly drew the arrow out.

"Aito, you drink first."

"Wh-what?"

"I said, you drink first."

"No."

"No?"

"You're the leader, aren't you?"

Bahm.

Ratty Aito.

"Ikki, drink."

"I don't…" Ikki mumbled. "You're the leader."

They are right. You are the leader. Do it now or they won't respect you.

I slid my gamgam into the slit and sipped. The blood was sweet. I had to fight the urge to spit it out. I swallowed and directed the others to drink. Tetsu complied but took an even smaller sip than I did. With each penetration the boar moaned in agony.

By the time Shun had finished my entire body was trembling and I couldn't look at any of them.

They are watching you. Stop punching your thigh.

I knelt down and started chanting "Namu May Mu". The others joined me and gradually the boar's moans faded and mir chest no longer rose.

"What's that noise?" whispered Tetsu, eyes wide.

For ratty hell's sake, what now?

There was a rustling coming from the bushes behind us. We stood up and drew our weapons. The bush quivered and shook then began to part.

Oh bahm.

A light-brown snout snuffled the blood-soaked ground. Golden striped fur caught the sliver of sun blinking through the habim leaves. Hopeful brown eyes slayed us with a soul-shattering stare.

"Move the body," I barked at Ikki.

"Move it where?"

"I don't care where, just move it. Tetsu, help mem. Put it with the others."

They dragged the carcass off to join the other slaughtered beasts.

Aito, Shun, and I watched transfixed as the five piglets explored the atrocity. One strayed from the others and began to sniff my feet. I knelt down and stroked its fluffy head.

"Is that a good idea?" Aito asked, watching me with horror.

"Why not? They're cute."

Aito and Shun looked at each other like I had smashed a coco on my head.

"What's wrong with you two? Pet them!"

Shun looked nauseous but obeyed. Aito, the ratty fool, shook mir head and said, "Not after what we have done to their carrier."

Lightning struck my spine. *How dare this sanctimonious slug lecture me on right and wrong? Why was mu talking about ratty carriers?*

I hate Aito. Mu could have tracked other boars and then I wouldn't have had to kill the tuskless one.

Aito was still staring at me with disgust. I couldn't bear it.

I charged at Aito and my hands were crushing mir throat when there was a loud crash from the bushes and I was propelled into the air. I landed with a thump, sprawled out on my back. My arrows cracked beneath me. The patter of fleeing feet and the guttural grunt of a furious boar clobbered my ears.

I sat up and the boar charged me again. I managed to roll aside, thankful it was another tuskless one, otherwise I would have been skewered.

They have deserted you.

I made a quick sweep of the area before the boar came for me again. There was no sign of Aito, the maggot, but Shun stood there slack-jawed with mir bow held in a limp hand.

"Do something, you ratty idiot!" I screamed at mem.

Shun shot mir arrow at the boar but mu may as well have thrown it for all the good it did. The boar attacked again and I couldn't move fast enough so it slammed into my left shoulder, shattering my bow. *Was Shun laughing?* Mu had definitely made some weird noise.

The boar struck again but this time I was ready. I let it trample my legs and when its trotters sank into my stomach I drew my gamgam from my loincloth and stabbed it in its side.

It screamed in agony, and congealed spit dripped from its mouth and oozed onto my face. My hand was drenched in warm blood. I wrenched my gamgam out and stabbed it again. And again and again until it slumped in a dead weight on my chest.

The suffocating pressure ended when Tetsu and Ikki returned and helped Shun lift the beast off me. Aito was fidgeting a few steps back, rubbing mir strangled neck as if it was going to excuse mem fleeing like a rat and leaving me at the mercy of the raging carrier boar. I should have snapped Aito's neck instead of only squeezing.

I got to my feet and appraised my pack. They looked terrified. Shun was transfixed by the boar. When I followed mir gaze I almost forgot I had caused the carnage. The boar looked like it had been eaten alive by a crocodile. It was riddled with puncture marks down one side. A mutilated pink tongue was lolling out of its mouth, the tip bitten off during the ferocity of my attack.

Ratty Shun.

"Hey," I shouted, shoving Shun's shoulder, "what the ratty hell happened to your aim?" Mu gasped like a fish out of water. "Answer me!" I screamed in mir face.

Then mu laughed at me. A freaky, hysterical laugh, but mu was *laughing* at me. It spread to the others. They were all laughing at me. Tears rolling down their cheeks. Clutching their sides. Laughing.

They are laughing at you.

I know.

They are still laughing at you.

Shut up.

They are laughing at you.

I KNOW.

I plunged into the ocean but I couldn't breathe salt. I scaled the mountain but I couldn't breathe cloud. I crossed the sands but I couldn't breathe heat.

Attack.

I can't breathe.

Attack!

I can't breathe.

I am clenching my gamgam. I am drenched in piglet blood. I am condemned.

Chapter Nine

KAORI

I can't believe. Belief makes it true. Mu could never do this. I know Kairi has done some horrible things before but this is something else. Something evil. Kairi may be many things but mu is not evil. Mu could not do this. Slaughter innocent piglets like that? No. Absolutely not. It is unbearable to think about.

Squeal. Stab. Splatter.

It makes my blood congeal in my veins.

No. This is not true.

How could this have happened? It is impossible. I should have been there. If I had been there it wouldn't have happened. It *didn't* happen. Mu would listen to me. Mu wouldn't have done it. Mu didn't do it.

If only I hadn't said what I did in the creation hut. I wasn't trying to goad mem. I wanted to teach mem a lesson for creeping around and spying on us. I didn't mean for this to happen. Any of it. I didn't know mu would go so far. I only wanted to hurt mem a little. Give mem a little shock. Not this. Who could have expected this?

And why did Saki have to come and tell me? Where the ratty hell was Aito? I have asked mem so many times to take care of my twin during their hunts. Aito has never said there were any problems in the pack, so what was different this time? Why didn't Aito try and stop Kairi? Why didn't any of the pack try and stop mem? There are so many things I don't understand. It doesn't make any sense.

Kentaro has woven memself into the floor; mu has not moved. I am swaying like a benme in a gale. The stench from the hollowed-out tortoise shells is nauseating. The perfume is clouding my thoughts. Nothing adds up. Why didn't the Experienced make it forbidden to slaughter a carrier boar? If they had, this would never have happened. Of course there will be piglets somewhere near a carrier boar. Stupid Takanori. Mu wanted this to happen. Mu must have. I can't believe this. Where are the piglets? I want to see them. How can we know what Takanori is saying is true?

Kairi, defend yourself! Say it is not true!

Why are you just standing there? Say something!

Where is the rest of the pack? They are as responsible. Why is Kairi alone? It is not fair. Mu shouldn't be alone.

Kairi isn't alone. I am here.

But... Kairi was so thrilled to show me the carrier in agony in the jungle.

Stop. Why are you thinking about this? It doesn't mean anything. Mu didn't kill the carrier!

But mu was revelling in mir pain.

So what? It is not the same thing. At all.

Kairi did kill the rat.

No, back then we were only unnameds. We didn't know any better.

But Kairi does get so euphoric after a hunt, the look in mir eyes after an afternoon of drinking boar blood is terrifying.

Stop being so disloyal. Mu can't help it; they ask mem to hunt.

They make us all do things we don't want to do. I am frightened every time I crawl into the snake cave. Frightened I won't return, terrified a snake will snatch my wrists in its jaw and flood my veins with venom.

But wait, a rural like Kentaro only milks goats and weaves megg. Mu is hardly suffering?

It doesn't matter. So what if I suffer more than Kentaro on this stupid island? Neither of us would do what Kairi has to.

Mu has stabbed five innocent little piglets to death. For no reason.

"Kaori, either regain control or leave!" Takanori shouts at me.

My arms are wrapped tight around my belly. My treacherous thoughts have become moans dribbling down my trembling chin. Takanori's cold scold snaps Kentaro from mir own dark reverie and mu cuddles me and we rock together in silence.

Kairi has not glanced in our direction. The side of mir face I can see is impassive. Mu is not even grinding mir teeth anymore.

"Do you have anything to say?" Takanori asks Kairi.

No reply.

The Experienced take an indignant breath and exhale in disgust together.

"Then we have no choice. Although the slaughter of carrier boar is not forbidden, the taking of life for no reason most certainly is. You savagely executed the piglets for your own pleasure."

At this, Kairi's bowed head flicks up. Takanori pauses. Mu waits but Kairi does not fill the silence.

"We must replace the stolen life with another." Naho's arm shoots out and grips Takanori's elbow. Mu shakes mem off. "It is the Maymuan way."

The Experienced murmur assents.

"It doesn't have to be," someone screeches.

All eyes swivel to the hysteric.

Me.

Bahm.

What can I say to overturn orbits of relentless rigid rule? Kairi has finally turned to look at me and I rub the nub where my little finger used to be.

"My dear fellow Experienced, please forgive the other half for mir inability to act as a Maymuan. Mu is as undeveloped as an unnamed."

Takanori has one eyebrow raised, daring me to continue speaking. I take a deep breath. I am sick of fearing mem.

"I said, it doesn't have to be." I am shouting but I don't care. "Why does anyone have to die? Has there not been enough blood spilt? What is the point of a trial without hope of redemption? Kairi did a wicked thing but taking mir life is also wicked. Who are you to decide who lives and dies?"

Takanori snorts and rises from mir throne. "So in your delusion, your other half can take life but I must seek your permission?" Takanori swells with righteous indignation and roars, "Who am I? I am the Experienced. I decide. If I say the sun will not rise then it does not rise. If I tell the moon to hide, it hides. And if this half needs to be sacrificed to restore balance on my island then mu will die tonight."

Takanori's face is terror itself flickering in flames from the fire pits as mu preaches from mir mount.

I back away and can only whimper, "Please... can't nobody be sacrificed?"

A lucky pebble is thrown in a river to make a wish. With a splash, hope ripples in ever widening circles. If you can restrain doubt until the wish rests on the riverbed, your wish will come true. But be careful what you wish for.

My wish rests; the water is still.

It is as though I have sucked the heady perfume from the chamber. Mist lifts, fog clears. Takanori sits down with a crunch back into mir chair to ponder my words, but Naho's eyes are popping out of mir head and mir hand is covering mir open mouth.

"No. No. NO!" Kairi screams. *"Don't."*

What the ratty hell is wrong with Kairi? Mu is swivelling from me to Takanori with bright, frantic eyes.

"No, no!" Kairi dives at me, seizes my arms, and shakes me. "Take it back, Kaori. Take it back!"

Naho runs over to help Kentaro's attempts to untangle me from Kairi's grasp but mu does not let go until Takanori clears mir throat.

"Nobody will be sacrificed."

My heart soars but Naho and Kairi exchange a look of terror. Kairi's body goes limp; Kentaro manages to prop mem up. It is over. The Experienced have finished. They are gravely nodding at each other with pursed lips.

The Experienced leave their perches and gather in groups to pick over the bones of what has happened here. We are no longer worthy of their attention. I don't understand how they can hold Kairi's life in their mottled hands and then brush mem off like the sooty hunmir ash which has settled on our robes.

They may no longer be surveying us but they are still cawing over something. Okay, so they may be upset they didn't get their slab of flesh but what is wrong with Naho and Kairi? They are also squabbling over something in hushed tones.

"What is going on?" I ask.

They stop arguing. They look very similar. They share an expression that seems to say, *Get lost, Kaori.*

"Take mem back to mir hut," Naho says with kindness and a tight-lipped smile to Kentaro. Naho pats the top of Kairi's head and a spark of jealousy courses through me. Kairi makes to protest but seems to run out of energy. Kentaro leads Kairi away.

"Naho?"

"For now let's be grateful Kairi is safe."

For now? How about, *Well done, Kaori. Congratulations on saving your twin?*

What am I, chopped goat's tongue? Unbelievable.

Naho drapes mir arm over my shoulder and I let mem guide me out of the opening because I am sick of being here, sick of not understanding.

I glance back into the Experienced chamber and shiver because Takanori is smirking.

I count the plaits of my roof again but the repetition does not calm my mind. What the ratty hell happened tonight? I have lain here since Naho walked me back to my hut and I can't make any sense of it. Why was Kairi so upset and why wouldn't Naho tell me what the glance between them meant?

Outside, the earth is squashed by someone trying to move in silence. I hope it is Aito. I could use some distraction right now. But I know it isn't. Mu could never be so discreet.

It is Saki. Mu peers hopefully around the opening and I accept. I like Saki, I really do. I just sometimes find mir attention overwhelming. Aito is more relaxed, mu makes me feel like mu is not mine. With Saki I feel too sure. Too certain mu will always be there. Saki is fearless in showing mir affection whereas Aito is a coward. In every way. I knew mu would not come tonight but still I hoped.

"What happened?" Saki says.

"I don't want to talk about it."

"Is Kairi alive?"

"Yes."

Saki kneels down next to me on the floor.

"Are you okay?"

"Yes."

"I was thinking of you. I came as soon as I could."

"I know."

It is not Saki's fault mu is not Aito. I feel bad. I don't deserve mem. And mu certainly deserves better than me. Saki smells of petals and sea spray. Fresh, joyful things, not roasted hunmir wood and fear.

"I just wanted to see if you were okay," Saki says, and makes to leave. I pull mem to me and my tongue enters mir mouth. Mu tastes like salt. Saki unwraps my robe and we begin a familiar ritual. My body relaxes as Saki strokes my skin and bites my neck. Mir mouth is like honey sting and girnum wing until mu reaches the pearl between my legs. Mir tongue circles; my toes and fingers scratch the floor and I chase my breath as wave after wave of pleasure fizzles and splashes inside me. I cry out and let go. Joy crashes over me.

We roll over and I kiss my way up Saki's leg.

"What the ratty hell is that?"

Saki tries to reach for mir robe but I won't let mem. I tilt my head. It can't be.

"What is that?"

"It's nothing. Leave it."

"It's an ankh, isn't it? What is it doing up there?"

On Saki's inner thigh is an ankh. Carved into mir skin.

By Saki. It is awful. It looks fresh and deep. Mir beautiful, tight, dark skin is slashed, slack, and peeled back, exposing sore pink flesh. The opposite of an ankh. Not life but ruin. Violence. Pain.

I hand Saki mir robe. Mu puts it on and I reach for mine too. I had hoped Saki was an escape, not another trap. I can't handle this. I curl up against the wall but mu does not take the hint to leave.

"Maybe you should go now," I say.

"You mean a lot to many of us, you know," Saki says.

The opening of the hut seems to gasp as a chill sweeps into my room.

"What are you on about? What does this have to do with me?"

"It is your sign."

"No, it's not. It is our sign. All of us who hunt snake."

Saki smiles mir patient smile. I want to reach for my dagger. Mu is making me feel like I am drowning. I want mem to leave but I am desperate to know more.

"No," Saki continues, "it is *your* sign. You are the best hunter."

Saki is speaking like mu hasn't mutilated memself and I am the one who has a broken mind.

"Why would you do that to yourself?"

"Because I love you."

Mir love is a stampede of boar across my gut.

"Kaori, many Maymuans idolise you. You must know. You are the best hunter on the island and, not only that, you are different... Both you and Kairi are. But you are *more* different. You inspire us in how you stand up to Kairi."

What mu is saying is not true. I don't stand up to mem. At all. Not in the way Saki is blabbering on about. Kairi is my twin. No one else in this horrid place understands. I don't stand up to mem because I am brave. I don't know how else to be.

If I threw a coco at Saki would one hand move to catch it or would both reach out instinctively? That is how I am with Kairi. We are together. Bound. Light and dark. Without mem, who am I? Who would I be?

"In the last hunt, Kairi tried to rattle you but you confronted mem. You didn't back down and then you caught more snakes than ever before! You are special, Kaori."

This is not good. This island is not a safe place to be special. I am normal. I am the same as any other Maymuan.

Wait.

Saki said, *Many Maymuans idolise you*. So there are those who don't.

This is not good.

"I don't know what to say to you." A cold shiver trembles through my body. "I think you have made a mistake."

Now I want mem to go. Mu doesn't. Instead mu says, "Open your eyes, Kaori! Haven't you noticed the ankhs around?"

I gulp. Yes, yes, I have. But I didn't know they were for

me. Hanging from huts. Etched into dirt. I have even seen ankhs woven into braids and now branding Saki's skin.

Me. Everywhere.

"Please leave."

Saki fixes me with an intense stare and tilts mir head to the side. "Why are you ashamed of being different? I wish I were different. I wish I were like you."

If we were the same then you wouldn't be different.

Stupid buha.

I rest my head on my raised knees until mu leaves.

This is not good.

Chapter Ten

KAIRI

Kentaro is my second skin. Mu is hard but I don't want mem inside me. Not tonight. I prefer mem wrapped around my entire body. Shelter from a relentless dusk. A cloak shrouding the inevitable.

"Are you okay?" Kentaro whispers in my ear. "Did something happen to your neck?"

The memory of Takanori slicing through the neck of the farmer in the white robe is sticking my hand to my throat. As if my fingers could protect me from mir blade.

"It's nothing," I say.

Kentaro squeezes me and I cling on tight. I hate that I need mem. I hate having an anchor to this island. And I hate Kaori. Mu has no idea what mu has done. Mir pride in the chamber was reckless.

I can't believe mu chose my trial as the moment to rebel. Why now? What's the point of rebelling if you haven't mastered the rules? I suppose I can't talk; sneaky snake

Takanori has plucked me like a bugir. After all I have done for mem.

Come and tell me.

I can't.

Tell me, Takanori, to my face.

No!

Coward.

"Where are you going?"

"I going to…" Why am I explaining myself to mem? I get up and stride over to the opening before I lose my nerve.

"Don't," Kentaro says.

"Don't what?"

"Don't go to mem. It will make things worse."

"I have to."

"You might be seen."

The night is black. In my sleeping robe I will be undetectable.

"Please don't go."

See? An anchor.

"I will come with you," Kentaro says, tossing off the thin gobu blanket we were cuddling under. Mu joins me at the opening.

Now that makes me laugh. As if Kentaro could come with me.

"You're not supposed to know I see mem."

"But I do know."

It was a weak mistake but the burden was too heavy to carry alone.

"I have to talk to mem. I have to know why." I kiss Kentaro and enter the night.

The trees shiver as I leave the refuge of the huts and enter the forest. Crickets rattle gnarled tree bark. Moist moss groans as I creep further into the depths. Stars peer through crooked branches, inquisitive eyes questioning my stealth. Owl hoots pepper the insect rattle. The forest pulses with unseen souls. I feel a warm prickling sensation in my spine. There is someone as unwelcome as I in this gloom.

"My dear May."

I run, scattering dead leaves and broken sticks until I fall into mir arms. I bury my head in the soft folds of mir robe. I try to be what mu wants but I am betrayed when my tears soak the red fabric. Mu holds me close until the trees flutter and remind us soon dusk will become dawn.

"What happened?" I sob. "You promised to always protect me."

Takanori pushes me away so we are no longer embracing.

"I have protected you. You are still breathing, aren't you?"

No thanks to you.

In the chamber it was too close. Death was by my side, mir rancid breath in my face.

Get a grip.

I can't.

You must.

Bahm.

Takanori wipes my tears away with fingertips like sand, erasing my truth with rough, careless scratches.

"That's enough now, May."

"Can't you call me Kairi?"

Takanori scoffs. "What, after a little bit of pressure you are afraid to be a May?"

I shrivel under mir disdainful gaze.

"I am disappointed in you, *Kairi*." Takanori rolls my name around mir mouth like a shrewd spider rolls a fat, juicy fly in its web before devouring it.

I wipe my eyes and stand straighter. Takanori smiles.

"You are special, May. You have a special mission. You are not like the others. You are not like that half-cockroach. Though I did admire mem tonight."

"You admire mem?" I say, unable to control the tremble in my voice.

"Yes, mu showed some courage tonight. Cockroach does not seem so inclined to feel sorry for memself."

"That's not fair."

"Perhaps, but when the Mu is more than the May, what else am I to conclude?"

"Kaori is not better than me!" I scream.

Ratty cockroach Kaori.

Takanori, as death did in mir chamber, leans in close. "You are May. You are the first and the last pure being on this island. You have the everlasting fire from the depths of the island within you. You will burn for eternity! Nothing can destroy fire."

"Well... water could," I mumble without thinking.

"What?"

"Nothing."

"Water could?" Takanori kicks me. "What is wrong with you? Why are you so pathetic? Water can? Fire can *fry* water. Are you afraid of water? Then why am I wasting my time with you? A coward can never rule this island. How many times do I have to tell you? You must be strong. You must be ruthless. And stop crying. Real May do not cry. It is embarrassing. I am embarrassed for you."

Takanori's admonishments ricochet around my body, perforating my organs. I don't want to be weak. I can't help it. I don't know what to do. How to be. I don't know how to appease Takanori but I know I desperately want to please mem.

"I am sorry, Experienced. You have given me a great opportunity but I have not been grateful. Please forgive me."

Takanori gives me a familiar look. It is the look of Kaori and the snake I forced mem to give me in the cave. Only a flicker, but I catch it. Then Takanori fills mir eyes with warmth and mu pats me on the shoulder.

"The island needs you."

Mu is going to make me do something horrible. Mir requests are never good for my soul. But I have no choice.

"Okay."

"Follow me."

I follow Takanori through the forest. Mu crushes any fallen leaves and twigs in mir path without a care for the racket mu is making. What will it be like when I have such power? I am sick of skulking around this island. I want to be free. Free to be myself in the open. The next best thing to getting off this island would be to rule it.

An owl hoots next to Takanori; its flat, open face and thin nose remind me of Kentaro. Takanori, without breaking stride, punches it off the branch and it lands with a dull thump.

Ratty hell.

I step over it.

Takanori has not glanced back so I pivot and pick it up. It is warm and alive, just in shock. Its little chest heaves, trying to catch its hoot. I ruffle its chalk-white feathers and stand it upright on the forest floor.

I pursue Takanori's path and soon we exit the dense tangle of forest and approach the neat hand-sown crop fields. Long lines of tall green cobs sway in the advancing dawn. Takanori dives headfirst into their heart but I hesitate. They tower over me with a sneer. Even the wiliest creature could be ensnared in their midst.

"May!" yells Takanori.

I enter the maize.

"Hold onto my robe."

I snatch the swell of Takanori's sleeve and mu guides me through the cobs like a goat leading its kid. Despite the rising light it is dark and cold between the cob stalks. My skin prickles and I instinctively reach for my absent gamgam. The potent scent of boar penetrates my nostrils. The cobs are fed boar dung so with each step the stench becomes muskier as the dark soil is disturbed. My heart thumps and blood rushes to my head, pounding my ears.

Attack.

But there is no foe.

Attack.

There is only Takanori. I yank on mir sleeve.

"A few more steps and we will be out," Takanori snaps.

The cobs end and we step into a large golden clearing. I blink as my eyes adjust to the creeping dawn. In the centre of the clearing is a huge tree. The thick branches lurch under the weight of dense leaves. It is impressive that it is still standing. The legs are buried in rich, dark soil.

"Wow," I say.

Takanori flinches. Mu is probably going to make me hack at its ankles until it collapses. I will do it. Maybe it is the right thing to do. It has too much pressure on its shoulders.

"I saw you," Takanori says, without looking from the overburdened tree.

Where? This could be anything. Silence is wise. I don't know if mu means stealing cocos or honeycomb. Or something with Kentaro. Or even with Kaori.

Bahm.

Takanori is pulling the silence until it is all sinewy and misshapen. I don't care. I am keeping my mouth shut.

Mu will break first because mu has obviously brought me here to do some sick thing and can't help but sermonise it.

"I saw you."

Off mu goes. I knew mu couldn't resist.

"That day when we lost the farmers."

Oh bahm.

"You shouldn't have been there. You shouldn't have seen."

Mu is not scolding me; there is pleasure in mir voice.

"How did you feel that day, May?"

"I don't feel. You have taught me well, Experienced," I say.

"Very good, but this time it is okay. You were still underdeveloped then. Weakness was to be expected. Tell me, how did you feel?"

I felt terrified and every night since you have chopped off heads in my hut.

"I felt okay. They must have done something to deserve it."

Takanori lowers mir head and narrows mir eyes.

"So even if you could have prevented their sacrifice you wouldn't have?"

What is the correct answer? What does mu want to hear?

"I don't know."

"For light to shine one must know shade. Sometimes a great leader must show mercy for our inferiors to know our power."

I don't agree.

"Yes, Experienced. I would have prevented the sacrifice."

"Correct."

What now?

104

"Look into the leaves on the tree."

The ascending sun has illuminated the dark leaves. Nestled amongst the branches are what look like huge yellow flower buds. It is difficult to see. Maybe they are more like plump honeycomb pods? The sun has brought with it a strange noise. Rasping squeaks like angry rats swung by their tails screech from the tree. There is something at each pod, poking and prodding.

"I don't understand," I say.

"They are gubaga."

I have never heard of such a thing.

"They are scavengers. They fly to this tree to build their nests and when their offspring hatch they will consume our entire crop field."

No way.

How is this possible?

I know every creature on this island. Where have they flown from? It was locusts who destroyed the crops. That was what the Maymuans where told. So, the thing poking at each pod is a carrier gubaga protecting its maymu?

"What are they? Are they like a girnum?"

"Have you ever heard a girnum sing such a wicked song? They are to girnums what Kaori is to you. They must be destroyed."

How? What does Takanori expect me to do? Pierce them all with my arrows? I haven't even got my bow with me. The Experienced have all my weapons because of the trial.

"Here, use these."

Takanori reaches into mir robe pocket and withdraws

one of my arrow heads and a bright green stone with red veins.

"It is a bloodstone. You can keep it."

Weird.

The stone warms in my hand and the veins glow iridescently under the green skin.

"Thanks." I make to put the gifts in my pocket but Takanori tuts.

"They are for now."

The stone goes cold.

"Strike the arrow head against the stone and save our crops. And the farmers."

"But the nests must be filled with little ones."

"And?"

"But after what you said about the piglets…"

"These are not piglets."

"But still…."

"But nothing. I have told you to do something. Do it."

The fate of the piglets has not left my soul and now this. I meet Takanori's stare and recoil as a forked black tongue flickers in a pink mouth.

"Strike."

If I don't, Maymuans die. If I do, these gubaga die. If the Maymuans starve again, Takanori will have to kill the farmers. No blood splashed on my skin. Whereas if I incinerate these creatures, each soul is on me.

Takanori will give the island to Kaori.

Never. Takanori despises Kaori.

It would be the worst punishment for you.

So?

Then it is exactly what Takanori would do.

"Don't do what you decided in the chamber," I say. If I blindly do what Takanori says, mu will think I am no more than a dirty carrier. I can't believe they create life and then hand it over and say, *There you go, Experienced, please take my strength.*

Why are they stupid enough to do that? If the carriers ever realise their true power and value, the Experienced are finished. Anyway, forget the carriers, what Takanori is planning to do instead of executing me is wrong. Even I know it.

"No."

Takanori refuses my demand without flinching. Mu is not at all surprised I asked. I knew as soon as Takanori said nobody will be sacrificed what mu really meant. Takanori can't penetrate my mind without leaving a bit of memself behind. I know how Takanori's mind works as much as mu thinks mu knows mine.

"Don't do what you decided in the chamber or I won't do what you are asking now," I say.

The forked tongue flickers once again but Takanori nods in agreement. The bloodstone begins to warm in my hand. My wrist spasms as I strike the arrow head against the stone. Nothing happens.

"Again. Like you are trying to slice it in half," Takanori pants with anticipation.

I saw at the stone and bright sparks shower my hand. I catch the sparks and make them a downpour of flames.

"Good, May! Yes! Now quick, launch them at the tree."

I drench the tree with fire and the clearing fills with agonized screams.

"Get them all." Takanori shoves me and points. "There are some flying away!"

My fire reaches for those fleeing. They are incinerated in the air. Gorgeous green-winged souls burned to a crisp. They shriek with agony as I strike again and again. The wind reeks of charred feathers and scorched nests. Torched bodies reduced to ash then dispersed by the gentle rise breeze.

Takanori is giddy with excitement. Mu is hopping from foot to foot in a perverse ecstasy. Burnt feathers smell horrible. As do burnt nests. And burnt souls. But still Takanori dances.

The tree is weeping from the cruelty. Its once brimming branches now flop in defeat. Enough. I suck the blaze back to me and stumble to my knees. I whisper, "Namu May Mu," into the cinder-smothered grass.

Takanori leaves me alone. I miss the souls' screaming. I even miss Takanori's sick celebration. The silence is too quiet. Too empty. Too much to bear. Dawn is over. The sun wakes impotent, unable to redeem the charred life below.

My throat is dry.

I need water.

Chapter Eleven

KAORI

Water tugs gently at my hair. Tender ripples fan my curls out like an oyster shell. The cool water soothes my scalp. It was aching before I untied my braids. I don't know why I keep braiding them so tight. It is like a loose curl is a secret I want to keep close, under wraps, to myself.

A head bumps my hips. I tap my gratitude on the hard dappled shell. The turtle is nudging me to sit up and appreciate the sunrise. It has been seven sunrises since my outburst in the Experienced chamber. Seven rises since I saw Saki's self-mutilation. I prefer to lie with my ears submerged in the cove and my eyes shut tight but the turtles won't let me.

The sun is hope. Regardless of our fear, pain, or doubt the sun rises. From the cove I have a clear view of it bursting from the land through the trees to nestle in the clear blue sky.

When the sun rises so must I. My sleeveless robe is covered in sand but I wrap it around my wet body anyway. I like the gritty feeling against my skin. I can't be bothered to fix my hair but I have to.

One of the many reasons I love this cove is the abundance of mimin. Their long stems wobble in the short grass by the shore. I carefully detach the big head and pluck the yellow petals. I put them in my pocket out of habit. I don't want to see Saki but I still store mir favourite fragrance. I scratch my fingernails over the dark bald centre of the mimin and fill my palm with seeds.

I find I can extract the most oil if I pound the seeds while imagining Takanori's face. Though thinking of Aito also works well. I can't believe mu has not been to see me. Stupid slug licker.

My oiled hair is easy to braid. By the time the turtles have swum to the rockier side of the cove in search of sea snails, I am done. Back to good old Maymuan conformity. I am finding it harder and harder to be here. The stuff with Saki has really freaked me out.

Everywhere I look now I can see ankhs. It is scary to think of influencing these Maymuans. I don't want their admiration… but I have noticed the ones without any kind of ankh. I can't help noticing. It is the other hunters who don't hunt snake. The Maymuans with rural duties hang tiny straw ankhs from their hut openings but who would want them on their side in a battle?

The Experienced and all the other hunters versus me,

the snake hunters, and the ones who make baskets and grow grain. We wouldn't stand a chance.

Why am I wasting my energy thinking this way? There is no *us versus them*. I am turning into my twin.

"You may as well come out, Kairi," I say.

Kairi jumps up from a cluster of mimin, bashing their heads and scattering their petals.

"Be careful, bonehead."

"How did you know I was here?"

"I could smell you."

"Very funny. Really, how did you know?"

"If you want to spy on people you shouldn't stink of hippo dung."

Kairi smiles despite mir best efforts not to.

"What do you want?"

"Nothing."

"Okay, well go and want nothing somewhere else."

"Why do you spend so much time here?" Kairi looks around, oblivious to the cove's beauty.

"Why do you spend so much time fumbling in Kentaro's robe?"

"I don't fumble," Kairi says with a smirk.

"Ew. You know what? I don't want to know."

"What's going on with you and ratface?"

Mu means Aito.

"Who?"

"Okay, whatever. I don't care anyway. But you should know if you ever get trampled, Aito will poo memself and cry like a carrier."

True. Not the carrier part – I hate how mu denigrates them – but mu is right about the full-of-poo part.

"You're the leader, aren't you? If your team is weak it is because of you."

Bahm.

Too far. Kairi looks hurt. But why? I have barely scratched mem. What is going on with mem? Why is mu here?

"Have you been okay, Kairi? You know, since the thing with the Experienced."

"Do you want to go and get honeycomb?"

What?

It is so random. Together? We haven't had a forage for ages.

"Erm, okay, yeah. If you want."

"But I don't want to be out all day, especially with you,"

Ha! There mu is.

Kairi has not gone after all.

"I was thinking we could take a shortcut down by the river. I can't be bothered to tramp through the forest."

Kairi tries to say it all casually, as if mu has only just thought of using the river as a shortcut. At least now I know the real reason mu needs me. I don't care. I want to go with mem. I pick up a piece of hard flat rock from the shore and we head towards the forest.

After the openness of the cove, the forest, even in the gorgeous rise sunlight, is dark, dank, and dismal. What must it do to a Maymuan to have an island duty which means they have to be in here all the time?

It must be even worse for Kairi, who has to pass through the forest to venture even deeper into the jungle. Creepy. I try and keep up with Kairi but mu is on mir terrain. I am not as sure footed on the dips and slumps of the undergrowth.

"Aaargh!"

We must be close to the river because I have sunk waist-deep into forest sludge.

"Help!"

"For mymig's sake," Kairi says, but mu is scanning the forest for something to dislodge me from this gunk. A bright-eyed yellow-feathered buha squawks from the tree above.

"Up there, look," I say, pointing frantically towards the buha. "Get that vine, throw it over the lower branch, and then I can hold one end and you can pull me out with the other."

Kairi scales the bent trunk and retrieves the vine.

"Are you ready? Because if you don't catch it I am not getting another one."

"All right, stop blathering and throw it." I am pleased to catch the stupid vine. "Pull!"

"Oh my ratty hell, this is worse than dragging a boar." Mir own mention of a boar seems to droop Kairi into a morose rut, making the vine go limp. I do feel sorry for mir sour memories but now is not the time. I am sinking further and further into this smelly sludge.

"Kairi!"

"Huh?"

"Pull the vine, you ratty idiot!"

Kairi wrenches the vine and I move a bit.

"I can't do it all, Kaori. Kick your legs and get yourself out."

"I can't move my legs."

"You can try."

"I can't."

"You are worse than Aito and Tetsu. They got stuck in this exact same spot but at least they could kick memselves out. Ratty traitors…"

I kick as hard as I can before Kairi becomes morose thinking about the pack and boars again. The mud belches and burps around me, Kairi yanks the vine, and I slip out and land with a plop on much firmer mulch.

"Thanks."

"You look disgusting."

All right, thanks Kairi.

"And you stink."

"So do you," I say.

"No, I don't."

I scrape a handful of sludge off my knee and throw it at mem.

"Now you do!" I shout, and run past mem towards the gurgle of the river.

The river is as bleak as the rest of the forest. The water is murky and covered in a glaze of scum.

"Where is the raft?" I ask innocently.

"What do you mean? Do your thing."

Kairi is spluttering. It is fun to watch.

"What thing?"

"Call them."

"Who?"

I should put Kairi out of mir misery but this is too good. Stupid Aito has been running mir mouth off again. There is no way Kairi will admit Aito taught mem something. I brought Aito here in secret.

Mymig mem.

Kairi is fuming.

Oh dear.

"Forget it then. Let's just go back."

"Forget it then. Let's just go back," I repeat in my best sing-song voice. Mu is going to blow.

Stupid idiot.

"Okay, well, erm... I'll see you later, Kaori."

Again I have an uneasy feeling. What is wrong with mem? Usually mu destroys me with snide remarks but I have the upper hand and I don't like it.

"No, no, I was kidding. They are here."

Kairi's eyes are shining and mu looks expectantly at the water. "What do we have to do?"

"Kneel down and whisper, 'Namu Oooh Ooooh'. They need to feel the vibrations."

Something may be wrong with Kairi but I don't get many opportunities to play with mem.

"Namu ooooooooooooooooooooooh," Kairi croons into the water.

"Move out of the way, slug brains." I shove mem away from the banks of the water and I dip my hands in. They do need vibrations but not from Kairi humming like a fool. Ha! I can't believe mu did it. I pulse the murky waters until the film of dark green scum bubbles and froths. Kairi yelps when a long, pointy pink nose pierces the gloomy membrane.

"Wow. Look, there is another one!"

Kairi is so excited, I feel a bit bad for playing tricks on mem earlier.

"Look, there is a *massive* one. You should ride that one, Kaori. You don't want to break the back of a little one."

I take it back.

There are at least ten river dolphins circling. Their protruding fins create little pink pyramids gliding on slimy moss.

"Pick one and get on."

Kairi of course picks the dolphin with the sharpest fin. Mu straddles the dolphin and starts clipping mir heel against the dolphin's side as if to say go. Honestly, how can mu be my twin? Mu is so impatient.

"Wait for me to get in the water. I have to tell them where to go."

Kairi looks at me with squinted eyes, daring me to ask mem to chant into the water again.

"Don't worry, only I need to go in. Stop kicking the poor thing."

I wade out and place my arms over the dolphins either side of me.

"Why do you have two? Are you really too heavy to ride one? Shame."

Think of the sweet taste of honeycomb at the end of this river and ignore mem.

"No. How can I influence the water and tell them where to go if I am not actually in the water, slug breath?"

"Hurry up then and let's go."

We ride the pink dolphins down the gloomy river. Kairi has a much better experience than me because mu is above the scummy water. I may have washed off the stinky sludge from my legs but it has been replaced with neck-deep foamy river gunk. Vile. At least this time I am not with someone I am trying to impress. When I brought Aito I forgot about the slop and slime but it did result in us disrobing under the waterfall.

Why am I replaying moments with that slug?

I should have brought Saki. But then mu would probably start carving ankhs around the dolphin's blowhole. Every Maymuan on this island is a freak.

"Watch out!"

Something lands with a plonk and a splash in front of me.

"Here comes another one!"

Plonk and *splash* again. What the ratty hell? I peer over the fin of the dolphin and, hopping up and down amongst the tall reeds on the banks of the river, is a small agitated monkey.

"Look on the other side!" Kairi says.

Bahm.

Several agitated monkeys, launching cocos at my head. This is exactly what I need now, to be stuck between two dolphins and have my head split open by a mad monkey's renegade coco. Kairi is enjoying memself, and as we ride further down the river the monkeys follow us. Kairi catches cocos, cracks them open, and drains the milk.

"Do you want some?" mu asks me, knowing I do, but I can't. "Suppose you have your hands full."

I hope Kairi catches a few in mir face. Mu is throwing some back at the monkeys which is stupid because then they have even more to lob at us. Despite the fact Kairi is the one goading them, they seem to be targeting me.

Why? The lone monkey on the opposite bank is chasing us down the river too. Whenever there is a hanging branch, mu scrambles across it but none of the branches reach further than halfway over the river.

"I think it wants help."

"What?" Kairi says, mid-slurp.

"The monkey on its own. I think it wants to get across."

"I'm not carrying it."

I didn't ask you to but I was about to.

"I don't think I can direct myself to the bank and grab it," I say.

"You won't have to grab it. If it wants a lift it will jump on your head."

And scratch my eyes out probably.

I duck as a coco whizzes over my shoulder.

"I don't know."

"Leave it then. They can't chase us the entire way," Kairi says.

"But then it will be stuck."

"So?"

"But I feel bad for it."

"Get it then and I will wait here."

Wait? You won't be going anywhere without my dolphin guidance, dear twin.

I direct my dolphins towards the stranded monkey. It springs even higher in the grass but no more cocos have splashed near me since I began to approach it.

I get close enough to see the poor, wide-eyed thing. I wait for the monkey to climb aboard but instead the reeds along the bank tremble. Many clawed hands reach out to grab me and drag me from between the dolphins.

"Aargh!"

The dolphins reverse but several monkey claws are stuck in my braids. The warm, sweet scent of their bristly bodies fills my nose as they leap all over my head and their jaws snap with fury.

"Stick your head in the water," Kairi shouts, and when my face is submerged I hear the dull clunk of a coco slamming into monkey torso. Kairi scoops up more cocos and whacks the monkeys until I am free. The dolphins don't need me to tell them to zoom down the river.

"Ratty hell!" Kairi says. "See? This is what I mean when I say you have to stop thinking everything is good and as it seems. They would have torn you apart and devoured every last lump of flesh."

I don't have a response. I can't believe the sneaky tricky monkey.

"You could have let them have a nibble of your belly. Would have done you both a favour."

"Watch out! Coco!"

Kairi ducks my imaginary coco. We both laugh and we don't stop until the river narrows. The dolphins have taken us as far as they can. We wade over to the bank and haul ourselves out of the water. The dolphins leap out of the river in farewell.

"It is good how you can control them."

Wow, a compliment.

"I have to wash this forest juice off," I say.

"Forest juice? That's disgusting," Kairi says with a smirk.

We trek towards the pounding sound of water drenching rock. I dive into the cool, clear lagoon and swim until I am directly under the waterfall. I sigh as the downpour rinses my skin, braids, and robe clean of smelly river and sharp, angry monkey claws.

"It's nice here, isn't it?" Kairi says with mir usual underappreciation of beauty.

Lush, languid frog-green tendrils caress the shimmering turquoise pool. Clouds bob in the mist of the waterfall, fluffy and plump. A place to rest, to catch my breath before the plunge. Deep below the lagoon, beyond the river and streams to the ocean, a voyage to retrieve an abandoned black pearl and return it to the light.

"Yes. It is."

I know I can come back here whenever I want, but I like to stand for a moment and absorb the sublime sight of the lagoon, so I never forget. Because one rise I will stand here and it will be the last time.

"I have never bothered to come to this part of the forest," Kairi says, interrupting my thoughts. "Which way is it from here?"

Kairi does have a spectacular talent for unceremoniously waking me from my dreams.

"Head that way and you will recognise the path again," I say, pointing back into the gloom.

We re-enter the forest and Kairi quickly gets mir bearings.

"Through there is the grassland," Kairi says, pointing at a ray of light shining through a slit in the dense undergrowth. The space between the trees becomes wider as we approach the light and we enter a dry golden expanse. A merciless sun burns the back of my neck and dries my robe as we peer at the tall, wide-branched trees dotted around the space.

Kairi makes a low whistle. We squint into the cloudless sky, waiting for a response. Kairi whistles again.

"What's wrong? Where is mu?" I ask.

"I don't know."

"Keep trying. It's too hot for me; I am going to sit under this tree."

"Well, I'm not standing out here getting burnt if you're going to lie down there."

"Shut up and keep whistling," I say.

I plonk myself down under the nearest tree. Kairi insists on sitting right next to me without whistling.

"Why aren't you whistling?"

"My mouth is too dry. You whistle."

"Maybe we should walk for a bit and see if mu is further out."

"Oh yes, Kaori, let's do that, because I really feel like getting eaten by a jungle cat. Weren't the monkeys enough for you?"

"Do you promise if we walk out further you will get eaten?"

Kairi smiles. Then screams, "Get off!"

I can't stop laughing. The whistle has been answered. A little genmo has swooped down on Kairi and is trying to peck mem to death.

"Do something to help!" Kairi shrieks, failing to swot away the determined genmo.

"You shouldn't cheat mem out of honeycomb."

"I didn't."

Mu must have. Genmo are kind creatures except when double-crossed.

"That's enough now. Come on." I hold out my hand to the genmo and mu struts up my arm and affectionately pecks at my ear.

"Shall we forgive mem?" I ask the genmo. Mu flies from my shoulder and gives Kairi one last jab on the forehead. Then, with a high-pitched tweet, mu whizzes through the air and lands on the branch above us.

"Let's go." I pull a well-reprimanded Kairi to mir feet and we chase the genmo from tree to tree. Mu chirps happily as we stumble over the bumpy terrain and try to keep up.

The genmo finally settles in the lower branches of the tallest tree we have passed so far. Mu makes another high-pitched tweet.

"Had to be, didn't it?" Kairi grumbles and begins rummaging in the dry undergrowth.

"It is no fun if it is too easy," I say, but I am a little apprehensive. The tree is so high I can't see the top. Looking up, the tangled dense branches seem impenetrable.

Kairi has collected random twigs and strands of long grass. Mu begins weaving a crude basket.

"This is when we need Kentaro," I say.

"I don't think this is so bad," Kairi says, holding up mir lopsided gaping attempt.

"Erm..." I don't want to wind Kairi up before my life depends on mem, so instead of replying I approach the tree. I stroke the gnarly bark. The tree has a long straight section but after about five times my body length it bends. Reaching up high, I whack the rock from the cove against the trunk. A chip of bark falls out and I use the hand hold to pull myself up.

"They are too far apart, Kaori. Make them closer together."

"Can't you reach up?"

"I have to carry the ratty basket as well. You don't."

"Shut up and reach up."

"I can see right up your robe."

"That's sick. Stop looking then."

"I can't. It's like watching a hippo climb a tree."

I drop a bit of bark on mir head.

It is much easier when we reach the bend. We can crawl up the trunk as long as we ignore the swarm of red ants biting our ankles and wrists.

"Are we there yet?"

"Shush, I am trying to hear the buzz."

We crawl further up the tree but I can't hear the tell-tale song of bees.

"Are we there yet?"

Would it be so bad to back kick mem off this tree? But I suppose I need the basket.

"Ouch."

"Are we there?"

The angry red lump on my hand with a stinger protruding from the centre says yes.

"Snap the thinner branch there," I say.

Kairi reaches out for a branch above mem and almost loses mir footing. "Not that one, bonehead! The one next to you with loads of leaves on."

This must be what it is like being a rearer.

"Feel the leaves. Are they dry?"

"Yes," Kairi says.

I wonder if we can get a spark off this rock but I haven't got my dagger with me.

"Can you get a spark off this?" I ask holding up the shore rock.

"No," Kairi scoffs, "I can't make fire out of nothing. Can you shower us with water from here?"

I could use the clouds but I don't think that is what mu wants to hear.

"What are we going to do then?"

"Move out of the way. I will stick my hand in and grab some." Kairi hands me the leaves and tries to barge past, almost knocking me off my perch.

"Look! It is crawling with bees. If you want stingers sticking out of every hole in your body then go ahead but wait until after I have climbed down."

Kairi screams in frustration. "What do you want to do?"

"We need to light this and get some smoke going." I wave the branch in mir face. Kairi rummages in mir pocket and pulls out a weird red and green stone and an arrow head.

"What's this?"

"Strike that against this," Kairi says handing both over to me. I roll the green stone in my hand. Red veins glow inside the green skin. It is beautiful.

"Where did you get this?"

"Come on! Rub that against it."

"Will you get me one?"

"Kaori, for ratty hell's sake, hurry up and light the stupid thing!"

I am trying but it won't work. Kairi takes my failure way too personally. Every time I strike the arrow-head against the rock mu flinches.

"You will have to do it," I say.

"I can't."

"Here you are." I try and hand them back to mem.

"I can't. Don't make me." Kairi is shaking.

"Okay, okay. Calm down a bit though. What's wrong with you? You're being a freak."

Mu is still shaking. My frustration with mem gives me more force and I manage to light the leaves. I am sick of spending time with mem and I want to go back. I give the stone and the arrow back to Kairi and mu puts them in mir pocket.

"Are you doing this or do I have to?"

Kairi ignores me. Mu seems to have got lost somewhere inside the smouldering leaves.

"Will you at least hold this so I can stick my hand in?"

Kairi shakes mir head.

Oh for mymig's sake.

I wave the smoking branch in the direction of the bee pod and the buzz becomes a hum. I can hardly see the hole through the thick smoke but I can just about make out a dark space which is not crawling with little yellow and black fuzzy bodies.

"Can you at least pass me the basket?" I hiss at Kairi but mu doesn't crawl over with it. Instead, mu holds it out, but I can't reach it.

I plunge my hand into the hole and pull out a chunk of honeycomb dripping with golden honey. I throw it at Kairi. It lands with a splat on the front of mir robe. Mu peels it off and places it in the basket.

Something is definitely not right because mu would either throw it back at me or start eating it straight away. I throw a few more pieces at mem. Some land in the basket but those that don't Kairi peels off in a dazed, detached way that makes my skin crawl.

We climb back down the tree. I deliver a golden grub-filled wedge to the genmo. Mu seems to read the mood because it gives a subdued peep and flies off with its reward hanging from its mouth. I pass a piece of honeycomb to Kairi and mu sucks it in silence. Mu doesn't even complain as I crunch my way through three pieces in quick succession.

"Your arm is covered in stingers," Kairi says.

"I know," I answer, "so is your chest." Stingers fill the gap in mir robe where I splatted the honeycomb.

I go and collect some guma leaves. When I return, Kairi is still mournfully sucking on mir honeycomb. Is mu not going to sort mir own stingers out?

"Should I?" I say, pointing at mir red raw chest. Mu doesn't respond so I carefully pluck out the stingers. I smear honey over the lumps and gently pat guma leaves on top to seal in the honey.

"Thanks," Kairi mumbles when I have finished.

I start plucking the stingers on my arm but Kairi reaches out and holds my hand. It hurts. I feel torment placed in my palm, an offering of pain so burdensome I fear my heart may crack from the strain. I open my hand. It isn't pain or torment; it is the green stone. I don't understand. Kairi closes my hand around the stone and begins plucking out the rest of the stingers from my arm. Mu smooths soothing honey and lays guma leaves on my damaged flesh.

Chapter Twelve

KAIRI

I don't want to be near the dolphins again. I would rather trample through the forest in the shadows. The lost bloodstone burns a hole in my pocket. I shouldn't have given it to mem. I should have buried it. Destroyed it. Takanori gave it to me because I am special.

You are special.

I shouldn't have given it away. It belongs to May. Kaori keeps trying to chat to me as mu stumbles and trips on the forest floor.

The sun is sinking but we will be back by the huts before it is laid to rest in the dark earth.

"Something has them all worked up," Kaori says as we approach the huts. The Maymuans are whispering to each other at their openings.

"They sound like crickets, don't they?"

Kaori's careless description is a vicious punch to my

stomach. They do sound like crickets. Crickets riddled with fear and glee.

Bahm.

Please, no.

I start to run.

"Where are you going?" Kaori yells.

"I have to get ghili. And Kentaro!"

"Ghili? Wait! Wait!"

I run from mem and sprint to Kentaro's hut.

"Where have you been? I have been looking everywhere for you. Have you heard?"

I can barely respond, the run has left me so breathless.

"With. Kaori. Get. Bag," I pant.

"What?"

"I was with Kaori. Get the ratty water bags!" I say, gasping for air.

Kentaro is not doing what I have told mem. Mu is staring with a dumb look on mir face.

"Get the water bags!" I shout.

Mu reaches for them.

"How many do you have?"

"We have our two and Kaori has one."

Mu made Kaori one?

"Mu saw mine and asked me to make mem one," Kentaro answers, reading my face.

"It doesn't matter. Go and get it from mem and take them all and fill them with goat's milk."

"Why?"

"What do you mean why? Because I said so!"

"But the temple... You know what they are saying is happening there soon."

"Yes. For mymig's sake, that is why you have to go now then meet me there."

"Where are you going?"

"To pick ghili!"

I race from the hut and barge through the filthy Maymuans who are beginning to swarm. I run in the opposite direction. The blaze in my lungs is scorching my insides. I leap over low hedges until I find the field full of dangling bright-red spears. I try and only touch the green stalks but the quantity I need means touching the red skin. My fingers are on fire. My eyes are watering but my pockets are full.

I have to get back to the Experienced temple before it is too late.

Chapter Thirteen

KAORI

What was Kairi on about? What use is ghili right now? Before I could unravel my tangled thoughts, a sea of bodies sweeps me down the mud path between the huts into the forest. At first, they were standing there, chattering like normal – well, not entirely like normal; they were jabbering at a higher volume and with more animated hand gestures than usual – then they began to form larger groups and, like a flock of nullos, they convened on the path and flew into the forest, swooping me along with them.

The cheerful chirrup of crickets has now become the ominous rattle of land snakes. Our frenzied throng throbs through the dark forest. My palms are sweating. I wipe them on my robe and smear the last residue of honey onto the fabric.

I try to smile at the Maymuan next to me but it is not

returned. I search for a friendly face but I can't find any. I see many familiar faces but no friends.

Crisp leaves crunch and dry twigs snap as they trespass over the forest thicket. Knotted wooden limbs flail in protest at their unceremonious invasion but they march on regardless. I am alone in this crowd.

Looking up, I see the falling sunlight cannot pierce the dense foliage. The branches and leaves have intertwined, scrambling over each other in their haste to squeeze the light from this place. Smothering us. Withholding all that could nourish and save us.

I stop but the flock refuses. I am dragged forwards until the leaves scatter and the trees thin. The forest spits us out and we land with a splat on manicured grass.

The Experienced temple looms.

I bump into the Maymuans surrounding me but instead of retreating from physical contact as usual, they close in tight. I fear I will be crushed to death, the air squashed out of my lungs by this herd edging towards the steps of the temple.

The pounding of a nunum triggers mass chanting. I would recognise the rhythm anywhere. The faint scratch that follows each pound; Takanori's sharp yellow fingernails clawing the taut snakeskin between each beat.

Everyone is chanting "Namu May Mu", shoulders lurch and sharp elbows nudge me into joining their rippling sway. Eager zealous bodies stink like boar meat left out for too long in the sun. Without the crowd around me I would stumble and fall. Silver bees swarm under my eyelids.

"Move!"

Someone is shouting and causing a commotion behind me. The Maymuans around me scatter and I stumble backwards.

"Catch mem quickly, Kentaro, or we will never be able to get mem back up."

Firm hands catch me underneath my armpits. I turn to thank Kentaro but it is Kairi. Kentaro is laden down with three megg bags overflowing with what looks like milk.

"What's that?" I ask, pointing at the bags.

Kentaro begins to reply but Kairi interrupts mem, "Here, take one." Kairi takes a bag for memself and hands me one.

"What am I supposed to do with this?" I ask.

"Get ready. As soon as they get up the steps we have to run behind them."

There are so many questions to ask, like why is Kairi's robe all misshapen and, more importantly, what is going on? But I am distracted by the fact that my armpits are stinging. Thankfully, the rest of the crowd is now avoiding us so at least the silver bees have dispersed.

Kairi is focused on the steps up to the pyramid. I catch Kentaro's eye and mu gives a stiff little nod with a grimace as if to say, *here we go*. Kentaro looks like Kairi. Whatever is about to happen, they are in it together.

The pounding of the nunum is shaking the ground as the Experienced approach. I peep between the lurching heads of the Maymuans. My stomach flips at what I see.

It can't be.

My mouth hangs open but no words come.

It can't be.

I shove the Maymuans out of my way and scramble, kicking and punching, to the front of the crowd. I can faintly hear Kairi telling me to wait but my body has its own agenda. I burst out of the front line and can no longer hope my eyes are deceiving me.

In front of the gaudy red-robed procession of Experienced is a little one, obscured before by the fully matured bodies of the crowd. Mu is stumbling over the hem of a far-too-long white robe. Mir fuzzy black halo is wobbling. Mir eyes are glazed but from mir mouth pours a heart-breaking melody. It is an unnamed.

The unnamed I saw practising joy in the temple.

I can't believe what I am seeing. My head swivels from mem to the Experienced. Takanori is engrossed in banging the nunum. What did mu say in their chamber? *Nobody will be sacrificed.*

Nobody?

My stomach flips.

Nobody.

An unnamed.

Oh bahm, this is my fault.

This is Takanori's revenge. *Nobody* will be sacrificed. The unnameds do not exist. They are nobody until they complete their temple training and are allocated an island role.

My shoulders slump, spilling some of the milk from the bag onto my foot. The chanting of "Namu May Mu" becomes a roar as the sacrificial party ascend the stone stairs. Following behind the Experienced are two black-robed Maymuans. One is holding a long silver sword. The blade's sharp edge glints in the setting sun. The other is carrying what looks like a pile of dark cloth.

Hold on, isn't that Naho?

It is!

I can't take any more of this. I have to leave. I can't be here.

"Go!" Kairi's fist punches the small of my back but I am stuck. "For ratty hell's sake, move out of the way then!"

Kairi and Kentaro push past me and race up the steps. I don't know what to do. Should I go? The crowd surges forwards, eager to observe the commotion, shoving me up the stairs.

I reach the two stone tortoise statues and there is absolute chaos on the top of the pyramid.

Kairi is emptying mir pockets of bright-red ghili into a huge smouldering copper urn. Kentaro is next to mem, screaming at the pack of Experienced to stay back. Takanori has the sword and looks like mu would like to skewer everyone with it. Naho and the other Maymuan are standing beside Takanori with stiff spines and slack mouths. The unnamed is teetering on the edge of the pyramid with a dagger in mir hand, still singing mir sweet song. The boom of "Namu May Mu" is resounding from the bottom of the staircase.

The chanting ends when thick black smoke wheezes from the urn.

I fall to my knees. Smoke claws at my eyes until they

bleed. A blaze-laced fog rams down my throat, making me gag. My skin is melting and dripping from my bones.

"Use the milk!" Kentaro splutters. I can just about make out mem splashing mir face with milk and pouring the rest down mir throat. I copy mem. It still hurts but I can see better and I can focus on more than pain.

Kairi is dripping with milk. Mu sprints across the temple roof and snatches the dagger from the unnamed. Kairi drags mem from the edge of the roof, away from the baying cries of the Maymuans who are being denied their sacrifice. Relief soothes the agony of the roasted ghili gas. I can finally exhale.

Swirling amongst the dense fog is the shrieking misery of the Experienced. Even the Experienced furthest from the urn are screaming. Experienced Takano is wailing and rolling from side to side on the floor trying to extinguish the flames under mir skin. Next to mem is Experienced Taketo. Mu is clawing at mir arms and legs, trying to skin memself alive. The torture from the spicy, noxious smoke has led mem to try and remove chunks of mir own skin with mir fingernails in a futile attempt at relief.

It is worse than when the rabbits near the cob field are struck by convulsions and die with swollen eyes and foaming mouths, pitifully flailing and thrashing, desperate for one more breath.

The Experienced closer to the urn are in a much worse state. Experienced Takahama is vomiting more than breathing. Lumpy rivers of supper and stomach lining are streaming out of mir mouth and nose. Experienced Takara and Experienced Takabe have lost control of their bowels.

Takanori, Naho, and the other Maymuan are on their knees, clutching their throats on the other side of the platform. The tears pouring from their eyes are unable to extinguish the effect of the fiery gas.

Kentaro is demented. Mu is trying to wrestle the sword out of Takanori's hand but Takanori has not loosened mir grip. Mu won't let go. Kentaro needs Kairi.

I crawl over to Kairi and the unnamed. "Go and help Kentaro. I've got mem."

I hug the unnamed close to my chest. Mu is still humming a little tune and seems blissfully unaware of the gas. I look into mir eyes but mu does not see me. They must have given mem a potent root-draught.

Ruthless ratty Experienced.

I splash mir face with some milk anyway and pour the rest over my head.

I can see Kairi and Takanori are on their feet, staggering and stumbling, still intoxicated by the gas. Their mouths are twisted and deformed from the ferocity of venom they are spitting at each other. Kentaro is circling the pair, ready to strike and snatch the sword.

Naho's mouth is moving but to no avail.

Mu keeps gagging on the remnants of smoke still billowing across the roof.

Chapter Fourteen

KAIRI

"Don't betray me, May!" Takanori screams. "And tell your little pet to back off!"

Kentaro needs to grab the sword now, for ratty hell's sake.

What is mu waiting for?

Grab it!

"You promised me. You said you wouldn't hurt mem," I shout.

"Don't be foolish, May, you know as well as I do this had to happen. Did you not hear your inferiors roar when you denied them their sacrifice? Perhaps I was wrong about you. You don't have what it takes to lead this island. The Maymuans hate you now."

It is not true.

No.

It is true they hate you.

"Shut up and drop the sword," I say.

"Poor May. You thought sacrificing an unnamed instead of your pathetic hollow shell would make them hate you? No, they would have feared you!"

"Don't listen to mem. It's not true," shouts Kentaro.

"This is why you are weak," Takanori says, jabbing the tip of the sword at Kentaro. "Let me kill the unnamed. Hear me, May, it is better to be feared than hated. Maymuans don't like the taste of hate; it is bitter and corrosive, but fear? Fear is a thrill. The Maymuans can't resist a sweet sip of terror. They are addicted and I am weaning them onto you. Stand down and accept your fate."

The unnamed's dagger becomes heavy in my hand. I don't know what to do.

"Don't listen to mem. Mu doesn't know what mu is talking about!" Kentaro pleads.

Takanori uses my doubt to leap back and catch us both off guard. Takanori lunges at Kentaro's chest with the sword. I dive onto Kentaro and the sword slices across my back. We fall hard onto the stone platform. Takanori leers over me.

Is mu going to kill me?

I have betrayed mem. I deserve it.

I wait for the cold metal to pierce my heart. I close my eyes. There is nothing except Takanori's ragged breath and Kentaro's deep moans. I squint up and Takanori has mir hand outstretched to help me up. I reach for mem but mu snatches my megg bag and pours the last of the milk over mir head.

"Kaori! Kaori, run!" I scream.

Before my words reach mir ears, Takanori is towering over them. Without breaking stride, Takanori punches Kaori in the face and mu falls with a sharp crack of bone against stone. The unnamed peers up at Takanori with curious innocence and a placid smile. Takanori roars, "Namu May Mu!" and with an almighty swing slices the unnamed's head clean off mir little body.

Silence I have never heard before descends on the roof. The unnamed stands suspended for one horrible moment and then slumps to the floor. Blood gushes from mir neck.

The sword drops with an unceremonious clang. Takanori picks the severed head up by mir soft black curls and growls like a jungle cat. Mu turns to me, triumphant, and thrusts the head up into the air.

Chapter Fifteen

KAORI

Which came first, the rumbling or the wail of my twin?

I am not sure, but the pyramid is trembling and my twin is screaming loud enough to disturb the foundations of Mu. The pyramid bobs as the land becomes water. We are sailing on soiled sea. As the waves roll, the unnamed's blood splashes over me. I am drowning. Mir headless body floats over. I seize hold of it and I don't let go. Mu is my raft. Mir corpse is my lifeline.

Takanori is cackling with laughter and shrieking, "Yes, May! Yes!"

The earth heaves, trying to toss our wickedness from this land. The urn has overturned, scattering glowing blood-orange embers across the roof. The earth has split open and demons are dancing, revelling in our evil. The ghili smoke finally dissipates and I can see my twin. It is Kairi underneath the island of Mu trying to throw the weight of us from mir shoulders. The soiled waves calm but the pyramid lurches, tugged by an unseen force. The land is sighing, weary of our failings. It has drawn in a deep breath, sucking us towards mem.

The exhale brings terror.

On the other side of the island, the land breathes out a craggy wide-mouthed mountain. Stealing from the earth, the ravenous mountain devours the landscape, swelling up until its appetite is satisfied and its peak can guzzle from the clouds. Fully satiated, it burps noxious black smoke, and red lightning sparks from its belly. A volcano.

Kairi has transformed the landscape of Mu.

Kairi looks at me and I clutch the corpse closer. Kairi blinks rapidly as if to refresh the image before mem. When it doesn't change, mu retches and surveys the chaos. Pools of blood, faeces, and vomit.

Kairi flees the carnage with Kentaro in mir wake. They descend the staircase and they are gone.

The Experienced are crawling about aimlessly, knees and palms in their own waste, trying to make sense of what has happened. Takanori struts to the rear of the roof, lifts up a hatch, and sweeps down a concealed staircase, clutching the severed head.

The remaining Experienced drag themselves to the hatch, leaving me on the roof clutching the headless unnamed, with Naho and the other Maymuan standing over me.

"You have to let go," Naho says. Mu looks horrible. Mir eyes are swollen from the ghili gas and mir braids are sticking out like the fuzzy legs of a spider flailing on its back.

"No." The body is warm but mir blood is beginning to congeal and become sticky.

"Kaori, give mem to me."

"No."

The Maymuan beside Naho draws Takanori's sword. I scream.

"No, don't be afraid. This is Miki. Mu is here to perform the sky burial. You must give us the body before it is too late," Naho says.

Too late? I loosen my grip and the unnamed's arms flop. I can't. I have to keep mem safe. That is my island duty.

Why has mu stopping singing? I look for mir sweet little mouth but it is not there. Mu has no head. There is no head. I am holding a body with no head.

I let go and Naho and Miki roll the body onto the cloth and cover it up. I scurry into the corner and curl up like a coco. I can't help but watch them.

Both chant as they straighten the copper urn. Naho rips the cloth and wraps it around mir hand so mu can pick up the scattered hot rocks. When the urn is half full, Naho throws in a handful of hunmir wood from mir pocket and the scent of the Experienced crawls from the urn, bringing bile to my mouth. Miki has soaked up every last drop of the blood from the unnamed and is carefully placing the soiled fabric into the urn. Hunmir wood scent becomes the heady, meaty stench of blood.

"Kaori, prepare yourself," Naho warns.

For what? It can't get any worse.

They uncover the unnamed and Miki cups mir hand over mir mouth and makes the squawk of a nabgar. Miki repeats mir call until the bruised sky is filled with the swish of heavy wings. Black beady eyes appraise their prey over cruel, red, hooked beaks.

Naho picks up the sword and chops off the unnamed's foot.

"What the ratty hell are you doing!" I scream.

Naho passes the sword to Miki and approaches my corner.

"Don't you come near me! You are as bad as the rest of them!"

Naho tries to hug me but mu stinks of fire and blood. I can't bear it. I punch and kick at Naho until mu backs off.

"It must be done. We cannot leave any trace of a soulless body," Naho says, as three of the nabgars swoop down on the foot. They screech, shoving each other with their wide wings. They peck at the foot until they each get their chunk of flesh.

"Don't be afraid. This is a sacred sky burial. Mu is returning to the sky."

Sacred? I envy the unnamed. I wish I were dead. I wish I weren't seeing this. I have never really thought about what the Experienced do with dead Maymuans. When I was an unnamed I never questioned the ceiling of skulls. I didn't think of them as being attached to necks I would ever care about. I never wondered what they did with the rest of the body.

Chop.

Miki takes another limb. The nabgars dive for more flesh. The poor unnamed. I should have taken mem when I first saw mem in the temple.

"Look, Kaori," Naho pleads, wanting me to indulge their barbarism.

I can't. I won't. This is sick.

Naho won't shut up.

"This will happen to us all. However we pass, whether it be sacrifice or natural, we must be returned to the sky. It is best to embrace it. Don't fear death otherwise you will be unable to live."

Mu must be joking. I don't fear death. I've never thought about it. But now? It's normal not to want to be hacked up on the roof of Takanori's pyramid and fed to scavengers. And as for unable to live? I would like to jump off the side of this pyramid. The only thing sticking my feet to the ground is the thought of Takanori chopping my head off my mangled body and proudly holding it up like mu did with the unnamed.

"I don't want to die," my treacherous mouth says, my fear betraying my pride.

"I know, but you will, and you must accept it. I know enough of the unseen life to not be afraid. Our blood nourishes the dark earth and our bodies soar like a girnum returning to its mate."

"I don't want to die like this. Promise me, Naho, please, please don't do that to my body."

Swish. Chop. Screech.

"Come on, be brave. I can't let Miki do this by memself. Come with me. Help me. Then you can understand."

I don't want to. I don't want to understand.

Naho observes me with pity.

"You saw mem, didn't you?"

I don't respond.

"When we were looking for Kairi, I remember you approached me from the far end of the hall where the unnameds were practising joy."

I nod.

"Then you must show respect, Kaori. Come. We will do it together."

I let Naho drag me to my feet. Miki looks surprised as we approach but mu hands me the sword and steps back.

Why do I have to do this?

I don't believe in the island, in Namu May Mu, or in their stupid rituals.

So why should I do this?

Naho wraps mir arms around mine and nudges me towards the mutilated body. Naho's fingers close around mine. We squeeze the sword. I scrunch my eyes tight shut when Naho raises my arms and slams them down in a swift chop. A piece thumps against the stone as it rolls away. Nabgars swoop. Their scrambling and scratching are sickening. I scurry back to my corner.

I don't feel better. I feel much worse.

Chapter Sixteen

KAIRI

The foundations of the Experienced temple tremble as the fiery core of Mu churns. I clamber over the crouching Maymuans who are wailing into the earth, pleading with Mu to explain why a volcano has been spat out of the land. Kentaro and I dive into the forest. Instead of returning to the gamgam huts, we head in the opposite direction and thrash our way towards the simmering mountain.

The air as we approach the base of the volcano is stifling and heavy with a rotten gas. Kentaro squeezes my hand, mir eyes wide with both fear and wonder. I release mem and lay my palms on the craggy rock my lava has erupted through. What churns within boils my veins. I realise I haven't taken a full breath since I poured the ghili in the urn. I rest my face on the hot rock and breathe.

"I am sorry," I whisper. "Namu unnamed."

Mir halo of black fluffy hair sways in my mind.

Mymig you, Takanori. May you burn inside my mountain for all eternity.

"Be careful," Kentaro calls.

My anger has shot a blast of red-hot embers from the volcano. They land with a thud and scorch the grass.

"Let's keep going," Kentaro urges. "The slash on your back is bleeding. I need to gather some guma leaves."

We trek around the volcano plucking leaves until a slope leads us down onto an empty beach. We sit on the sand, preparing the guma, but Kentaro can't settle with mir back to the forest.

"No one will follow," I say.

Kentaro swivels to check again. "How do you know?"

"The Maymuans will be too scared. At least at first."

"But what about the Experienced? They are not going to let you leave Mu."

"We haven't left Mu," I snap. I wish we could. I look out to the horizon.

How can I get there?

Kentaro stares at me. "We have! Okay, we are still on the island, but if we don't go back to our huts right now then we are no longer Maymuans. You know that as well as I do."

Kentaro is right. It is over. We are not Maymuans. I never was. Even if I'd wanted to be they wouldn't let me. I am not allowed their balance.

Takanori says I am May.

Let it be.

"What about Kaori?" Kentaro asks.

"What about mem?" I shudder, remembering mir holding the slaughtered unnamed. "Cockroach Kaori will find a way to survive," I spit, with a venom that shocks Kentaro and surprises myself.

Kaori and I will never be whole. I must stand alone. No more twins.

I understand now all Takanori has taught me.

Fire must rule. I don't need water.

And as for Takanori, I don't need mem either.

Chapter Seventeen

KAORI

"Come and sit over here next to me."

I shake my head. I like my corner. It is where I feel safe.

Saki sighs. "I suppose I will have to come to you."

Mu has said the same stupid things every ratty rise for over a moon cycle: "Sit here", "Let's go for a walk", "Why don't we go to the cove?"

Why don't you leave me alone?

Saki sits down next to me on my woven mat. The scent of mimin petals on Saki's dark skin brings the cove to my hut. A scented respite from the stale unwashed air.

"How are you?" Saki asks. Again. Same thing every rise.

I ignore mem. Again.

"You look better."

I don't.

We sit in uncomfortable silence. Fruit flies buzz around the mango Saki brought at the last rise. They swarm in the hollow of my single bite, enjoying the sweet juice which churned in my stomach.

"Why do you come back here every rise?"

Saki's brow furrows. "Why?"

"Yes, why?"

"Because I love you."

"You love seeing me like this?" I say.

"No, of course not! I love you and when I enter your hut I hope this will be the rise you won't be like this anymore," Saki says with a kind smile.

"Sorry to disappoint you."

"You never disappoint me."

Mu is disgusting. Why is mu being so patient and calm?

"I am *this* so you may as well stop coming."

Saki holds my hand. "You will get better, Kaori. What you saw has unsettled you, but it will pass."

I get up and kick the overripe fruit so hard it splats on the gamgam wall. Saki flinches.

It will not pass. I will not let it.

"I am not like you."

"Oh Kaori, not this again, please, I have told you I'm sorry, but I don't feel the same way about sacrifices as you do."

Don't feel the same way?

This sick buha thinks what happened to the unnamed is fine. "Kairi took too many lives on the hunt and the Experienced had to restore balance," mu says. How was chopping off the head of a sweet little unnamed balanced?

"So you could have chopped off mir head?" I say.

"Kaori, come and sit back down. I have a lot to tell you."

"Answer me!"

"I have told you I couldn't but I am not an Experienced so I don't have to."

"So that makes it okay, does it? It's fine as long as you don't have to get your hands dirty? I was covered in mir blood!"

Saki sighs again. "You shouldn't have been up there."

"Bahm you! How can you say that? I was up there and I saw it! I saw it all and you don't understand." I am shaking.

Saki scrabbles up and pulls me in for a hug.

"You don't understand," I sob into mir robe.

"I know, I know. I'm sorry, I really am," Saki says stroking my back.

How am I going to get through this? Some rises I wake up and for a moment I feel peace. I think of going to the cove and playing with the turtles and I plan the rest of the day. I will go to the preparers to pick up my portion of food, then I'll meet Kentaro and Kairi and head to the beach to cook our portions together... and then I remember. Mu had no head. I was lying in a pool of blood clutching a headless little unnamed. I cut mir leg off and fed it to nabgars. Naho is a savage. I am a savage.

I haven't seen or heard from Kairi or Kentaro since they left me on the roof, drowning in the unnamed's blood.

Saki and I sit back down. I want to keep ranting and raving but I am exhausted.

I rest my head in Saki's lap. It feels nice and I try to enjoy it because I know Saki will start going on again.

"I have to tell you about Kairi."

There mu goes. I have barely begun to relax and mu wants to speak about ratty Kairi.

"I don't want to know," I say.

"I am not sure you have a choice."

"What?"

"Listen, I know this has been hard but Maymuans are beginning to pick a side."

The bitter taste of ganba juice floods my mouth.

"What do you mean?"

"Well, erm…"

For ratty hell's sake, mu is the one who brought it up and is now going all Maymuan coy. Vomiting with no mouth.

"I don't have the patience for this. Either say it or leave," I say.

"I know, I'm sorry. I don't want to hurt you, that's all."

"Well, don't say it then."

Saki chews mir words then bleats like a goat, "The boar hunter pack live with Kairi."

What?

It is impossible. The Experienced would never allow it. We all have to live here, in huts. Well, except for the rearers and the carriers, and I suppose the unnameds and the Experienced. But everyone else lives here, in gamgam huts. Together. In unity. To care for each other. And watch over each other. Watch each other like nabgars.

I shiver.

"Are you saying Aito lives on the other side of the volcano with Kairi?"

Saki nods.

Oh bahm.

But the pack didn't stand with Kairi in the Experienced chamber. Why would Kairi want them there?

The fruit flies are devouring the splattered mango pulp from the walls.

"That is... I don't know what to say. When did they go?"

"About fourteen rises ago."

"Fourteen rises? Why didn't you tell me!"

Saki, to be fair, refrains from answering the obvious. I wasn't listening. I haven't been listening to mem for over one moon cycle. Ever since... I can't think of it now. I can't believe Aito is with Kairi!

"But Kairi hates Aito," I say.

"It is not just Aito. All of them have gone – Shun, Tetsu, and Ikki are there too. I suppose Aito couldn't be the only one *not* to go."

Saki says it kindly, giving Aito the benefit of the doubt. Saki has never been threatened by my relationship with Aito. But I don't understand. How could mu *not* be jealous of my time with Aito? Saki doesn't see anyone else. I wouldn't like it if mu did.

I once asked Saki why mu isn't jealous and mu said my freedom is what makes my choosing to spend time with mem so precious. Saki is a better Maymuan than I am. The truth is that Aito is a pathetic maggot. The only reason mu would leave the huts is because mu is more afraid of my twin than of the Experienced.

Oh ratty hell, what if the other Maymuans start to feel the same?

Kairi more powerful than Takanori? Surely not.

"How do you know?"

Saki looks at me like I have sprouted jungle cat whiskers. "I told you, I have been going and watching them."

"But it could be dangerous if they saw you!"

Saki seemingly tries not to roll mir eyes. "If I don't, how else can I tell you what is going on? Maybe you should come with me next time if you are so concerned for my safety."

Ouch.

Mir rebuke bites like red ants. Saki is usually so calm I often forget mu is also an exceptional hunter.

"What do they do over there? Are there even boars on that side of the island?"

Saki shakes mir head and scrunches up mir nose in disgust. "They hunt anything."

"Like what?"

"Anything! I have seen them enter the forest and drag out a stag," Saki says, eyes wide.

"A stag? But we are only allowed stag when the moon is half."

"I know but they drag it out by its antlers, collect a pile of branches, light them, then roast the poor thing alive and eat it."

"Without preparers?" I say.

"Of course without preparers. Did you hear what I said? Roasted alive!"

"But... are they even chanting before?"

"I don't know. I can't hear them but I haven't seen anything that looks like respect. They go into the water too and fish out whatever they can. They definitely don't chant because they shove whatever they pull out straight into their mouths like they are plucking berries not souls."

This is very bad.

"Could you wipe this, Saki? It is making me feel sick," I say, pointing at the fly-covered mango smearing the wall. Mu goes to pick some leaves from the back of my hut. I will clean it myself when mu gets back, I just needed to be alone for a moment to absorb what mu has said.

Kairi is spinning out of control. If the Experienced find out, there will be sacrifices every sunrise and sunset for the next orbit.

Saki returns with the leaves and together we wipe away the sticky pulp. I leave my hut for the first time in a full moon to follow Saki behind my hut where we dig a hole to bury the mess. The dark earth between my fingers feels good.

"I stink, don't I?"

Saki scrunches up mir nose and nods.

"I think I would like to go to the cove."

As we pass the huts, dark eyes stare. Some with kindness, many without.

I reach for Saki's hand. We shouldn't in front of others. Most Maymuans seek pleasure outside of their creating duty, and often with those who it is impossible to create with.

It is tolerated if discreet.

Holding hands with Saki is not discreet but I don't care.

I won't make it to the cove if I don't.

The cool water washes away the dirt from my skin and soothes the pain in my heart. Saki crushes mimin seeds and I rub the oil into my skin until it shines. Saki massages the last of the oil into my scalp. I sit between mir legs and I let mem braid my hair.

"Why are some of the Maymuans mad at me?"

Saki pauses, sectioning the hair at my right temple.

"You have such beautiful hair," Saki says, bouncing my curls in mir palm. "They are so full of joy it is a shame to tuck them away."

"Saki!"

"Sorry. They are not mad at you."

"They are. Did you see the looks on their faces as we came over here?"

"It's because you wouldn't let go of my hand," Saki says, pulling my hair taut, forcing it into a tight croprow.

"No, it wasn't. They were giving me sly eyes before then."

I lean back into Saki's lap and kiss mir chin.

"Why?"

"I don't know."

I tickle mir chin with my tongue.

"Okay, okay," Saki giggles. It is a lovely sound. "It may be because you didn't go to the cave."

I thought so. I missed my island duty. Seven rises ago was the full moon; I should have been snatching snakes from black water. Instead I was wallowing in my hut.

"I couldn't... I wouldn't have known what was snake and what was water."

"*I* know that, but they don't. I think they felt you had forsaken them."

"Forsaken?" I despise those sanctimonious Maymuans, I really do. "But I have provided enough snakes over the entirety of my duty to cover for missing one hunt."

Saki doesn't respond.

"Don't you think? I always catch loads! How many do they need? There must be some of my last catch still in the smokehouse."

"Yes, but it doesn't work like that, does it?"

"It should."

"But it doesn't. We all have an island duty and we all have to fulfil it no matter what. Also, were you listening to what I said in your hut? They are picking sides. Those who display an ankh want to follow you, but you have to be capable of leading them." Saki pushes me a little so mu can stand up. "There you go. I'm done."

I touch the braids. They are already giving me a headache. Saki weaves them even tighter than I usually do. Thoughts of ankhs burn my mind.

I have to be capable of leading the Maymuans where?

"Thanks." I look at Saki. Mu is beautiful, mir full lips and dark eyes framed by long, heavy lashes. "Do you think I should have gone to the cave?"

Saki covers mir mouth and mumbles through mir fingers, "No."

I don't believe mem.

I wish I didn't care what mu thinks but I do. I start to cry.

"Oh Kaori, I mean it. I really didn't want you to come to the cave. It would have been the correct thing to do but I honestly didn't want you to. I know it wouldn't have been safe for you. So no, it was wrong, but I am glad you didn't come with us."

"What about everyone else?"

"What about them? I don't know what was in their minds. Naho came over the hill alone and we went without you."

Naho *had* come to my hut but I had been curled up in the corner in my sleeping robe. Mu hadn't even said anything. Mu had just left.

"I suppose Kentaro wasn't there either." I say.

"No."

"So I wouldn't have had a torchbearer anyway."

"True," Saki says with a sad smile. "Anyway, let's talk about *now*."

I am not going to see Kairi.

"I think you should go and see Kairi."

At the back of my mind I have been planning my route to the volcano ever since mu told me where Aito is.

"I have to think about it."

"Okay," Saki says, reluctant to let the topic lie. "What do you want to do for the rest of this rise?"

"I'm really hungry."

"I'm not surprised. Let's go over to the preparers. I am sure they will give us something."

"Thanks, Saki."

Mu gives me a look so full of affection I fear I will cry again.

"I love you."

Now Saki is crying. "I love you too."

Chapter Eighteen

KAIRI

Takanori pushes two terrified unnameds onto my beach. Takanori has been visiting me here every rise since the sacrifice. At first, I resisted mem. But only at first.

"I don't need you anymore," I said, all those sunrises ago.

"You need me more than ever, May. Don't you see this is exactly what was destined to happen. You are a treasure, May, *my* treasure." Takanori smiled.

"This is my island," I said.

"Not yet."

"This part is." My volcano belched a plume of black smoke.

"But what next? Are you going to spend the rest of your days over here with your little pet?" Takanori sneered.

"Kentaro is not my pet!"

"Okay, okay, but really, May, you are so much more. You were born to lead, but you can't lead without any followers." Takanori gestured to the lonely landscape.

"What are you saying?"

"I think you should at least have your pack join you, don't you?"

Shun and Ikki were the first to appear from the forest. They told tales of how the Maymuans were in awe of the volcano but Takanori had declared it a gift from Mu. Our absence had been dismissed as exile for disrupting the sacrifice.

Tetsu came next with further news of secret whispers amongst the Maymuans, particularly the hunters. "Kairi created the volcano and mu lives inside it!" they said.

Aito scuttled over last. Mu only wanted to talk about cockroach Kaori and how mu had not fulfilled mir island hunting duty.

After Aito arrived, Takanori kept bringing me other useful things, like my weapons, and tools to hack the trees and shred vine for building huts.

Each gift was delivered with a drop of poison. "The bellies of those bright-blue frogs in the forest pond could have a devastating effect on a reluctant Maymuan. Shame there is no way to effectively deliver a targeted dose of their venom..." Takanori muttered, with a pointed glance at my quiver of arrows.

~

Takanori strolls slowly over with the unnameds, to where me and my pack are waiting on the shore. If mu is shocked by our appearance mu hides it well. Not even a flicker of surprise crosses mir shrewd face in response to the physical transformation we have undergone.

The unnameds, however, stare at our new skin.

I survey the shivering unnameds. They have more orbits than the slaughtered one who haunts my dreams. These two would surely have a naming ceremony soon. Whatever their orbits, now is not the time for weakness. If they are to stand with me they must be strong. And controlled.

"By the next rise you will share my skin," I say. At this even Takanori cannot feign indifference. Takanori fixes me with a nabgar-like glare.

"Are you sure, May?"

I return mir glassy black stare. "Yes."

Chapter Nineteen

KAORI

Girnums twitter as I pace the misty dawn alone. At the cove, the turtles bump my thigh in reprimand for abandoning them, but after I crash enough waves for a tummy-filling sea snail apology they are happy to bob next to me.

We watch the sun as it rises past the trees. It now has to ascend another obstacle before it can settle in the sky. Kairi's mountain is sticking out of the forest like broken bone through skin. Natural but abnormal. There is no place on Mu from which the volcano would not be visible. Kairi has transformed the face of this island, and only by burying my head next to the turtle eggs in the warm sand will I be unable to see it.

I chase the scent of rotten eggs through the tangled vines of bush beneath the volcano. I use my dagger to slash my path to Kairi. I have no idea what I am going to say to mem. I squeeze the bloodstone in my pocket for courage.

Mu is my twin. I will not fear mem.

The volcano wheezes, huffing another blast of stomach-churning stench into the air. How can they live under this? It stinks. Approaching the volcano is terrifying enough, never mind sleeping under it.

The once smooth land stolen for its creation is now craggy and jagged. A mutilated flank desperate for soothing lava from the throat to relieve and calm. I shudder at the thought of an eruption. Kairi uncontrollable, humiliating Mu. At the base of the volcano the trees thin and the earth is black. My feet are covered in ash. My ears tingle when waves crash on a nearby shore. I scramble through the last of the forest. A charred-meat breeze ruffles the leaves. The beach is in sight.

Crack.

An arrow is quivering in the bark of the tree to my right.

"Hey! Don't shoot! It's me."

"Who?"

"Kaori."

The undergrowth shakes and out pops Aito. It had to be, didn't it?

"Thanks for checking before releasing, bonehead."

Aito has the grace to blush.

"You shouldn't be here."

"Neither should you! If my twin said, 'Stick your head in the crater,' would you? You are pathetic."

Aito is blinking and spluttering, the scrawny maggot.

"And what the ratty hell are you wearing?"

Aito puts mir hands in front of mir crotch but it doesn't

172

disguise the fact mu is only wearing a loincloth. Kairi must have convinced them they are on an eternal hunt.

"Where is mu?"

"Who?"

"I don't have time for this. Take me to Kairi," I say.

"No."

"What do you mean no? Take me to mem now."

"I can't. Only Maymuans who want to join us can step foot on the beach," Aito says, shielding mir eyes from the bright sunlight shining through the trees.

"Don't be ridiculous."

"I mean it, Kaori. You can't be here."

"So you really think Kairi is going to be happy you turned me away?"

Mu would be but Aito can't be certain. Aito wipes mir sweaty forehead with the back of mir hand.

"What the ratty hell happened to your arm?"

Aito's arm is covered in poorly healed purple welts. It looks as if mir arm has been lashed by a frenzied whip. I can't help but reach out but mu recoils from my touch.

"Did Kairi do this to you?"

"It's nothing. Why are you here?"

I have to give Aito a reason to lead me to Kairi. "I have something important to tell Kairi, from the Experienced."

Aito's eyebrows shoot up. Mu really is an idiot.

"Okay," Aito says and leans into me. Mu reaches over and pulls out mir arrow from the tree. The puncture hole is black; the flesh beneath bark is usually white. I squeeze Aito's injured arm and mu squeals in pain.

"What do you think you are doing firing poisoned arrows at me? You could have killed me!"

"I didn't know it was you," Aito whimpers. I squeeze tighter.

"Who do you think you are? Who are you to fire poisoned arrows at anyone! Who gave you the right to take life?"

Tears are streaming from Aito's eyes, but I am squeezing not only for the arrow, but also for the betrayal and cowardice mu has shown me since Kairi killed the piglets.

Mymig you, Aito.

And mymig you, Kairi.

"Take me to my twin." I release mir arm and mu staggers from me.

"You two are as wicked as each other," Aito says and turns back into the undergrowth. I follow mem and mu leads me out of the bush down a sandy, shrub-littered slope to the beach.

There are more bodies on the beach than are in the pack. Five are standing around two others who are kneeling. As we draw closer I see Ikki, Tetsu, and Shun. I recognised the shapes of Kentaro and Kairi as soon as we came out of the woods. The other two I don't know. I can't believe it! They look like unnameds who have only just left the Experienced temple. They are small and trembling. How has Kairi smuggled two unnameds out of the temple?

Kairi's beautiful black skin has gone. Mir entire body is covered in the same welts as Aito's arms. Kentaro's torso is the same. Ikki, Tetsu, and Shun have a slashed arm each. Despite the heat on the beach, I shiver.

"Look who I found," Aito says to the pack with pride. *Idiot.*

Kairi is not impressed. "What the ratty hell did you bring mem here for?"

I can't help but snigger. Aito looks dumbly from me to Kairi. "But I thought you wanted... mu has a message for you."

Kairi stares at me and I am sure mu almost smiles. "From who?"

"The Experienced," Aito says in the hope of redemption. Ikki and Shun glance at each other but Kairi snorts with derision.

"We are in the middle of something here," Kairi says with a wave at the kneeling unnameds. "Keep mem over there and if mu starts, jab mir with an arrow."

"I need to—"

"What did I say, Kaori? Shut up and I will deal with you later."

I try and address Kentaro. "Kentaro, I need—"

Kentaro shakes mir head and nods at Aito to drag me away. Kairi considers the trembling unnameds and says, "Actually, tie Kaori to that tree. And gag mem."

Kairi turns mir back to me and I see that the long gash from Takanori's sword is surrounded by more of the strange welts. The deep wound has been stuffed with chewed guma leaves and grain. Maggots writhe in Kairi's injury. Aito drags me to a lone benme tree whose neck droops at a forlorn angle.

"Don't do this, Aito. It's not too late. We can leave this place. You don't have to do wh—"

Aito ties a vine tight across my mouth. Any attempt to speak results in incoherent drool. Mu continues to wrap vine after vine, bonding my body to the bark.

"You shouldn't have tricked me, cockroach," Aito hisses, tying the last vine tight against my throat with a vindictive knot. Mu re-joins the pack. I can't move or speak but I can still see and hear.

Kentaro is holding a large version of mir megg water bag. The bag is swollen with liquid. Ikki is eyeing the bag as if it may explode. Even Shun, who I have heard from both Kairi and Aito is quite fearless on their hunts, can't stop glancing at it.

Kairi reaches deep inside and draws out a translucent blob of fungi-shaped flesh. An inner blue orb glows, crackling with pure concentrated energy. Long purple shimmering tentacles dangle, writhing with impatience, longing to lash skin.

Ratty hell, this terrible creature must be what has transformed Kairi's skin.

"Hold mem," Kairi says.

Ikki and Tetsu grip the shoulders of one of the unnameds. Aito and Shun seize the other. Kairi stands over the first, and the terrified unnamed begins chanting "Namu May Mu" and Kairi almost drops the jellyfish in anger.

"You do *not* chant 'Namu May Mu' here! Do you understand?"

The unnamed begins rocking back and forth on mir knees.

"Hold out your arm," Kairi demands.

The unnamed peers up at Kairi with a heart-breaking look of fear. I can't stand it. I thrash against the vines binding me to the tree and I try and scream through my gag.

"It will either be your arm or your face," Kairi says.

A reluctant arm rises. Kairi flicks the jellyfish and the tentacles scorch the poor unnamed's defenceless skin. Mu screams in agony and rolls onto mir side, pitifully trying to wipe the tentacle burn from mir arm.

The other unnamed is panting, trying to suppress mir terror. The unnamed's eyes are scrunched shut but mu has stuck mir arm out as a wicked offering to my twin. Kairi strikes again. The unnamed screams and rolls over and joins the other writhing in agony.

Kairi turns and approaches me with the jellyfish. I can't even panic properly; my chest can't rise and fall and my throat can't swallow the fear in my mouth because the vines holding me are tied so tight.

"Do you know what we call this type of jellyfish?" Kairi asks, swinging the tentacles close to me. "*Kaori...* It suits it, doesn't it? A fat blob from the sea which is occasionally useful."

Kairi drops the jellyfish and mir tentacles draw grotesque shapes in the sand as they flail, searching for skin.

Kairi jumps and lands with a sickening splat on the jellyfish's head. The blue light is snuffed out. Blobs of luminous shattered soul speckle the sand.

Kairi returns to the prostrate pair. The pack splits. One half led by Kairi, the other by Kentaro. They lift their loin cloths and piss on the Maymuans. It provides no relief. They continue to sob into the sand and only stop when they crawl to the sea and allow the water to soothe the burn.

Kentaro unties the vines binding me to the tree. Mu removes the mouth gag and it is difficult to prioritise which thought to verbalise first.

"What the ratty hell are you doing here?" I say.

Kentaro's face has changed since leaving the main island. Mir round face has become more angular, sharper. And mir eyes are no longer kind. Mu gestures for me to follow mem.

"Answer me!"

Kentaro turns to face me with the aggression of my twin. "You saw what we do here. If you don't like it, then leave."

"Why are you speaking to me this way?" I have to bite down hard on the inside of my cheek to prevent myself from sobbing. I don't know what is worse, the initiation ceremony I just witnessed or Kentaro's wretched transformation. How can Kentaro throw away all of our memories? Toss them into the wind and *poof!* Gone.

Mu is treating me worse than the bag of snakes we take

to the smokehouse. At least we appreciate them as we accept their sacrifice for the greater good. But it is more dangerous here under Kairi's volcano than it ever was in the snake cave.

Kentaro has marched off and I can either leave or follow mem.

I follow Kentaro to an extraordinary cluster of huts. They are huge structures – smaller than the Experienced temple but bigger than any Maymuan hut, smokehouse, or preparer barn I have ever seen. All the island huts are one level and built from gamgam with woven benme roofs. These huts have two levels and are wrapped in what looks like megg. They are incredible.

"Wow, did you design these?" I say.

"Yes, aren't they brilliant?" Kentaro says, mir eyes shining with a familiar excitement. "I thought if I can weave the megg and it can hold water and milk without spilling a drop then what else could it do? When it rains no water leaks in and—" Kentaro's chin dips and mir cheeks blush as mu remembers I am no longer a friend.

"I miss you." I reach out for mir hand.

"Don't. It's too late."

"No, it isn't. Look at your skin, Kentaro." I choke on my words "It's terrible. Please come back with me. Please."

Kentaro says no more and merely leads me into the largest hut where, of course, Kairi is waiting.

"Why are you here, cockroach?"

Cockroach? What is this cockroach thing?

"What?"

"Why are you here?" Kairi shouts.

"I... I wanted to see you."

"Why?"

"Why? How about because the last time I saw you I was holding a headless unnamed and you made a ratty huge volcano, that's why!"

Kairi stops pacing around the large space and gestures for me to sit down. I kneel and face Kairi and Kentaro. Although it is as if I am on trial, my chin trembles to see them both again. They are the only others on this island who have a sliver of understanding of how I feel about what happened on the roof of the temple.

"Are you hungry?" Kairi asks.

"No," I say.

"Kentaro, get mem some of the leftover meat."

"I don't want your stupid meat."

"Is what I offer not good enough for you?"

"Did you chant before you slaughtered it?" I ask.

Kairi smirks.

"What the ratty hell do you think you are doing over here? Have you lost your mind! You can't kill whatever you want. And are those unnameds? What do you think you are doing here, making your own island? Are you insane!"

Kairi glances at Kentaro and they both smile. Snakes stir in my stomach.

"Takanori will never let you get away with this."

They both laugh.

"It's not funny! What you did to those unnameds was sick. What is wrong with you? Kentaro, say something!"

"Mu doesn't have to explain memself to you," Kairi says, placing mir hand on Kentaro's knee. "We have made our decision. It seems to me you are the one who needs to make peace with *your* decision."

"What decision? What are you on about?"

In my hut a breeze can squeeze through the tiny cracks and spaces where the gamgam doesn't quite fit together. But here, wrapped in megg, I can't breathe.

"Are you really going to spend the rest of your existence with those filthy Maymuans?"

"You are talking as if you are not one of them! We *are* Maymuans."

Kairi winces as if I slapped mem with the back of my hand.

"I am not a Maymuan."

"Yes, you are! And no volcano or jellyfish will ever change that."

"I am not a filthy Maymuan!" Kairi screams.

Kairi is drunk on boar blood or something because what mu is saying is nonsense. Of course we are Maymuans. We may be the only twins, but we are twins born on Mu.

"So that's your plan? You are going to become a new creature? What are you, a boar? A snake? A ratty genmo!" I scoff. "You are as mad as Takanori. And what about the Experienced? Where do they fit into your stupid plan?"

"I don't need the Experienced. What are they anyway? Only the longest living things. They have never been the strongest. In fact, they are the weakest creatures on this island."

"Not in the eyes of the Maymuans."

"Well, maybe it is time to gouge out the eyes of the Maymuans," Kairi snarls.

I recoil from mir horrible words.

"Even if you don't think of yourself as a Maymuan, how can you talk like this in front of mem?" I say, pointing at Kentaro, who has been nodding along like a freak.

"Kentaro is not a Maymuan."

Oh for ratty hell's sake! This is getting ridiculous.

"So you're not a Maymuan because you are a twin, but somehow Kentaro, who is not a twin, is *also* not a Maymuan because...?"

"It is not how you are born. It is what you choose to be," Kairi says.

"That's convenient. What am I then?"

"You are Mu."

"And you're May?"

"Yes, we are Mayans."

Mayans? What the ratty hell is a Mayan?

"There is no such thing as a Mayan."

Kairi wraps mir arm over Kentaro's shoulder and they smile with drunken pleasure. "We are Mayans."

Aito stumbles through the opening. "They are back on their feet now."

"Good. Take them to your hut," Kairi says.

"My hut?"

Kairi arches one eyebrow. "Yes, your hut. We will begin building them their own from the next rise."

Aito doesn't have the guts to defy mem. I almost feel sorry for mem.

"One other thing, tell Kaori what you are."

I already know: a coward.

"Sorry?"

Kairi sighs with impatience. "Are you a Maymuan?"

"No," Aito replies, "I am a Mayan."

The lava flowing beneath the volcano churns, the hut trembles, and a putrid stink burps from the craggy mouth.

"Take mem back where you found mem," Kairi says to Aito. I stumble to my feet, unable to walk straight under the weight of all I have heard.

"And Kaori"—I meet Kairi's unblinking stare—"next time you come, Aito will shoot you."

I look from Kentaro to Aito. Their jaws are set. They each give a curt nod.

Bahm.

Chapter Twenty

KAIRI

I watch Aito push and prod Kaori up the slope back to Mu. Before Kaori returns to the forest, mu takes a final sweeping look, from the unnameds still recovering on the shore, to my hut.

"Make sure no one else can wander over here," I bark to Ikki, Shun, and Tetsu who are standing beside me also watching Kaori leave.

"Do you think someone else will try and come?" Kentaro asks, stepping out of our hut to stand beside me.

I don't know.

A cloud passes before the sun, bringing a chill.

"If anyone else comes with no intention of joining us, you must shoot them," I say.

The pack nods.

Chapter Twenty-One

KAORI

"You have to go back."

Naho hasn't been anywhere near me since I refused to take part in our snake hunt. What was the over-dramatic word Saki used? *Forsaken*. Since I have "forsaken" my duty, Naho has disappeared but, like a true nabgar, at the whiff of vulnerability mu appears, waiting in my hut for my return from the volcano.

"No," I say.

Naho smacks the gamgam wall in frustration.

Wow. Why the sudden concern and un-Maymuan passion? Maybe this idiot is also a Mayan.

"Listen, I don't want to talk to you about this. I went and I am not going back. Kairi has gone mir own way and I think it is best if we leave mem over there. I'm sure it will fizzle out in the end."

I ignore the memory of the sturdy huts and maimed recruits.

Naho scowls and taps mir foot. "You must go back. It is clear now Kentaro will do whatever Kairi wants – even give up being a Maymuan. You are the only one with any hope of getting through to Kairi before it is too late. If Kairi does not return to Mu..." Naho shudders. "You have to convince mem to return."

Mu is really getting on my nerves now. Who the ratty hell is mu to come in here—without, may I add, even a single mention of the sky burial—and demand I crawl back to Kairi?

"Hold on, Naho, why don't *you* go? You are very good at telling me what to do. 'Don't cry', 'Fulfil your island duty', 'Keep an eye on Kairi', 'Chop off an unnamed's foot!' I am sick of it. I am sick of you and all the Maymuans. Why do *I* have to do everything?"

Naho puts mir head in mir hands and I don't know if mu is upset or angry. Or both. Naho sighs and seems to shrivel deep into the folds of mir robe. "I am sorry you feel I am asking you to do what I wouldn't do myself. But you must know there is a reason it has to be you."

"And that is?"

"You are half of a whole. You *have* to stay together."

"Kairi doesn't want me. It doesn't matter what you say, mu has already decided."

Naho shakes mir head. "You can fix this."

"Fix this? Are you suggesting *I* was the one who broke it?" I am screaming now. Naho is pushing me too far and I can't take much more. "Kairi does whatever mu wants – mu always has. Instead of spending your time following me around this island, maybe you should have focused on mem."

"Maybe I should have," Naho says in a flat monotone. "I am sorry, Kaori, I thought I was doing my best."

"Well, you were wrong!" I roar. There are tears in Naho's eyes but I can't stop. "You always tell me to be quiet, stop doing this, stop doing that. Why me? Why didn't you tell Kairi? You treat me differently to mem. *Why?*"

"I—"

"I haven't finished! It is because I am a *carrier*, isn't it? I know it is. Kairi can do whatever mu wants because mu will never carry life. Well, neither will I, Naho. I don't want a maymu! I think it is disgusting how the carriers give their maymus to a devil like Takanori! I am afraid. I am afraid the maymu will take all my strength and I won't hunt anymore. Kairi can hunt forever. Be strong forever. Why should I give my power? Why are you always trying to control me and tell me I am less than Kairi? I hate it."

"That is not what I believe. Where is all this coming from?"

"From you! From the island! I ratty well hate it."

Naho frowns. "I'm sorry you feel this way."

"You don't get it, do you? I am sorry for cursing, but please listen to what I am saying. It is wrong to treat me differently to Kairi. All the other Maymuans can be both, why is it only me who has to be half?"

"Kairi is half too."

"But mu is the stronger half!"

"No, Kaori."

"Yes! Mu is the sun and I am the moon. Without the sun, I can't be seen. I may as well not exist."

"No."

"No what?"

Naho almost smiles. "No, Kaori. Now you listen to me. You have got this all wrong. Mu is and always has been the greatest force on this island. May takes, it consumes, which is necessary, but it is more important to know when to stop. Enough. Let the land heal. That is Mu. We have both. As do you and Kairi. You are not half. You are whole and always have been. But Kairi has indulged mir May for too long and I am sorry if you have felt I have indulged your Mu. You are both. Be both, be more May than Mu if you want, but never be ashamed of Mu; it is your power. If you don't want a maymu that is your choice but, Kaori, please know you would be a great carrier. You could be a great carrier to us all. Don't give your maymu to the island. You choose."

I sob into my hand. Now I feel guilty. Naho's words are lodged in my throat, making me gag. Maybe I have gone too far in what I have said, but it's easy for Naho to tell me to return to Kairi – oh, and while I am at it, transform this ratty island and orbits of rigid Experienced rule! If it is possible then why hasn't mu done it, or anyone else?

Naho reaches for my hand. My palm welcomes mir warm, familiar touch. "I should never have asked you to do what I haven't had the courage to do myself. It is the curse of those who have seen too many orbits."

"No, you don't have to... you know. I don't really mean what I said, I am just tired of it all."

"Don't worry." Naho smiles. "It is going to be okay."

Chapter Twenty-Two

KAIRI

"What is it? What has happened?" I ask. Kentaro looks like mu is about to pass out in the opening. I run over to mem. "What happened?"

"I... er... someone in the..." Kentaro mutters, legs buckling. Mu leans against the wall and closes mir eyes.

What is going on?

"Tell me what has happened!" I screech, shaking Kentaro until mu rattles.

Shun enters. "A Maymuan has been shot in the forest," Shun says, finally explaining what Kentaro couldn't.

"Who?" I ask, my eyes darting from Shun to Kentaro.

Kentaro groans and slides down the wall onto the floor.

I sprint out of the hut and up the slope into the forest. Aito, Ikki, and Tetsu stand over a body with an arrow jutting out of the stomach.

I look at the face. Mu blinks.

Oh ratty hell.

"Quick, carry mem to my hut," I shout. They stand still, staring, "Now!"

Aito and Tetsu pick up the limp body. Ikki remains staring at the shadow left imprinted on the grass. I poke mem. "Come on!"

Back in the hut, Kentaro looks relieved to see the body moving but I shake my head at mem. No one could survive the frog venom.

"Go and get Kaori," I bark to Aito.

"I can't walk back into Mu. The Maymuans will destroy me."

I will destroy you.

"Go now!"

A low, painful moan roils the hut. Aito's face pales.

"Mu doesn't have long. Go. Now!"

Kaori staggers into my hut. Broken twigs are caught in mir hair and in mir robe.

"Aito won't tell me what is going on," Kaori pants. Aito appears in the opening looking as dishevelled as Kaori is from sprinting through the forest.

"What is it? What happened?" Kaori asks, searching each solemn face in the hut but no one responds. The pack avoid her frantic eyes and the two unnameds try and melt into the wall.

"Kairi, are you okay? What is it?"

Mu has run all the way here thinking there is something wrong with me. I suppose in a sense there is.

Another terrible moan. A familiar voice. Kaori's face crumples. Mu staggers. I hold mem up. I want to say it is as not as bad as it sounds. I can't because it is. Kaori knocks me out of mir way and tracks the moans to the back of the hut.

"Oh my..." Kaori drops to mir knees and clutches Naho's sweaty palm.

I stand over them. Kaori searches Naho's body until mu finds the cause; a snapped arrow shaft protruding from a stomach.

"I thought it was best to break the arrow but I thought we should leave the head in otherwise blood will... you know," I say, holding up the feathered end of the shaft.

Kaori blindly reaches out for the other half of the arrow. I give it to mem. I don't know why I thought it was better to snap the arrow. I suppose wrenching out the entire arrow was too much like hunting. I could taste sweet blood from Naho's body sipped through my gamgam and then the arrow was in my hand, snapped.

Kaori is looking from the stump in mir hand to the other end jutting out from the robe, trying to clumsily restore the two.

"Our three hearts together," Naho mumbles.

My stomach flips.

"Mu keeps saying weird stuff. I don't like it."

Kaori glares. "You don't like it? What the ratty hell did you do to Naho?"

Kaori hurls the broken shaft at my face.

"It wasn't me," I say.

"It *was* you. Who else would be sick enough to smear the tip of their arrow with frog poison?" Kaori hisses.

"I didn't shoot mem!"

"You may as well have!"

Naho writhes on the floor. "Stop, stop this."

Kaori kneels. "Shush, be still."

"Don't fight, never fight," Naho mumbles.

"Was it you, Kentaro?" Kaori says, spit flying from mir twisted mouth. "How can you stand there not saying anything? Naho has never done anything to you."

"It wasn't Kentaro," I say.

"Let mem speak for memself."

Kentaro has to clear mir throat. "It wasn't me. And I'm sorry. For both you and Naho. I know what mu meant to you."

"Stop speaking as if mu has gone. Mu is still here!"

Kentaro glances at me; we both know Naho will not be here much longer.

Kaori gently draws the glyph of an ankh on Naho's forehead.

It is the second time I have seen an ankh tonight. The first time was on Naho's right hand, carved into the soft piece of skin between mir thumb and finger. On the left, in an identical position, was what looked like a healed burn. A blotch of pink flesh on black skin.

Naho splutters. Mu is trying to say something.

"Kentaro"—Kaori can barely speak—"please go and get some gebun seeds."

Kentaro looks to me for permission but I shake my head. "There is no point. Nothing can stop the spread of the poison."

"For the pain," Kaori hisses. "Mu is trying to say something and I would like to hear it."

But what if Naho says something *I* don't want to hear?

I nod at Kentaro anyway and mu leaves to forage for gebun. The rest of the pack have made themselves as small as possible by the opening of the hut. Aito, Shun, and Tetsu have made sure to make a space between them and Ikki. Ikki looks ready to bolt – mir heel is pounding against the wall and mir eyes are darting from Naho to the opening.

Naho continues to mumble, groan, and sigh on the floor until Kentaro returns with a handful of seeds. Kaori cracks them with mir teeth and tucks them gently between Naho's top lip and gum. Gradually Naho's panting and writhing calms.

"Come closer."

Kaori scowls at me and shuffles closer but Naho looks past mem and a limp hand beckons me.

"Both of you."

I don't like this. Kaori gives me a nasty, sly eye as I kneel down next to mem.

"I can barely see you," Naho whispers. "Lean in."

Kaori and I bump heads as we peer into Naho's wide,

feverish eyes. Naho raises two clammy palms and lays one on my face and the other on Kaori's.

"My precious twins." We don't breathe. We concentrate on Naho's quivering mouth, not wanting to miss a single word. "It's me. It's always been me... I am your carrier."

For a moment there is only silence.

Then Kaori is wailing. But so is my blood.

Volcanic smoke pours through the opening. Lava floods my veins. I can't see. I stumble. I scramble across the walls. Scratching. Clawing my way to revenge. I grab the bag, splashing sea water on the floor. My hand is shimmering blue.

It is not true.

It is. I know it is.

Naho has chased me around Mu for many orbits. And I laughed at mem. I spat at mem. Now I have killed mem.

Tentacles sting my arm, lashing my flesh. Naho's flesh. Our flesh. The smoke clears.

Ikki.

I throw the monster at mir face. It lands with a squelch.

"No, Kairi! What have you done!" Aito shouts, Ikki's flailing body at mir feet. Ikki's screams are smothered by the jellyfish. I look to Kaori; mu will know what to do but mu is in mir own cage. Oblivious to mine. Oblivious to even Ikki's agony.

Everyone else panics until Kentaro slides my dagger from my loincloth. Mu stabs the jellyfish and extinguishes the blue orb. The beast slides from Ikki's ruined face.

"Take mem outside and cover mem with guma leaves," Kentaro says, compensating for my lack of command. The pack drag Ikki's twitching body outside.

"Take them as well," I say, nodding to the two horrified stranded unnameds, "and don't come back until I say. You too, Kentaro."

Kentaro hesitates but obeys and leaves the hut.

I kneel again at Kaori's side. I check no one else is in the hut and I wrap my arm around mir shoulder and pull mem in close. Naho looks up at us through glazed eyes and smiles.

"Why didn't you tell us before?" I demand, but Naho continues to smile.

"What is wrong with mem?" I ask Kaori.

"Nothing."

"Why is mu smiling like that then?" Naho's expression is churning my stomach.

"I don't think Naho is really here anymore. Look... the light is dimming in mir eyes."

"Why didn't mu tell us before?"

"Because it is forbidden," Kaori says.

"Did mu tell you?" I search Kaori's face for the truth.

"No."

"Hmm..."

"What do you mean *hmm*? Just because Takanori tells you things mu shouldn't doesn't mean Naho did the same for me. I can't believe... all this time..." Kaori is sobbing again.

Naho is saying something over and over, "Takanori... Takanori."

"Kaori, focus." I squeeze mir arm. "Naho is trying to say something. Stop crying and listen."

"I can't help it."

"Well, *try*, for ratty hell's sake."

"Okay," Kaori whimpers wiping snot on the sleeve of mir robe. "Naho, it's Kaori, can you hear me? What about Takanori?"

"Takanori..."

Spit it out.

Bahm. Mu is unbearable!

"Paired."

What? Kaori and I exchange a look of confusion. What is Naho on about? Paired?

"Do you think mu is too far gone now?' Kaori whispers.

"I don't know. Ask mem what paired means?" I have to know.

"You ask mem!"

I lean in. "Naho, what's paired?"

"Takanori..."

Yes, we know this part, what else!

Naho points at memself, then at Kaori, and then at me.

What?

"Four hearts."

"No!" Kaori screams. "No, no, Naho. Please, no." Kaori is rattling Naho's limp body, trying to shake out another answer.

"Get off mem!"

"No, it can't be, Kairi. No, no, not mem. Anyone but mem."

"What do you mean? What does four hearts mean?" My heart thumps in my throat.

Kaori retches and spits. "Naho created us with Takanori."

The floor of the hut dissolves and I fall.

I fall deep into the fiery heart of the island.

Takanori and Naho are my... No.

Yes, May.

Why? Why did this wretched carrier have to confess? It is wrong. It is forbidden. No. Not Takanori. All the things I have done for mem... All the wickedness.

I am not mem.

You are me. You always have been.

Naho is whispering something to Kaori. Mu is tapping the ankh on mir hand again and again. Then Naho ends. Everything ends. Naho's hand flops and mir soul flees.

Naho has gone.

I wait for Kaori's wail but it does not come. Mu is staring at what is left of Naho but I don't think mu is looking at mem. Kaori has also gone, but to where I don't know.

"Kaori?"

No reply.

We can't just sit here; it is dangerous to preserve the shell of a Maymuan. We have to destroy the shell immediately otherwise an animal or other non-Maymuan soul will try and possess the body.

"Kaori," I say, as gently as I can, "you know we have to... deal with Naho."

My words strike Kaori like lightning on the ocean.

Kaori pummels and shoves me. "We are not cutting mem up."

"I didn't say anything about cutting mem up!"

"What do you mean 'deal with mem' then?"

Kaori forgets we are not on Mu. I have as little appetite for chopping Naho's head off as Kaori does.

"We can do whatever we want. This is my island; we deal with the body however I say."

Kaori's face flickers with hope in an eerie echo of the last expression I saw on the face of the unnamed before Takanori decapitated mem.

"Can we bury mem?"

For ratty hell's sake! No, of course we can't.

Kaori has to ask for the impossible. I can't have a Maymuan buried in the foundations of my empire. And then what? Whenever a Mayan dies will I have to bury them as well? Build huts on the shifting sands of decomposing Mayans? I shiver. No.

"No."

"Why not?"

"Because it's not"—*think quickly and make it good otherwise Kaori will be hysterical*—"good enough... I know. Why don't we use the ocean?"

Kaori frowns but then mu says to memself, "Yes, yes, I think it could be lovely and Kentaro can build a raft and we

202

can chant and shroud Naho and cover mem in flowers and I can guide Naho to tranquillity."

I don't want chanting. I don't want flowers. I don't want Kentaro making rafts and I don't want Naho's rotten shell washing up on the shore after a few rises.

"Okay."

Kaori claps mir hands together. "Get Kentaro to start making the raft. Is it okay if I wrap Naho in this blanket?"

No, Kentaro made it for specially for me.

"Okay."

"Do you think I should wrap Naho with more gebun seeds? They smell strong and will ward off any evil souls."

For ratty hell's sake, Kaori, wrap mem and get it over and done with!

"Okay. I will get the pack to go and pick some more."

Kaori is not memself. Mu is too calm, but all I can do is wait for the inevitable storm.

~

"Why am I doing this?"

"Because I asked you to," I say.

Kentaro is weaving strands of megg through tall, thick stalks of gamgam.

"It's not right."

"What does it have to do with you?"

Kentaro stops tying the knots securing the gamgam together. "You are forcing me to make a raft to sail a

Maymuan shell on! It's not right; Naho should be with the Experienced. It is the Maymuan way."

"We are not Maymuans."

Kentaro continues fixing the raft. "But—"

"There is no but; it's what Kaori wants."

Kentaro's head jerks back in surprise. "What Kaori wants? Since when have you cared what Kaori wants?"

Mu is jealous!

I don't need this now.

As if this night is not awful enough.

"You like Kaori. You spent enough time with mem in the creating hut. And you knew Naho well. Why are you being so nasty all of a sudden?"

Kentaro's face falls and mir chin trembles. "I'm sorry, I didn't mean it like that. It's just, I taught myself to hate mem and now, well, now mu is here and even though it has been horrific I have kind of liked mem being here and I do feel terrible about what happened... It's just been... you know... So much has happened."

I know exactly what Kentaro means. I feel the same way but it is futile. We have started down a path and we must continue.

"Listen," I say, grabbing Kentaro by the back of mir neck, "we can't cry. Real Mayans don't cry. What has happened has happened and there is nothing we can do about it. Finish the raft. We get rid of Naho, Kaori goes back, and we keep growing our side of the island."

Kentaro wipes mir eyes.

"That's it; we have to be strong. I will lead with you by my side but we have to be strong, do you understand?"

Kentaro nods.

"Finish up and drag it to the shoreline."

I kiss mem and head back to check on Kaori.

"Where's your pack?"

"I asked them to go and pick as many morgons as they can find."

Kaori has tightly wrapped up Naho's full body, including mir face, in my blanket. It looks horrible. Although it is Naho who is bound, I can feel the cloth clinging to my skin, squeezing my arms in too tight. Kaori has left no space for my mouth. I can't breathe; the cloth is too close. I try and bite through but I can't pierce the gag. It's hopeless.

"It looks nice, doesn't it?" Kaori puts mir hands on mir hips and surveys mir horrible handiwork.

"Hmm."

Thankfully the pack return with arms full of plucked morgons. Aito has collected a lot more than the others.

"Where's Ikki?"

No one replies.

"Where is Ikki? Mu needs to be here."

Shun shuffles from foot to foot. "Mu is not in any state to join us."

"What?"

The pack glance nervously at each other. Kentaro appears in the opening and surveys the awkward scene,

"These ratty idiots won't answer me. Where is Ikki?"

"Ikki?" Kentaro says.

"Yes, Ikki. Am I talking to myself or what?"

What is wrong with these freaks?

"You threw a jellyfish at mir face. Mu is recovering in mir hut. I don't think mu will be joining us for a while."

Oh bahm.

I forgot. I forgot about maiming Ikki.

"Oh, right. Okay. Is the raft ready?"

"Yes," Kentaro says, still looking at me with an odd expression.

"Kaori, are you ready?"

"Yes."

"Then let's get this over with."

The pack and I carry the bound body to the shore and lay it onto the raft. Kaori begins the chant of "Namu May Mu". At first mu is alone but after Kentaro and I join in the pack follow with suspicious enthusiasm.

Kaori has filled a bag with morgon flowers and mu begins tucking them around the body. Mu holds out the bag and we all take a handful and place the fragrant blooms until the raft is full. To my horror, tears sting the back of my eyes.

Do not let them fall.

This was my carrier. My vessel onto this island. Naho made me. And Takanori made me. Mu made me.

The beach is lit by the moon. Its light shines a path from

the shore to the horizon. Kaori gives the raft a firm push and lays mir hands in the water.

Naho sails the moonlight.

"Namu May Mu" becomes a whisper.

The peace is shattered by Kaori's scream.

"Look, Look!" Kaori shouts, pointing at the looming dark shadows blemishing the pure moonlight. "It's nabgars! We have to do something!"

A wake of nabgars are leering over the raft. One swoops and pecks at the body, scattering many of the morgons.

"Do something!" Kaori screams.

Aito runs off, ratty maggot, but the others stand there, gaping at the attack of the scavengers. The nabgars circle, plotting how best to ravage the body without losing it to the ocean. Another nabgar swoops but before it reaches the raft it drops like a stone and splashes into the water.

Aito has returned with mir bow and arrow and mu has just taken out the nabgar. I am amazed mu can shoot from this distance and in this light.

Ratty hell.

"I can't shoot them all," Aito says. "What shall we do?"

"Light it," Kaori says to me. "Set fire to the raft."

Mu must have lost mir mind. First mu wants to preserve the body forever in the sand and now mu wants to incinerate it.

"Light an arrow and fire it at the raft now!"

The nabgars have made Kaori hysterical. Kentaro shrugs as if to say *why not?* It would solve a lot of problems, but will Kaori change mir mind?

"Fire one now!" Kaori cries, rummaging in mir pockets and pulling out the bloodstone I gave mem.

Aito wraps the end of an arrow with leaves and holds it out to me. Kentaro hands me a dagger and I strike it against the bloodstone and the arrow catches fire. Kaori snatches the stone back and squeezes it tight in mir palm. Aito makes to fire the arrow but I snatch it from mem, and after a moment of hesitation mu hands me the bow.

We gawp as the fire flies through the air and lands on the raft, setting it alight. I stoke the flames high into the sky and the nabgars disperse with a disgruntled squawk.

The pyre burns fast. The flame recedes into the water and ash is carried by the cool night breeze all the way over to us as we stand on the shore.

A flake of ash lands on my hand. I barely touch it and it disintegrates. I look to Kaori and see mu is mesmerised by mir own ash-sprinkled robe.

Kaori pinches a flake and dissolves it on mir tongue. Mu swallows and stares out past the horizon.

An eerie silence falls as the waves cease to crash on the shore.

Kaori takes a deep breath and inhales, heaving the water towards mem.

The pack and I flee as the ocean is wrenched from the sea bed and smashes in to the sky. The clouds swell and lightning flashes. White-hot veins pulse through the night. Black becomes purple. The clouds groan in protest at the abnormal volume of water Kaori has thrown at them. They rumble and roar until a bolt of lightning shatters the dark and the downfall comes.

The water crashes to the earth, forcing us to bow down as it tries to drown us on the sand. We crawl to my hut, leaving Kaori alone in mir madness. Inside, Kentaro coughs up the sea and we all gag on Kaori's power. Rain batters the megg. The walls are like cicada, disturbing our minds with their incessant rattle. The unnameds have shrivelled up and are rocking on the floor.

Aito retches from the flood but admires Kaori from the opening. "Mu is incredible."

The pack murmur their agreement. Kentaro is trying to remain stony-faced but mir wide eyes betray mir terror. We all gather at the opening and watch Kaori. Purple rain is pounding mir shoulders but mu has no humility. Kaori owns the sky. Mu uproots shocking white tree roots and scrawls them across the night. The air crackles and thunder booms, rattling benme trees already bent under the weight of merciless rain.

Kaori turns and walks towards the forest without even a backward glance at us. Mu leaves mir monsoon. Aito tries to chase after mem but the rain is too sharp. Aito has to return to us, gasping in pain and dizzy with awe. "Kaori is incredible!"

For five rises the rain pours. At first, we waited, all sheltered in my hut, certain Kaori would soon stop falling.

By dusk on the second rise we had to crawl out and seize the fish flailing on the sand and shove them in our hungry mouths. Fish, crabs, and shell-pocked kelp lay like a blanket of lost souls across the shore. Rain pounded them, trapping but also keeping them alive.

Finally, now the sky is dry. The fish are rotting and Takanori is in my hut.

"Were you afraid of a little rain?" I ask.

Takanori glares. I don't care. Why has mu waited so long to come and see me? Mu should have come as soon as the skies split open not after they sealed. My island is devastated.

At first it seemed like Kentaro's tight weaves could withstand the water. But by the third rise of relentless rain the megg began to sag and water poured through the gaps. Kaori flooded our sanctuary.

Kaori is everywhere, dripping from the roof, the walls and pooling on the floor.

"You should have called for me not cockroach," Takanori says.

I know this, but it was Kaori who came first to my mind not Takanori.

"Where is Naho's shell?"

Oh bahm.

"Before the monsoon I put mem in Aito's hut and I was going to send Shun to get you but... the monsoon... it swept the body out to sea."

Takanori taps a long yellow fingernail on mir cracked lips.

210

"I'm sorry. It all happened so fast. Kaori went crazy and we didn't have a chance to get to Naho."

"What about Ikki?"

"What about mem?"

"I saw mem piling up mounds of washed-up seaweed as I came here." Takanori raises an eyebrow. "It appears as if mir face is sliding off mir skull."

I repress a shudder at Takanori's monstrously accurate description.

"Is there anything else you would like to tell me?" Takanori asks.

I have thought of nothing but speaking to Takanori since the monsoon began but now I want mem to leave.

"That's it. That's what happened."

Takanori licks mir lips with a forked tongue. "So Naho passed. Without a word. Not even to cockroach."

"Yes."

Takanori pounces. Strong fingers squeeze my throat and sharp nails puncture my skin.

"What did Naho tell you?"

I shake my head and Takanori's grip tightens. I could fight mem but the breath stolen from my brain is a relief. I seek the darkness and Takanori's grip brings it closer.

"Get off mem!"

Kentaro shoves Takanori and the light returns.

"How can you treat mem like this, knowing mu is yours?"

Bahm.

Kentaro, for ratty hell's sake!

Takanori laughs. "I told you to get rid of this pet."

"Get out!" I shout, and point at the opening. Kentaro looks at me with surprise. "Get out!"

"But I—"

I stand and scream, "Get out!"

Kentaro leaves and Takanori and I share silence. I rub the pain in my neck and Takanori smirks.

"What did Naho say?"

"You heard Kentaro." Takanori does not even blink. My pain is rising. I swallow but the hurt will not go down. "How could you... how could you not tell me?"

"No one knows who their carrier is."

Tiny flies purr over the pools of stagnant water dotted around the hut. Their calm and purposelessness infuriate me.

"I am not talking about Naho, I am talking about you!"

Takanori still does not react.

"All of the things you have asked me to do. If I had known..."

"What?" Takanori snaps. "You wouldn't have done them? Or you would have done more? Yes, Naho and I created you, but so what? How many times do I have to tell you it is not how you are born but what you choose."

My head is spinning. "It matters."

"May, you are forgetting all I have taught you. If you let this distract you all we have achieved will be in vain."

I punch the wall and dirty rain splashes from the megg.

"Is that all Naho said?"

I wish Takanori would shut up and go back to Mu.

"Yes, I think so."

"What do you mean you think so? Were you with Naho the entire time?"

"Yes, except..."

"Except what?" Takanori has a disturbingly hungry look in mir eyes.

"Why don't you tell me what you want me to say?"

"I am asking for your sake, May! It is important. Did you leave cockroach and Naho alone together?"

"Not alone but..."

Why should I tell mem? It was nothing anyway. And it looks like it would get Kaori into some deep dung. Takanori is salivating at the prospect of what I have to say.

Mymig mem, I am not saying anything.

"It was nothing."

Takanori cocks mir head and appraises me. Mu knows. Mu knows I am lying.

"I found this." Takanori reaches into mir pocket then spreads mir palm. It is the bloodstone. "It was on the trail from the volcano to here."

Did Kaori drop it or discard it?

"How did it get there?" Takanori asks.

"I told you, it was crazy here. I must have dropped it."

"On the trail?"

"Yes."

Why did Kaori throw it away?

I did everything mu wanted for Naho. And Kaori has destroyed my island.

Ratty, ungrateful cockroach.

I snatch the stone from Takanori.

"Actually, Naho may have said something to Kaori."

"What?" Takanori practically pants.

"I couldn't really hear but Naho definitely pointed at the ankh on mir hand. Did you know it was there?" Takanori doesn't respond but leans in so close I can feel mir breath on my face. "Anyway, mu kept tapping it again and again."

Takanori lurches up and nearly trips over the hem of mir robe in mir scramble out of the opening.

"What's the matter?" I yell after Takanori. "What does it mean?"

Chapter Twenty-Three

KAORI

As if losing Naho wasn't bad enough, now Saki has gone.

Nothing even really happened with Aito. I was amazed when mu sneaked over to see me.

Aito arrived two rises after my downpour started. My rain was lighter by then, no longer able to break skin but mu still arrived pummelled and disorientated.

"What the ratty hell are you doing here?"

Aito stands, dripping wet, at my opening. Mu is gasping from the onslaught of rain. I can't leave mem standing there. Mu is pitiful, shivering in mir loincloth.

"Quick, get in."

I pull Aito through the opening and cast a wary eye out along the path but I haven't seen any Maymuans since the rain began. I throw Aito one of my robes but instead of putting it on the idiot uses it to wipe mir wet body. It is a disturbingly pleasant sight.

Don't even think of it, I tell myself.

But my body is not listening.

Mu is no good for you and how can you think of such things after Naho's passing?

My body doesn't care and continues to tingle.

Say something!

"What are you doing here?"

Good, be strict with mem. Mu can't just walk back in like this.

"I... I... think what happened to Naho was wrong."

Of course it was wrong, you ratty idiot!

"You sneaked over here to state the obvious? What you have created over there is vile! And if you hadn't abandoned Mu, Naho would still be alive."

"That's not fair."

My lust is subsumed by rage. "It's not fair? Naho is dead! Mu is dead!"

"I know, I know, Kaori, I don't know why I came, I just..." Aito's trembling chin drops to mir chest. "I wanted to see you, that's all. See if you were okay."

"Are you moving back to Mu?"

Aito's head flicks up. "What? No."

"Then get out."

"Don't be like that."

"Like what? You don't have the guts to stand up to my twin. How can you stay over there with those freaks! They are freaks, Aito. You can't just make a new island. It's not normal."

"We're not freaks."

"Get out!"

I shove mem but mu grabs my wrists.

"I care about you, Kaori."

"I don't care!"

"I don't believe you."

Aito kisses me and I let mem. I enjoy mir tongue and I get lost in mir mouth.

"Can you believe this rain! Sorry, I haven't—" Saki gawps at Aito's fingers tangled in my braids and our bodies fused together. "I..."

"Saki!"

Saki reverses out of the opening.

"Saki, wait!"

Aito grabs hold of my arm. "Let mem go."

"No, get off me. I have to go. I have to explain."

"What about me?"

I break Aito's hold and chase after Saki.

Saki refused to see me after that. I have been to mir hut every rise since and mu won't speak to me.

Nothing really happened with Aito. I suppose Saki would say, what if mu hadn't turned up when mu did? But I thought Saki wasn't bothered about Aito anyway. I told Saki that Aito has gone back to Kairi.

It's over. I am not going to see mem anymore.

It *is* over, I just haven't told Saki that Aito was waiting in my hut when I returned from chasing mem. How Aito held me while I cried. How Aito removed my robe and we lay together on the floor and used each other's bodies to escape reality. Mu never needs to know that.

So now I have no one.

First, I lost Kairi and Kentaro, and then Aito, Naho, and now Saki. Even the turtles hate me. My monsoon shifted the sand, exposed their eggs, and a flock of nullos devastated their maymus. I am alone in the cove surrounded by shattered shells.

I am so sick of this. All of it.

I have loaded my robe pockets with pebbles as I brood over wading out to sea. It can't hurt more than living on land. Then I could be with Naho in eternity, not stuck here on this stupid ratty island on my own. I should go and do it, right now, but I can't stop picking over the last words Naho said to me.

"Truth," Naho said as mu prodded the mark on mir right hand. I had never noticed the ankh hidden in the crease of Naho's hand before. It was terrifying when it spread like a webbed frog foot and revealed mir secret. An ankh on the right hand and a burn scar on the left. Naho alternated between saying "Truth," and tapping the ankh, and saying "Peace," then rubbing the burn and the ankh together.

Mymig ankhs.

What do an ankh and truth have in common?

Naho may have been telling me to find the true meaning of life. Truth plus ankh, but why wouldn't Naho say that then? It would have taken as long to say "Find the meaning of life," as it did to repeat *truth* and *peace* again and again.

Also, it is not like Naho to waste words. Find the meaning of life?

For ratty hell's sake, what did mu mean? It's weird. Ankhs?

Well, they had been hanging everywhere, but since Kairi left Mu, the Maymuans are cautious where they place their loyalty. *Cowards.*

Did Naho mean me to find my way back to the Maymuans? It would make sense; I do need to regain their respect, but Naho said "truth".

It doesn't fit. None of it does.

I wonder if Naho knew about the ankh on Saki's leg. Maybe mu was telling me to be loyal to Saki. I think that is just my guilt.

What then? Where are ankhs? Ankhs which both Naho and I would know about? On our obis when we hunt snake, I suppose, but I haven't tied my obi since Kairi was my torchbearer.

Hold on…

When I went to get mem from the cave and I dismissed mem, Kairi said there was an ankh. Above an opening. When I pushed back the water.

∾

Clouds of sand swirl around my feet as I sprint from the cove.

I scurry pass the weary Maymuans peering cautiously up at the sky in fear of another soaking. I squelch over soggy forest leaves. I reach the Experienced temple and I feel I am being watched. Takanori is standing between the two tortoise statues at the top of the staircase, leering over me like a nabgar.

What the ratty hell mu is doing up there I don't know but I ignore mem and proceed to the beach.

I skid down the grassy hill and gulp the salty air. The chalky white cliff face looms above me.

Bahm.

Torches hang in brackets waiting to be lit but I don't have the ratty bloodstone. I lost it during the monsoon.

Come on, breathe. No fear. Every full moon I enter this cave so I can do this without moonlight. I can do this.

Namu May Mu.

Inside the cave there is enough sunlight shining through the moon crack to cast shadows. I would prefer the dark. Black silhouettes stalk my path and leer over my shoulder. The air is moist and leaves a rotten yolk on my tongue. The rancid scent of mould plugs my nostrils, making my search for the snake pool impossible. I can't smell the dark water. I have to trust the memory of my feet.

Finally I hear squid ink splash rock. The pool should be still but instead it is aping my pounding heart. I have to calm down or the snakes will be frenzied when I step into the water. I can't remember how far back the opening Kairi pointed out was. If I push the water too far back it will make a wave on the roof and resentful snakes will shoot down from the ceiling with snapping jaws.

Breathe. Breathe. Namu May Mu.

I enter the water. A snake brushes my ankle. I throw the pool away from me. Too far. Snakes spray from the roof and slam, stunned, onto the dry basin floor.

Breathe. Be careful.

I draw the water towards me so it rests after the opening.

Kairi was right.

Above the opening is an ankh chipped into the rock and inlaid with shimmering pearl. I can clearly see the bottom of a staircase so there must be some source of light at the top.

Strange.

My heart thumps again.

Breathe.

As I approach the opening the snakes in the basin begin to uncoil.

Wait? Did the basin move?

I rub my eyes. The floor beneath the opening pulsates. The rock undulates and slithers. Two bright orange slits blink.

Ratty hell, there is a huge snake!

It must be twice the size and length of me!

I stagger back up to the edge of the pool.

Bahm. What should I do?

The sly eyes blink again. I scream.

Get out. Go back. Quick. I don't know what to do. What should I—Argh!

The eyes are advancing. The snake is zigzagging across the basin straight for me. Its mighty jaw swings and its sharp white fangs quiver.

I dive out of the basin. With a crash, the water smashes back into place, scooping up the furious snake.

I don't have the luxury of being afraid. I have to know what is beyond the ankh.

I shove the water back again and sprint to the opening. Snakes shower from the roof, their thrashing tails whipping my face. I slap and kick them away. As I enter the opening I steal a glance at the wall of water and spot the orange-eyed snake suspended within it. I shiver as mu calmly surveys me, biding its time.

I stagger up steep stone steps and when I reach the top the water crashes back to its natural place. The staircase floods but the water rests on the top step.

I enter a dimly lit room. In the corner, sunlight shines through a gap in the roof onto a polished bronze plate. The plate is flat on the floor, reflecting the light back up to its source.

I wonder if I... Yes!

I angle the plate against the wall and the light shines from the bronze to an identical plate in the opposite corner. A warm red glow fills the space. The walls are inlaid with slivers of blazing copper.

On my left, the wall is full of strange glyphs and to my right is an opening leading to another staircase. What are those drawings? I don't want to turn my back to the opening but the images are so unusual I am pulled towards them. They are not Mu glyphs; they are a style I have never seen before but I find I can understand. They don't spell anything. Instead, they seem to depict moments... events. They don't make sense.

The first is what looks like a red-robed, grey-haired Experienced leering and trying to unwrap the robe of a Maymuan. The Experienced is salivating and the Maymuan is crying and trying to defend memself. It is awful. It makes ants crawl under my skin.

The next set of glyphs show the attacked Maymuan but with three hearts scrawled on mir chest.

Three hearts? I lean against the wall for support. The copper flecks become swarming flame dragonflies.

Oh my...

This room is the history of Mu. No, it is much more than that. It is *my* history.

I chew the inside of my cheek until it bleeds and soothes my parched throat. The bronze plate screeches as it loses its grip on the wall and lands with a clang on the floor, plunging the room back into darkness. I wedge it firmly on the rough rock wall.

I have to see. I have to know.

Breathe.

The next drawing shows the Experienced with mir arms spread wide, dangling a maymu from each hand. The two maymus are identical except the left is on fire and the right is dripping water. It's me and Kairi! Scrawled under the

223

watery leg are glyphs I can decipher. They say *Aset*. Under the fiery leg they say *Ra*.

What, or who, are Aset and Ra?

There are other glyphs beneath them. Almost like a mouth or some kind of river. I frown.

In the next drawing, a lightning bolt strikes the twins, now grown.

"You are half of a whole," Naho often said, but I didn't listen. I didn't understand.

Next, boars, monkeys, barmuna, and other poor souls burn in a terrible fire, their faces twisted and contorted in agony.

I scurry to the next wall where water soothes the burnt land.

A monstrous smouldering volcano bursts from a pool of water. I can't breathe. These drawings are unbearable, becoming worse and worse as they go on.

I have to know what's next.

Maymuan corpses are sprawled across the sand, their bodies mangled. Arms for legs and legs for arms. Piled high are dead deer and dolphins. The sea is black; the sky is purple.

This isn't Mu. It can't be.

There is one wall left.

What is our fate?

I turn towards it. Sharp nails in my arm spin me around.

"I have been expecting you."

Takanori.

"Get off me." I wrench my arm from mir claws. "How?"

"You are in my temple."

What?

Takanori gestures to the opening. "My temple."

How fitting for the Experienced to live above a pool of snakes. So, every time I have crawled into the cave I was hunting beneath the temple? All those times the little unnamed was right above me, living, practising joy.

"I hate you."

Takanori laughs. "Are you enjoying the prophecy?"

Prophecy?

"Did you draw these?" I wouldn't put it past mem to have painted these this rise.

Takanori laughs again. "No. I am flattered you credit me with such imagination but I think even you can see these have been waiting here for a very long time."

I hate Takanori but what mu is saying is true. The glyphs are incredible in detail and must have taken a life cycle to draw.

"What does it mean?"

Takanori considers my question. "It means you are the beginning of the end of Mu."

"I... What are you saying?"

"You and Kairi are the end. You saw the prophecy."

I turn to look at the wall I have not yet seen but Takanori seizes my shoulder and spins me back around.

"There is nothing there for you."

"How does it end?" Sweat soaks my top lip. I am afraid of Takanori's answer.

"You don't need to know. All you have to understand is it is ending."

"It isn't. It hasn't all come true."

Takanori scowls. "What is missing?"

"The catastrophe on the beach."

"It has begun. Kairi is making sure of it. Mu is slaughtering without respect. And Naho was slaughtered on the beach, wasn't mu?"

Naho.

Keep mir name out of your filthy mouth.

"What you did to Naho was sick."

Takanori bristles. "I didn't do anything Naho didn't want me to do!"

"That's you attacking Naho in the first drawing!"

"It wasn't like that. Naho would do anything for the island. Even create you two abominations."

"How did Naho know mu was creating us?"

Takanori lifts mir chin in a defiant gesture horribly reminiscent of Kairi.

"Oh my!" I say. "You saw it! You saw the prophecy and you made it come true!"

"No," Takanori splutters.

"You did! This didn't just happen. You made it happen! You attacked Naho in order to make twins like the prophecy says!"

"I did not," Takanori spits. "It was fate."

How could Naho be around this vile tortoise after what mu did to mem?

Takanori trembles with rage. "Afterwards, I told Naho

226

there were three hearts beating in mir body but mu didn't believe me. I told mem it was as foretold. Mu had provided a great service."

I am going to be sick.

"When you arrived, Naho thought mu could keep you. Can you imagine! Naho thought we would all live together in the temple and be unlike all the others. Of course not! I don't know why mu ever thought it possible. I sneaked Naho into the temple and showed mem the prophecy. I showed mem how pointless it was to love you but mu wouldn't give you up. Naho insisted to be allowed to follow you and Kairi around the island."

"Shut up!"

"I allowed mem but look what happened. Naho is dead because of you twins. Everything you touch you ruin. You are the end. The prophecy has been fulfilled."

"No! Shut up! Shut up! I hate you!" I sob and sink to my knees.

"Thank you, you and your twin, for being so pathetic and predictable."

Takanori kicks over the bronze plate. I hear Takanori swoop up the staircase and I am alone on the floor.

Oh Naho, I am sorry. I am so sorry.

I roll over and lie exhausted, flat on my back. The prophecy flashes again in my mind.

You are the beginning of the end of Mu.

I sob into my hand. We can't end like this. *Why didn't I listen to Naho?* I never understood how important it was to be whole. My skin prickles. A snake. There is a snake near.

I hear it. The rustle of scales slithering across rock.

I look to my feet. Orange eyes. A collapsed jaw.

My legs are in its throat. Fangs scratch my hips. A forked tongue caresses my lower back. I sit up while I still can.

How many have I snatched from your pool? How many have I sent to the smokehouse? How many have I eaten?

Two orange slits blink. Another swallow and I am forced to lie flat.

My arms are free – I could try and push out, could try and place a hand on either side of the scaly face or grab a fang for leverage.

No. Let it be.

I throw my arms up over my head. My braids trail over the lip and I am swallowed whole. The mouth closes and I slide into its belly. Warm fleshy insides cocoon my body.

We move. I slither down the stairs and ease into the dark pool.

Scroll Two

Chapter Twenty-Four

KAIRI

"Has there been any sighting of, you know?" Kentaro whispers.

No. We wouldn't be strolling around my island if there had, would we? Idiot.

"No."

"It's been ages... What if mu has really gone for good?"

Kentaro has asked me some variant of this question every rise since Kaori disappeared.

You would think he hadn't been harvesting and weaving kelp incessantly for six moon cycles in anticipation of her return. Kentaro knows Kaori will return – she has to in order for us all to finally get off this ratty island.

And why is he still using *mu*?

"Mymig it, Kentaro! How many times do I have to correct you. Stop using *mu*!"

"Sorry." Kentaro winces. "Do you think *she* will ever

come back?" He casts a furtive look around as if Kaori is about to spring up from the long grass.

"Yes and you will be ready, won't you?"

Kentaro frowns but then regains his composure and tugs at my hand. "Come on! I can't wait for you to see them!"

I can't help but smile at the return of his enthusiasm. He has done well. They all have. We are leaving Mu. Forever. Takanori wanted me to rule Mu by fire with him in my ear but I want more. Ever since I saw the gubaga nesting in the tree I have longed to see their origin. There must be land beyond Mu and I am going to find it. And Kaori will be the crucial element when she finally reappears.

Witnessing her fury over Naho's death has shown me how to escape Mu. By water. We are almost ready. All I need to do is decide whose death will make her even more furious than Naho's.

I let Kentaro lead me towards the forest. It feels good to walk hand in hand across my island with Kentaro. Every Mayan we pass pauses to show respect. A nod or smile. I collect them like boar tusks to adorn my neck. Their expectations do not weigh on my shoulders. I wear their dependency like a gobu robe. A comfort.

As we pass the clearing beneath the volcano, the rural Mayans tug at the lush, leafy stalks poking out of the earth. A big white bulb pops out of the ground like a shiny tooth wrenched from dark gums. The ash from my volcano settled and nourished the ruptured land, providing a rich soil full of oversized vegetables, which has been extremely useful because there must be more Mayans over here now than there are Maymuans on Mu.

Lava warms my veins as I recall the fear on Takanori's face when he realised he was no longer in control. Takanori kept providing unnameds – drip, drip, drip – just enough for my island to develop at the pace he wanted, a trickle not a flood.

But the unnameds came at night, lonely in the heart of the Experienced temple without their missing familiars. Whispered words sailed on a warm wind until an alluring lullaby hummed across the island, heard in the darkest, most secret places. The carriers came next, seizing their chance to reclaim the flesh ripped from their bodies.

As we stalk across the forest, one of them, with a writhing little mayu in her arms, beckons us.

"Hasn't mu grown!" Kentaro says. I crush his fingers. "I mean, he's grown, *him*," Kentaro splutters. "Don't you think he has grown?"

I drop Kentaro's hand like a hot bloodstone. How can I expect the others to obey the new rules if Kentaro continues to say whatever he wants? He came up with *he* and *she*, for mymig's sake!

"Don't you think you should be a bit more careful with the carriers?" Kentaro says, two moon cycles after Kaori disappeared. We lie together on the warm beach watching the sun return to the ocean.

"Why?" I ask.

Kentaro stops running mir fingers over my shaved scalp and I rise from mir lap and turn around to face mem.

"Why?" I ask again.

"I just think... you can't trust them."

"I don't need to trust them." I don't trust them. All the Maymuans are tainted. Especially the carriers who give their maymus to Takanori. The least tainted are the unnameds. The only truly pure are those born under the volcano who have never known Mu. "Anyway," I continue, "don't worry. They only want to reunite with the souls snatched from their bodies."

"I know but I think—"

"You don't need to think," I snap. "You stay by my side, that is all you have to do."

Kentaro sighs and stares out to the horizon.

"What? You think they will go from absolute subservience with Takanori to rebellion with me? I, who have given them the thing they want the most, their maymu!" I laugh. "What power do they have? No Mayan respects them. Even the Maymuans don't like them. Do you honestly believe the unnameds even remember their carrier? We would have a bigger problem with the rearers but they haven't even bothered trying to come over."

"But that is how *you* feel. It is not necessarily how all the Mayans think. I know I'm not supposed to mention it, but on Mu"—I snarl and Kentaro hesitates, but I want to hear what mu has to say so I relent—"on Mu, some of the rurals would say there is power in passing a maymu."

I roll my eyes. "Yeah, there might be, but then the next thing they do is hand it over and scuttle back to the island as if nothing has happened. And if they are so powerful, why aren't they allowed to become Experienced?"

"Well, most of them don't live long enough," Kentaro says, stating the obvious.

"Yes, but even if they did they wouldn't let one sit in the chamber and make any rules, would they?"

"No, but there are Experienced who are like Kaori, who could have had a maymu but didn't."

Ugh, why is mu bringing Kaori into this? "I doubt any of the Experienced who are in the temple now were like you two, going up to the creation hut and only pretending to create."

"Oh, so you do accept that is what we did?" Kentaro says, seizing mir moment to give me a little kick. I suck my teeth and mu continues. "Anyway, we had a carrier join our hands once. There weren't enough rurals to complete all the farming duties so the Experienced let some carriers join. Mu could coax so much milk from the goats it was incredible. And mu had"—Kentaro searches the sand for the correct glyph—"an unusual energy."

I stare at mem. "And what happened to mem?"

Kentaro scoops up sand and lets it drain through mir fingers. "Mu died. The temple said mu lost too much blood during mir sixth passing and never should have returned to the island but Kanta swears mu saw mem hanging from a benme past the cobrows."

I shiver. Kanta is a liar. It is forbidden to destroy your own shell.

Mymig, I sound like cockroach Kaori.

"Don't be so paranoid. You're making me want to hang from a benme."

"And also"—Kentaro frowns, ignoring my attempt to shut mem up—"I... I don't like the way they look at you."

The creeping dusk casts a shadow over Kentaro's face. I pause to consider mir words. I know exactly what mu means. I don't like how they look at me either but Kentaro can't possibly know my reason.

"They stare at you," Kentaro continues, mir voice almost a whisper, "dead in the eye without flinching. I don't like it."

No, neither do I. They remind me of the carrier boar crashing through the habim. That creature wasn't afraid of me either. In sleep I can taste its warm saliva dripping into my mouth as I pierce its side. I hear the guttural moan as I drink from its wound. On my island, the unnameds from the temple and the others who have deserted Mu to join me know their place.

Every Mayan is united by a jellyfish-lashed arm but there is something about the carriers. Something inside them which is not quite right. They are grateful to be reunited with their maymus and I have even allowed carriers to reclaim their unnameds.

Maybe it was a mistake. They have gratitude but I feel like they don't give me full credit. They seem to think they had some role in it. As though I hadn't released them. It is as if they fought and earned their freedom. Which is ridiculous. They didn't. They owe me.

I rise and pace around Kentaro.

Mymig it. I don't need this. Why couldn't Kentaro keep mir stupid thoughts to memself?

"What do you suggest I do? Kill them all?"

Kentaro flinches. "No."

I kick sand at mem and shout, "So what then? Why are you always bringing me problems?"

"I'm sorry, I'm so sorry. I just..."

"I just, I just," I mimic, pleased to see the humiliation on Kentaro's face. But it only flashes for a moment, then Kentaro closes mir eyes and inhales heavily through mir nose.

"You need to separate them somehow. Make them different to you. To us."

I survey Kentaro. Maybe I should be more careful around mem. Mu has changed since we moved here. Mu is stronger, fiercer. And mu doesn't flinch when mu looks at me either.

"How?"

Kentaro draws up mir knees and rests mir chin on mir mottled arms. Mu gazes out over the water to the last of the sun. "Well, you did say we need to stop saying *mu* if we are Mayans."

"Yes, and? Are you saying we should refer to everyone as *may* except the carriers?" I ask with a sneer.

"No, not *may*. We are all Mayans now, but we need a new way to address each other instead of *mu*, *mir*, and *mem*... Simple, like those terms, but not them... Do you know what I mean?"

I murmur in agreement.

"But not only the carriers. I think everyone who can be a carrier should be one thing and everyone who can't be a carrier should be something different. Obviously, you and I can't be carriers so our group will automatically be the most powerful."

Darkness swarms the beach. I catch my breath.

Ratty hell, what an incredible idea.

"Hello, Kairi," the carrier says, bowing deeply to me. "Kentaro." She gives a curt nod and before Kentaro can respond she shoves the writhing mayu into his arms.

I stifle a laugh at the surprise on Kentaro's face. I know this carrier. It is Ayana. She used to be a water hunter until she became a carrier, and was the first to escape from the heart of the forest. She arrived dripping with sweat and cradling a huge belly. Three rises later, the first Mayan was born. She wanted to call him Kai and I agreed.

She looks well. I wish all the carriers would tie their gobu like her. The wrap skirt drapes gracefully over her hips, as does the gobu she has hung from her neck and bound around her chest. Even the initiation lashes on her arm are lovely, like long strokes of a fingernail across wet sand.

A bright-red necklace of morgon flowers sways as she

reaches for my hand and pulls me towards three young Mayans hunched over a fallen log. I recognise them too.

Ayana is unmistakably their carrier – they all share Ayana's fluffy cloud of dark hair and her strong, broad nose. They were unnameds who escaped from the temple. Ayana insisted on naming them as soon as they arrived.

The smallest of the group, Hana, is poking a stick into the dark gap between the log and the forest floor. After a few vigorous pokes she is rewarded with eight hairy legs scuttling towards her. The others squeal in excitement.

"Quick, squash its back. Watch the hairs," the one with the most orbits, Riku, says.

Hana scowls. "I know. Shut up and let me do it."

"It's getting away, quick!" says Haru, the last of the trio.

"I've got it," Hana says. "Move out the way, you are too close."

Riku moves closer. "I'm not. Ouch!"

"I told you, idiot."

The spider, in a desperate attempt to save itself, extends one of its long legs to flick hairs from its back towards Riku. The hairs land and he screams in pain and frustration as they sting his arms. I am impressed as Hana and Haru work together to catch the spider. She bends the spider's legs back with the stick and he wraps it carefully in a benme leaf.

"Excellent," I say and they spin around and jump to their feet in excitement.

"Kairi! Kairi! Kairi!" they squeal.

Ayana smiles. "Show Kairi how many you have caught."

They point to a small pile of wrapped spiders.

"There is enough for one each. Shall we eat together?" Ayana says, addressing me.

Before I have a chance to respond they scream, "Yes! Yes! Kairi! Kairi!"

I glance at Kentaro but he is still struggling with Kai.

"They"—Ayana blushes—"*we*... would appreciate it."

"Okay," I say.

The little Mayans scatter to collect dry wood and Ayana and I begin to clear a small area for us to sit down. Above, tall gamgam trees bend to embrace each other, green leaves entwining. Below, warm air hums with mosquitoes. Ayana pulls a ganba skin from the fold of her skirt. She rubs it slowly down her leg. A tang of citrus catches in my throat as I watch her.

"It's easier to use this with your mouth closed," she says with a wink, passing me the skin. I quickly rub it on my ankles, wrists, and neck then hand it back, ignoring Kentaro's outstretched fingers.

Ayana smiles as she sweeps away dry leaves, but then a dark cloud descends. "I know you don't like that I keep asking... but has there been any sign of Reo?"

On Mu, Reo was paired with Ayana. Together they created Riku, Haru, Hana, and Kai. After Kai was born, Ayana, barely rested and still bleeding, crept onto Mu and returned with Reo, only for Reo to vanish three moons later.

It is not a great loss. He isn't much of a Mayan. He was a preparer on Mu but I don't need them here. Everyone can harvest food and everyone can prepare it. Reo is useless and never found himself another duty. He followed Ayana around, all dreamy-eyed, doing whatever she asked. They never should have been paired. She is much stronger than he is.

"No, no one has seen mem— I mean *him*," I say, avoiding Kentaro's glare at my tongue slip.

"But it doesn't make sense." Ayana kicks a stray cone, ignoring or oblivious to my carelessness. "He hasn't been seen for over a moon cycle now."

"We *will* find him. I promise."

Ayana squeezes my shoulder and stares deep into my eyes. "I know you will."

Kentaro clears his throat. "Can I...? Would you?"

He tries to pass Kai to Ayana but she ignores him and claps her hands together in praise of all the firewood the little Mayans have collected.

Hana skewers the spiders and passes us one each. Ayana finally relieves Kentaro of Kai.

Haru draws a bloodstone from a small pocket in his loin cloth. I grimace, replaying Takanori's horror when he realised I had discovered the source of the bloodstone supply. Dirty, dusty tortoise thinks he can keep secrets from me.

The little Mayans who play in the river returned with tiny pieces embedded in the soles of their feet. We tracked the stream back to the mine so now every Mayan has a bloodstone and can strike it to make fire whenever and wherever they want. Not fire like mine, of course.

Ayana lays a gentle hand on my knee. "Are you okay, Kairi?"

"Yes," I say. *Mymig you, Takanori.*

"You seemed lost for a moment."

Kentaro growls and crosses his arms in front of his chest. "He is not lost."

Ayana removes her hand and watches as Haru sparks his small dagger against the bloodstone and ignites the firewood.

Riku, who has finally stopped scratching, glances hopefully at me. Heat builds in the back of my neck and flows over my shoulders and down my arms. I raise an eyebrow at him, flick my finger, and with a roar the fire soars as high as the trees surrounding our clearing.

They shriek and roll onto their backs, watching my flames burst through the green canopy to lick the sky.

Frazzled leaves drizzle down and Kai begins to cry. I reach for him and he calms in my arms. Together we catch the ash and I smear it across his brown skin, drawing tiny stars on his legs. Ayana smiles but Kentaro scowls. The flames recede and we roast our spiders until their singed hair fills our nostrils and air screams from their joints.

"Did you see her smirking when you were holding Kai?" Kentaro hisses. He hasn't stopped whining about Ayana since we left the fire.

Ratty hell, he is making my ears bleed.

"You shouldn't—"

"Who are *you* to tell me what I should and shouldn't do?" I say, and Kentaro stops dead on the path.

"He is not your maymu!"

"Maymu?"

"Mayu! Whatever!" Kentaro snorts and clenches his fists. "You don't get it. She is... I think she's... she is seducing you!"

I laugh. "Don't be ridiculous. Is that what you are worried about?" <u>I pull Kentaro in close and kiss him.</u> "Come on, Ken-kun"—Kentaro relaxes a little at my affectionate nickname for him—"we need to get to the shore before the sun sets. I want to see what you have made."

Kentaro thankfully stops whining and resumes leading me to the shore. I walk a step behind so he can't see my face as I ponder Ayana and Kai. Kai *is* mine. Not like I was to Takanori and Naho but mine because I want him to be.

He is pure Mayan. He has never known Mu so he will always be special because he was the first pure born. I like the feel of his pudgy legs. His two-toothed smile. How he slurps coco milk and bashes the shell against the trunk.

Ayana is... I don't know what she is, but I suppose she will always be the carrier of the first Mayan. At night she penetrates my dreams. Together we follow a genmo to a tall honey tree and scale it together. We suck the sweet golden juice from the comb. After, we sit in the shade of the branches and I braid her curly hair.

I bump into Kentaro, who has stopped where the dirt

243

path becomes sand. He turns to me with a huge smile and arms spread wide and says, "Look!"

They are incredible.

A row of enormous sailing pods hang from clusters of benme trees. The pods are large enough to sail all the Mayans from Mu. It has been an extraordinary six-moon effort. The spines of the trees bow in submission from the immense weight they hold. Swarms of Mayans fill the shore, each pack buzzing with duty.

Many are waist-deep in the ocean, wrenching long, murky green strands of kelp from the sea bed. Others receive the kelp and stretch the strands, doubling their width and length. Another pack weave the green strands and pass them to others who seal the wooden carcass of the pods with the dark veiny skin from the sea.

Kaori gave us this gift. She can't know, but after she destroyed our beach in fury over Naho's death, the monsoon deposited mounds of kelp on the shore. Before we had only ever chewed scraps of kelp as a snack, but when Kentaro saw the piles and unravelled the length, he began experimenting with it as a hut material.

We wrapped the huts in woven sheets of kelp and when it next rained we remained dry inside.

The packs bow to Kentaro as we pass, then they remember to give me a cursory bow too. My eyes narrow as I watch Kentaro evaluate them with praise or reprimands. He reminds me of someone. Me.

"What do you think?"

"It's okay," I reply stiffly.

Kentaro laughs and gives me a little shove. "Only *okay*?"

"Did you work out how to seal them from the inside after everyone is on board?" The thought of being encased in one of those pods makes me queasy. It was bad enough in the kelp-wrapped hut, the walls pulsating from the rain. I can't even imagine what it will be like out at sea.

At least we will no longer be on Mu. The Mayans are prepared for the sea to swallow us and spit us out towards a new land. Kaori and I can no longer hide our powers. Not after the volcano and the monsoon. I have told the Mayans what they need to know. *We are leaving by sea when Kaori returns. It will happen soon. Be ready.*

I think the Mayans expect a face-to-face final duel between Kaori and me, fire against water, but it will not happen this way. I won't even see Kaori. But I will detonate her. And she will drown and destroy the island. That is certain.

"Yes, I will—Sorry, I mean, *you* will have to choose a leader for each pod and I will train them how to weave the entrance closed. Your pod will have a red cloth to fly outside when we sail. All the others will have white cloth."

I control my face but I am impressed. "What about food?"

"The carriers have been drying out strips of mango, coco, and deer." Kentaro directs one of the Mayans who swiftly returns with deer for me to chew.

"And the water?"

"We have been working on funnels to capture the rain and collect it in basins inside the pod." Kentaro's chest puffs with pride. I am proud of him too. I could say so but instead I squint, looking up into the trees at the ropes tied to the upper branches preventing the kelp orbs from rolling out to sea. Kentaro follows my gaze.

"They will either snap from the impact of the first wave or, if she is *really* demented, she might uproot this entire row."

I shiver.

"What about the oars?"

Kentaro heads towards the nearest pod. "We are going to trial them now. We used gamgam to make them because it is strong and flexible so they shouldn't break. Do you want to be inside or watch from here?"

"Where will you be?"

Please say outside.

"Inside."

Then I can't ratty well stand here like a stupid carrier, can I?

Kentaro instructs a pack to cut down one of the pods and with great difficulty and many strong Mayan bodies, they push it until it bobs on the water.

The pack look to Kentaro for orders. When he flicks his hand and they file into the pod I make to follow but Kentaro holds me back. "You should know he is watching."

My blood burns. "Where?"

Kentaro jerks his head to further down the beach, past the pods where the sand curves up the dune leading to Mu. At the foot of the hill I can make out two of my pack who are always stationed there to monitor anyone coming in or going out of Mu. But at the top of the hill, red robes ripple in the strong sea breeze.

Takanori.

"He has been nagging me to deliver his pod," Kentaro says. "I told him they are not ready yet but he doesn't believe me, so he has started watching us. He has been trying to interrogate any Mayan he can get his hands on but they ignore him."

I am sure a Mayan snub has been as well received as a jellyfish tentacle down his throat. Takanori has no choice but to follow us off Mu. If he doesn't there will be no island left for the Experienced to rule.

I almost feel sorry for the Maymuans who have stayed with the Experienced and those over there with their stupid ankhs pining for Kaori. They have no idea what is crashing towards them. And how Takanori intends to abandon them. I turn my back to Takanori and enter the pod.

Inside it is eerily green and the sunlight warms the kelp, making the pod humid with thick umami air. The seabed coats my tongue as I swallow frantically to try and calm my racing heart. I can't breathe. I am in a hostile womb. I need to get back on land. I am not safe on water.

"Are you okay?" Kentaro asks. I pretend to look around the pod with interest. There appear to be three levels. A ladder leads up and another ladder leads down. This first level is empty.

"Where are the Mayans?"

"They have gone below, ready to row. But look," Kentaro says, gesturing around, "this level is for docking, above is where we will store the food and other resources, then all the other space is for the Mayans."

Kentaro climbs the ladder and I follow him up. He points to an elaborate series of deep wooden holes spread across the walls. "We copied the structure of honeycomb. Each Mayan will have their own cell to lie down in."

I hope not for too long. My lungs are collapsing so I scramble back down the ladder to the only source of breeze: the entrance. Kentaro goes to seal the pod but my hand betrays me and I seize tight hold of his arm. He looks at me in surprise but stops.

"I suppose we can keep it open for now. I'll tell them to start rowing. Wait here. I have to show them how to insert the oars." Kentaro disappears down into the pod's depths and I try to control my breathing.

It is okay. It is okay.

I want to jump out of this pod and feel the cool water on my ankles and the firm shoreline between my toes.

You are pathetic.

Redness flutters in my eyelids.

No! No more.

You are pathet—

No! Never again.

The pod shudders as the oars enter the water. After a moment of ominous lurching, the pod steadies and we glide across the water. Cheers rumble the wooden planks beneath my feet. Kentaro returns beaming. He happily skips over to me and we embrace.

"You are wonderful," I say.

Kentaro leans back in surprise to peer at my face.

"Don't tell anyone Ken-Kun," I say, squeezing him tight, "but you are."

We kiss.

"Soon we will be free."

Kentaro nods, tears shining in his eyes.

I cling to Kentaro tighter than I should. I close my eyes to block out the pulsating green walls but they are replaced by a cage of red.

"You must do one thing," I whisper into Kentaro's ear. "Give Takanori an incomplete pod."

Chapter Twenty-Five

KAORI

Green rock. Red sparks. Bloodstone. Consume the island. Ash trees. Ash creatures. Ash water. Black in my palm. Thirsty. Oil coats my throat. *Don't swallow. Don't accept. Go deeper. Dive. Dive.*

Naho is on the bed. My heart. Our heart. Morgon is mir skin, black and red. Burnt.

I'm sorry.

Namu may mu.

Shakes head.

Finger on my lips.

No more.

No may. No mu.

I lie. Naho buries me.

She. She. She. She. Who is she? You and I.

Then what is May? He. He. He is he.

Why? Incomplete is weak, I say. *Together. Too late. Too far. Time to part.*

251

Time for change.

Time for the end.

Time to begin.

I am afraid. So is he. Am I wrong to understand the fear that hides inside he?

~

I know. You must return. I am not ready. It is not about you.

We are ready.

Come with me. I am here. You are not alone.

The future stirs in your belly. You are the carrier of one and all.

The water is dirty. No, disturbed. It was never clear. It will settle again. Some calm, others agitate.

This is eternal.

The challenge is choice. Choose those who do not fear the shadow they cast. Who do not deny.

I am afraid.

You should be.

Fear is responsibility. And honour.

Never trust those who claim to live without fear for they wear a mask which also shrouds their heart.

Chapter Twenty-Six

KAIRI

Kentaro and I part, our bodies shining with sweat and pleasure. I drop from all fours onto my stomach and roll onto my back to gaze up at Kentaro. Soon we can emulate the gubaga and seek new land to rule together. Kentaro fetches a bag of water and we sip from the megg.

Footsteps approach. Kentaro strolls naked to the opening and moonlight turns his black skin blue.

It is Shun and, looking particularly horrible bathed in the silver light, is knobby-faced Ikki.

"What's going on?" Kentaro asks, eyes swivelling from Shun to me.

I rise and reach for my loincloth and nod at them. Shun and Ikki bow and retreat from the door.

Kentaro makes to block my exit.

"I have to go and see him," I say.

"Who? Takanori?" Kentaro says. "Why? You have been

so many times this moon cycle. He is not listening to you. He still came and watched from the hill, didn't he?"

"I have to keep him calm." I squeeze Kentaro's hand. "We are so close. I can't let anything or anyone interrupt our plan."

Kentaro steps aside. "Be careful."

Shun, Ikki, and I make our way swiftly to the shore.

We approach Aito and Tetsu, who are positioned by the Mu hill. They rise quickly from their slumped positions and stand erect in a pathetic attempt to hide their negligence. I draw my bow and an arrow pierces the sand where a moment ago Aito's legs were languishing. He retrieves it with a shaking hand.

I snatch the arrow from him and stab it at Tetsu's face.

"Do not let anyone pass here. Do you understand?"

"Yes, Kairi," they snivel in unison.

I lead Shun and Ikki not up the hill but around it, continuing along the shore until we reach a rocky bay swarming with coarse shadows. My skin gasps from the shock of the cold as we wade across a dark body of water. We approach a craggy hollow, its jagged lips glinting in the moon's light. I strike my arrow tip against my bloodstone and pour fire into the mouth.

Lying prone on the glistening rock tongue is Reo.

I kick his foot and he begins to stir.

"Get him up," I say.

Shun and Ikki drag Reo into a sitting position. Shun hands me the megg bag he is carrying and I tip water down Reo's throat. He splutters and wakes. I stroll to retrieve a sword leaning against the wall.

"I see you still haven't had the decency to do what I ask." I slice my finger down the sword until my blood stains the blade. "This should be your blood." I hold the blade before Reo's eyes and smile as he shivers. "What is wrong with you? Do you have no pride?"

Reo's teeth chatter. "I don't want to die."

"We will all die. Most of us won't be fortunate enough to die by our own hand. It is a gift I am giving you." I have thought a lot about the carrier Kentaro told me about who may have destroyed herself. Why was her act forbidden but the farmers were allowed to maim themselves? As always with Takanori, *power.* I understand.

"I want Ayana. And my maymu," Reo moans, the hysterical edge to his voice echoing around the hollow. His body trembles against the rock floor.

I squat down and look into Reo's frenzied eyes. "They don't want you. They are not maymu. They are Mayans now."

"I am a Mayan!" Reo screams, rising and waving his welt-covered arm. "I'm a Mayan! Please!"

Shun kicks Reo back to the floor.

"No," I say, "you are not a Mayan. Mayans choose. You were *taken.* Without Ayana's courage you would never have come here. I don't need cowards."

"No, please," Reo sobs, tugging his tangled, unkempt hair. "I love them. Please don't take them from me."

"You love them? But you never fought for them. Riku, Haru, and Hana were in the temple. You didn't free them. *I* did. You never fought for Ayana. *I* did. I have freed you all."

"I know, I know, you are special, Kairi. We never had your courage." Reo crawls and seizes my ankles. "Please forgive me. I just want to be with them. I don't care about anything else. Please." Reo collapses at my feet, convulsing with cries.

I catch a look of unease exchange between Shun and Ikki. I don't care. There is no way this maggot is living on my island.

"Get a grip on yourself. You are pathetic. Look at you! You are a disgrace. They wouldn't even take you back on Mu, you are so pitiful."

Reo gazes up, eyes shining, sensing a reprieve. "Send me back to Mu."

I can't believe it! "After all you have said, you would leave them and return to Mu?"

"Yes," Reo says, his voice clear for the first time.

"See!" I say with triumph to Shun and Ikki. "This is the kind of Maymuan I am dealing with. He is not worthy to even breathe the same air as a Mayan."

"Maybe he could go back," Shun says but, shrivelling under my glare, he hastily adds, "They love cockroaches there."

"No," I say.

Reo resumes wailing again. "But I... I just want to be near them. I promise I will never see them again, but I want to live through the same time as them. Please don't take that away from me."

Ikki sighs and shrugs as if what Reo is saying is reasonable.

"Do you have something to contribute?" I hiss into Ikki's mottled face. He holds my stare for a moment then turns away to raise an eyebrow at Shun.

"What about you?" I shout. "Do you think he should scuttle back to Mu?"

Shun hesitates. "You could send him back with the other three and keep Kai and Ayana."

How dare Shun say such a thing in front of Ikki and Reo!

"Yes!" Reo pleads. "Keep Kai but give me the others!"

Mymig you, Shun.

My fire crackles and splutters, flooding the cave with flame.

"Been watching me have you, Shun?" My face is close enough to splatter specks of spit on his face. "Think you know me, do you?"

Shun flinches. Sweat soaks his top lip as the cave becomes a furnace. "No, no. You asked and I was saying—"

"Go and get Hana," I demand.

"What?" Shuns say, astonished at my request.

"Get. Hana," I repeat. "I want her last moment before I slit her throat to be the sight of this coward on his knees, sacrificing her life for his own."

The blood drains from both Shun and Ikki's faces. Neither moves.

"Go now!" I roar.

Reo makes a strangled sound like a boar when an arrow first pierces its throat. He reaches out to me. I hand him the sword. He wipes his eyes with the back of his hand and addresses Ikki and Shun. "Tell my maymus and my carrier what I gave tonight."

The tip of the blade flashes in my firelight then the sword enters his stomach and, with a sickening rip of flesh, Reo disembowels himself. He slumps to the floor. I step on the blade to stop it clattering. Sweat pools in the crags of Ikki's face. Shun screams when Reo's leg twitches.

"Leave."

Ikki and Shun exchange another uneasy glance.

"I said go!" I scream.

They flee and land with a splash in the cold pool below. I watch the blood seep from Reo. My fire scrawls shapes on its surface and I see Ayana reflected in its sheen.

I leave the cave and enter the cold water. I immerse myself until I am fully submerged. Water fills my ears. It hisses, "You killed without purpose," and coils around my legs. I flail and thrash until I return to the night. I can't breathe; the cave chokes on smoke from my smouldering fire.

I flick my finger to reignite the hollow and cremate Reo's shell, but nothing happens. There is no heat in my body. The water has extinguished my power. I wade as fast as I can to the shore but the water won't let me go.

Finally, I land, panting. I scrub fistfuls of sand onto my arms until I am red raw and burning from the friction. With a roar I blast fire into the hollow until it explodes and the cave collapses. Fire leaks from the rubble and skates on the skin of the water, deftly resisting her clutches.

Steam sizzles, while I lie and let the salt sting my torn flesh.

Chapter Twenty-Seven

KAORI

W ater floods my mouth. I can't breathe.

Get out, Kaori.

I can't.

Help me. Help me, please.

Naho rests in the grave we share. There is not enough space for me. Every word is water down my throat. Eternal training. Fiery drowning.

From my stomach a kick. *Push.* My hand breaks the sand. *Push!*

I thrash and I am free. I need air.

Naho's closed eyelids flicker. She smiles.

Light shimmers above. *Swim.*

I am delivered.

∼

A sliver of light penetrates the dark, cautiously at first. Then a long straight ray bursts my cocoon. I blink as the aperture stretches open wide. My first breath is musty.

"Oh my... Kaori!" The words are too loud, as is the splash of water against rock.

Strong hands drag me from my skin. My legs buckle. I crash onto the damp floor. Strong hands pull again. I clamber to my knees. The water calls me. I crawl to it.

"What are you doing? Can you hear me?"

I can, but I ignore the question. I reach the rim of the basin and listen to the water gently lap against the side. I run my finger over the edge and plunge my hand down into it so I can lick the salt from my palm.

"Be careful!"

I am pulled back from the rim but when released I lean over again.

"Are you crazy? It is full of snakes! Don't you remember?"

I dive into the water.

It feels like I am back inside. The water squeezes me tight and I twist and turn until I rise and break the surface. I splash and slosh until I am awake.

I swim back to the edge of the basin and reach for Saki's outreached hand.

"I can't believe it! Are you okay? You're here. You are really here!" Saki is panting out of a slack mouth. A bloody dagger drops from the tips of her fingers and clangs on the floor, echoing around the torch-lit cave. *Her* fingers. Not *mir*, as before. Her. This is Kairi's doing. It is not enough for twins to be torn apart, now he has severed the Maymuans into two. The terrible consequence of splitting pounds my mind. But here Saki stands, a dagger at her feet, and suddenly nothing else matters.

I turn around.

There it lies.

I gaze at the blood oozing from the space between the dimming orange eyes and I blindly reach for Saki's hand, squeezing it tight. We approach the body I left behind. The snake is slit from its throat to its twitching tail.

"I didn't know what to do," Saki whispers, "I have been coming here every rise since you disappeared. It's crazy out there." She nods to life outside the cave. "I was sitting here and then"—she gulps and stares at the snake—"it slithered out of the pool. Those eyes. I didn't have time to think; I stabbed it and it stopped but..."

I give her hand another squeeze.

"Its belly was... kind of pulsating. It could have been anything in there. I don't know why I cut it."

"It's okay. Namu May Mu."

Saki flinches. "We don't really say it anymore."

"Oh, I know, but I thought you might want to. I'm sorry."

"You know? How?"

"It doesn't matter."

The dull orange eyes blink. I squat down next to the head.

"Are you insane? It doesn't know it is dead yet!"

I lay my head on its wound and whisper, "Thank you."

Saki approaches in mesmerised horror. The snake lurches forwards and snaps its jaws at her leg. Saki screams and jumps back, almost toppling into the basin. I leap up and grab her before she falls. I glance back at the snake and its orange eyes burn no more.

Saki is shivering. I guide her to the space beneath the bracket holding a burning torch and we slump in silence for a moment on the wet stone floor.

"I can't believe—" Saki says, but I interrupt.

"I know. There is so much to say, but first tell me what has happened here."

Saki sighs. "On Mu?"

I frown. "Where else?"

"On May."

"We are separate now?"

"Yes." Saki lets out a horrible kind of laugh which echoes around the damp hollow. "They chose. I did try and warn you. Most are on May now."

"What about the Experienced?"

"They haven't done anything to keep us together." She scowls. "They stay hidden in the temple. We don't really see them anymore. The rearers returned to Mu without any little ones. They said the carriers escaped with their maymus and went to May. There are rumours there aren't any unnameds left in the temple. They have all gone to…" She won't say Kairi's name. "He."

I nod.

Saki glares at me. "Aren't you going to ask me what *he* is?"

"I know."

"What do you mean you know? Have you been over there?" She is furious. "Making a new life with Aito while I have been sick with worry over here?"

"Don't be ridiculous."

"Then what do you mean? How can you know?"

"In there." I nod towards the snake. "I saw things. I can't really explain it but I know some things. Things that must have happened on Mu."

"But you have been gone for over six moon cycles!"

My stomach lurches. *What?*

Saki continues, "I hope you saw what will happen next because it is pretty ratty awful out there."

Six moon cycles! I struggle to get to my feet. My body is heavy and unbalanced. Saki holds out her hand. I take it but she pulls me back down.

"What's that?"

"What's what?" I ask.

"That!" she shouts, pointing at my stomach.

My stomach is protruding as though I have a large coco under my skin.

"I don't know. It must be from"—I hesitate—"being in there. It will go down, don't worry about it."

Saki seems ready to shout again but I haven't got time for her concerns. I scramble up the damp wall.

"Come on, Saki. I will show you what is next."

We walk to the edge of the pool. With a great roar, I force the water back to reveal the hidden opening. Saki gasps and points, shocked to see the ankh etched above.

Inside my stomach something stirs, writhing in rhythm with the snakes that litter the basin. My hand instinctively cups the curve of my belly and the squirming ends. I seize Saki's hand and drag her into the basin.

"What are you doing! It's not safe, Kaori, we haven't prepared. Are you crazy?"

The snakes slither, zigzagging towards us. The closest rise together and caress the air, their tongues flickering, their black eyes shining.

Saki twitches in my grip but I hold on tight. "Wait," I hiss.

I walk towards them. More splash from my water wall and slither to join the nest of snakes undulating in a circle around us. The basin is quickly covered by so many snakes that rock is replaced by glistening scales.

Ignoring Saki's whimpers, I continue to advance. The snakes move with me, circling us, but without attacking. Together we approach the opening and the snakes part to allow us entry. Saki trips in her haste to run up the stairs. I whisper my thanks, then with a crash I return the water and we enter a darkened room.

The room is not cold, but I shiver as I feel for the overturned bronze plate. I don't want to see what is drawn on the final wall, but I must. After all, I lived inside the snake; I know that cowering in the shadows is not an option. The river is flowing and we must follow its course. But I can choose not to drown.

I tilt the plate until a warm red light replaces the darkness.

Saki gasps. The illustrated walls are as magnificent as I remember. I raise my finger to my lips in warning for silence and whisper, "We are in the Experienced temple." I peer up the stairs where Takanori last crept up on me. I gesture to the prophecy. "This is the story of Mu."

Saki traces the path I took six moons ago.

And together we see.

Chapter Twenty-Eight

KAIRI

Screams fill my beach. Kentaro and I run to the commotion. Dried food lies abandoned in the sand as the Mayans leave their duties to shriek at the sky.

"Look," one yells, "the moon is eating the sun!"

We can't look because it burns. Those who try for too long must run to the sea to cool their eyes.

"What is this?" Kentaro says, his voice trembling.

I don't know, but it makes my stomach churn. I steal a glance and see half of the sun is already gone. Mayans cry around me. More stream from the forest to witness the massacre.

As the sun is consumed, the sand fills with prostrate bodies. Mayans lie overwhelmed by the death of their sun. I shiver as darkness falls. All is black. There is no beach, sea, or forest. Mayans wail. Their anguish is joined by a sudden rattle of cicada.

Day has become night. My sun is her moon.

Stars twinkle, laughing at our confusion.

Darkness remains and the Mayans fall silent. Together we raise our heads and search for our sun.

Please fight her. You must fight her.

A flame ignites around the moon. Hope murmurs from Mayan mouths. I push through the anxious bodies and thrust my arms into the sky. I scream until my throat tastes blood. My Mayans continue my roar. We stand together, screaming for our sun.

I stare at the ignited moon until finally my eyes burn. I run to the water and I am surrounded by the splash of others. I don't need to open my eyes; my skin can feel its return, warm on my shoulders. The salt water hides my tears. The cicada rattle is replaced by Mayan joy.

Kentaro wades over to embrace me. His body is still trembling. He whispers, "Maybe what we are doing is wrong."

"No," I say, "but we must be ready. She has returned."

Chapter Twenty-Nine

KAORI

Saki's legs buckle as she tries to process the terrible glyphs. I drag her to the final wall. Kairi's volcano has erupted. Red sparks blister the clouds and lava gobbles up Mu. Dense black smoke clogs the sky, snuffing out the sun. The heat from the glyphs melts my skin. Now my legs tremble.

"This can't be how we end, because of *him*," I whisper, resting my sweating forehead against the volcano.

"It isn't because of him or mem or anyone else," Saki says. "It is because of you."

I join her at the next glyph.

A huge frothing wave smashes the volcano. Frantic in its jaws are Maymuans, gasping for breath, desperate to survive. Deer, barmuna, and boar churn in the cruel water, their bodies reduced to vacated shells.

We stagger to the final glyph.

"I don't understand," Saki says.

I do. The glyph is still. No Maymuans, no life. Only water and sky. A horizon.

Saki's eyes are wide with fear. "What does this mean? Where is our island? What has happened to Mu?"

It has gone. Scorched and drowned. Takanori's zealotry complete. Beneath us, agitated snakes splash their fury at our stupidity.

"I won't let this happen."

Saki looks at me with pity. "It's already begun."

"No," I say, desperate to convince myself. "Kairi may burn the island but I will put out the fire. We can rebuild. We will survive."

We will. We must.

"But look!" Saki gestures to the glyphs. "It is foretold by those who came before us. We must respect their wisdom."

"What is wrong with you?"

Saki flinches from my screams and glances towards the staircase, but I don't care if Takanori hears me. I don't care about anything but making her understand.

"We *choose*. So what if someone painted these? We can choose, Saki. I choose to survive. If you still, after everything that has happened, want to blindly follow Takanori, then you may as well just go and jump headfirst into the ratty volcano and get it over and done with."

"But everything on these walls has happened. I have heard tales of prophets who could foresee. How else could our past have known all that has happened here so far?

They must have created this as a warning but it is too late. Our entire existence and all the ways the Experienced have wrapped us up tight are unravelling. You know as well as I do that Kairi will detonate the volcano."

She is right, he will, but what could he possibly do to make me trigger a tsunami?

Naho's face flashes through my mind. And the monsoon.

"But now I know what is going to happen, or what is *supposed* to happen, I can keep control of my emotions. I promise you. There will be no tsunami."

"You can't promise."

"I can." I kneel and seize Saki's hand. "I promise you,"

Saki grimaces and flicks my hand away, "You can't promise anything when it comes to Kairi. I finally understand what you have been telling me all this time. Kairi *is* you, and you are Kairi."

I don't have time to indulge her doubt. The volcano could erupt at any moment. It's like my feet can feel the churning of Mu's fiery heart. We have to act. Now.

"And," Saki continues face flushed with anger, "don't treat me like I am a maymu! I know what is in there"—Saki points to my stomach—"and how it got there."

I get off my knees and can't help but stroke my bump.

"You created with Aito," Saki says, finally bursting through the membrane that has separated us since I left the snake.

"Yes," I say.

Saki sobs, "I suppose it doesn't matter anyway. Your poor maymu will never see Mu. No one will survive this."

"Don't give up, Saki. Please. We must keep going. We choose. Listen to me, if we get as many Maymuans as we can and bring them to the temple, we can crowd the upper level and we will survive the waves I'll summon to quell the lava, but you must hurry."

"What about the Mayans?"

"They made their choice."

"Kaori!"

"What do you want me to do, Saki?"

"Do you think Kairi has seen these glyphs? I don't understand. If he blows the volcano and then you drown Mu, how will he survive?" Saki asks in desperation.

"He can't have seen the glyphs." I remember how shocked he was to see the ankh above the opening in the snake cave. "It is not about the prophecy, he just wants to destroy Mu. Takanori has filled his head with all kinds of poison since he was an unnamed. Kairi knows if he blows the volcano I'll have no choice but to flood Mu. He probably thinks I have no control like him and his ratty fire but I know what to expect now, so how can I lose control?"

Saki still has an infuriating look of scepticism.

"Look at the tsunami!" I say pointing at the wicked glyph on the wall. "Do you honestly believe I am even capable of creating a wave like that? I don't know exactly what Kairi has planned but he will have a way to escape and you can be sure it doesn't include saving any Maymuans."

Saki finally nods in agreement.

"Let's go." I head towards the staircase leading up into the temple.

"What about Takanori?"

No matter what happens, from now on Takanori's reign is over.

Chapter Thirty

KAIRI

"Grab his legs!" I say.

"Don't do this. Please. Please!"

Legs writhe and flail in the undergrowth, desperate to cling to life. Thorns shred skin and branches are stripped of leaves in the chaos. Hesitant hands struggle to keep hold. Aghast eyes condemn my heartless betrayal.

"Shut him up or you will be strung up beside him."

Finally they hold him tight and defeat stills the limbs.

"Why, Kairi, why me?" he pleads.

You are the only one she cares about.

I shove her bloodstone down his throat and bind his mouth with gobu, smothering his pleas.

"Good. Make sure he is left somewhere she will find him."

Chapter Thirty-One

KAORI

The chamber is empty except for the stench of hunmir-smoke-stained walls. Saki is drawn towards a discreet opening overlooking crashing sea waves. The chamber is full of luxurious colourful fabrics and gold trinkets. I despise Takanori and the Experienced.

"Kaori, quick! Look."

The salted air at the opening brings little comfort as I absorb the extraordinary scene below.

An enormous round boat is bobbing on the shore. It is as if the sea has spat out a huge seed pod. It is dark green like seaweed. Maybe this strange pod is covered in seaweed? Sunlight is caught in the kelp skin so it looks mottled like Kairi's. Piercing the side are long sticks of gamgam which must have been used to steer and row.

I lean further out of the opening to look closer, but the protruding oars withdraw from the water and are sucked into the pod. The green husk heals itself as if the oars had never punctured the skin.

Saki clutches my arm tight as an opening appears. From the green pod a swarm of mottled armed Mayans pour out, led by the unmistakeable figure of Ikki.

I shudder as the scent of Naho and morgon petals fill my nose.

The last of the Mayans disembarks carrying oars and, after a quick look over his shoulder, Ikki sends them sprinting into the trees. Saki and I exchange a puzzled look. What the ratty hell is going on?

A flash of red draws my eye and I watch as Takanori and the Experienced greet Ikki. They enter the pod and again it seals itself seamlessly. Then the opening returns and they step back onto the shore. The Mayans roll the pod until it is perched on the sand. Ikki bows to Takanori and leads all of the Mayans into the forest. The Experienced chatter excitedly around Takanori. I strain to hear but no words are carried on the breeze up here.

I lean forwards but something drags me down and I land with a thump on the stone floor.

"What is wrong?"

The colour has drained from Saki's face. "Look towards the back of the flock of Experienced."

I peep out of the corner of the opening and see Experienced Takafumi staring straight up at us.

"Go! You have to go!" I push Saki towards the opening leading into the temple. "Quick! Get out before they find us here. Hide down the hallway and when they pass, run outside and get as many Maymuans as you can to come to the temple."

"I can't leave you here with them."

I grab Saki's face and kiss her. "Go!"

Chapter Thirty-Two

KAIRI

O nce this begins there will only be one end. The severance of twins. Her death will make me whole.

I ignore the trembling of my fingers as I place my palm on the ragged base of my volcano.

I am the beginning and the end. The heart and the destruction.

Betrayal. Blood. Honour.

No longer blood tied.

Torn at birth. Torn in death.

Heat rises. My body rumbles. May rise. May rise and claim Mu. Red robe.

Mymig.

I was never yours.

Hate. Pain. Humiliation. Ruined skin, ruined island. Scratch. Until red blood pours from my wounds. Rip and tear until blood flows from my rock. Drown these hypocrites. Perfect. Balanced. Dead. Fired arrow pierced through three hearts. Condemned from creation.

Kaori and I never stood a chance. Not in this time. Not here.

Tears stream as lava overflows.

Chapter Thirty-Three

KAORI

The temple trembles as Kairi's volcano boils. I close my eyes and two familiar unnameds appear.

I strum the bugir scars on my fingers. A sweet tune plays. Tears sting my eyes. Did it have to be this way? My empty little finger tingles as my melody envelops my body and holds me tight.

I am so sorry.

The two unnameds look at me in confusion. "Sorry for what?" says the she with the missing little finger.

"Sorry for everything," I say.

The he stares at me. "You can't be sorry for everything."

"Why not?"

They both giggle. "You're silly," says the she. "You can't be sorry for everything. How can you be everything?"

Beautiful twins Kaori and Kairi roll about laughing then run off holding hands, leaving me alone.

~

"It is over, Kaori."

I turn to face Takanori. He draws near, brandishing the sword that severed the unnamed's head. The rest of the Experienced scuttle through the opening but do not approach.

Takanori smiles. "There is no place for you. Here... or anywhere."

I step back towards the snake staircase, keeping my eyes on the sword.

Takanori laughs and leans the blade against the wall. "Don't worry about this ending you. You are already over. This is a little reminder of all the trouble you have caused."

Rust floods my mouth.

Don't let him in your mind.

Is this how he intends to turn me into a tsunami? It won't work. I didn't kill the unnamed. Takanori did.

The foundations of Mu continue to rumble but I stand straight.

All of the Experienced laugh at my pride but Takanori scowls. "Do you have no shame?"

"How dare you speak to me of shame," I say.

Takanori stares at me for a moment then smirks, "You really are so predictable. You and your twin. Are you going to save everyone, Kaori?" Takanori sneers, and I am disappointed to feel myself blush. Takanori continues, "Of course you will. Saviour Kaori. And drown them all in the process. Your twin thinks he has chosen all this. Detonate a volcano and escape Mu. He has no idea he is following the prophesy glyph by glyph. It is pathetic. You both are."

The Experienced don't flinch when Takanori mentions the prophesy. They knew. They all knew.

"You are despicable. You have seen the glyphs. You know what this devil did to Naho. You have desecrated her and desecrated Mu." The Experienced gasp and Takanori squirms. "May you all burn in my twin's flame."

Experienced Takafumi screeches, "Use the sword!"

Takanori's hand twitches but he can't touch the blade.

I smile. "Seems there is a place for me after all," I address the Experienced. "It will be pretty difficult for my empty shell to raise a tsunami."

The only sound is the ragged breath of Takanori. I step towards him. "Before the moon rises Mu may fall, but one thing is certain. There is no place for you."

Splashes echo around the chamber. For a moment Takanori smirks.

I shake my head. "Sorry, Takanori, this is not your precious tsunami. You should never have built your temple on water."

Takanori scrambles for the sword as black water floods the staircase and soaks our feet. The Experienced watch in horror as a tide of snakes ascend the stairs. The snakes slither around my legs and torso, caressing my swollen belly.

I stroke the nearest scaly head and we gaze into Takanori's terror. He severs the first to attack but many follow. Fangs pierce his calves and poison buckles his knees.

Snakes squeeze the air from Takanori's lungs. When he attempts a breath, a long red snake enters his mouth.

Takanori's body slumps and I turn my snake eyes to the Experienced. I undulate into the air, ready to attack. The Experienced splatter to their knees. The snakes advance as the dark water pulsates with their collective cowardice.

"Get up."

The Experienced look in terror at each other and stumble to their feet.

"Take off those ridiculous robes."

They shed their red skins and stand as they should always have, in basic underclothes. There are too many Maymuans who worship the temple. For now I still need the influence of the Experienced to get them to safety.

"Maymuans are coming. You are to protect them. This is your last chance. Raise your heads and never forget." The Experienced follow my pointed finger to the red snake slithering out of Takanori's right eye.

Chapter Thirty-Four

KAIRI

Ikki kicks up clouds of sand in his haste to reach me and report back. "I delivered the pod to Takanori," he pants, brushing remnants of sprinting through the forest from his braids.

The rest of Ikki's pack emerges, clutching long gamgam oars.

"He didn't notice they were missing?" I ask.

"No, I only showed them how to reseal the opening. They didn't ask about the oars."

I nod and Ikki is dismissed.

Good.

Stupid tortoise too stuffed full of pride and delusion to realise he won't be escaping this hell he has created. Shame I won't have the pleasure of seeing with my own eyes Takanori and the Experienced bobbing aimlessly over their precious drowned island in the tomb I have provided for them.

I watch as Ikki runs to join my Mayans on the shore who are making final pod preparations. The sand trembles above the churning of my lava. The beach buzzes with life, fear, and expectation. Pods line the shore packed full of warm Mayan bodies, ensuring our future.

Tiny fingers graze my arm.

"We are boarding now," Ayana says, trying to keep hold of a squirming Kai. She shields her eyes with her hand and squints past the pods to where the ocean meets the sky. "Where are we going?"

I reach out and take Kai. He is heavier than I remember. He giggles when I squeeze him too tight. "Far away from here."

Ayana frowns and traces a finger down Kai's unblemished arm. "Destroying the island will never erase our past. Many will carry Mu in their hearts."

"Will you?" I ask.

Ayana's face is unreadable. "I suppose the more important question is, will you?"

Despite the glare of the sun from the kelp-coated pods, I shiver. Kai starts to cry. "You should board now." I return Kai to Ayana. "I am sorry we never found Reo."

"Are you?" Ayana asks.

I don't know what to say. We stare at each other for a moment, then she leans in and gently kisses my mouth.

Chapter Thirty-Five

KAORI

Outside the temple is chaos. Maymuans trample over each other in their haste for sanctuary. The air is thick with the smell of rotten turtle eggs as Kairi's volcano splutters and belches smoke cast orange by the setting sun. Screams ring out as the volcano hurls its first warning sparks high into the air. Red-hot embers descend, setting trees alight.

Panic escalates. Never mind the volcano, the Maymuans will not survive each other if they continue to fight for entry to the temple. Where are the Experienced?

"Takafumi! Takafumi! Get over here and help. Now!"

Takafumi squeezes his way over to me, his face shining with sweat. "They won't listen to us. They don't recognise us this way."

The under-robe Takafumi is wearing barely covers his thighs. *Mymig it.*

"Put your robes back on."

Takafumi raises an eyebrow. "Excuse me?"

"You heard me." *You ratty piece of dung.*

He fails to fight the urge to smile. He bows and says. "Of course, Kaori."

Control your breathing, he is not worth it. Focus on now. There's Saki!

"Here!" I wave my arms. "I'm here!"

Saki breaks away from the herd of Maymuans she was leading. She doubles over trying to catch her breath. "I think this is the last of them."

"I ratty well hope so," I say. "The top level looks full."

"When are you going to flood it? Once these last Maymuans are in the temple you should do it."

"I'm not sure."

"Not sure about what?" Saki looks at my face and screams in frustration, "Oh no, please don't, Kaori. You said yourself Kairi will have made a plan."

"But what if some of the Mayans have changed their mind? They might be in the forest right now."

"I just came through the forest!"

Saki is looking at me like I have inhaled too much volcano smoke.

If I don't check then I am no better than Kairi.

"You told me yourself the top level is already full," Saki pleads, "and do you think the Maymuans will be happy to see you lead Mayans into our temple?"

The earth shakes as the volcano clears more embers from its throat in preparation to spew lava.

I almost tumble over but I don't respond. Saki sighs with resignation. "I'll go."

"Absolutely not. You must stay here. Help the Experienced keep order and when the volcano erupts, I promise I will return."

"Let me come with you."

"No. You have a duty here." I push her towards the last of the Maymuans entering the temple. "Be careful."

Chapter Thirty-Six

KAIRI

All but my pod is sealed, yet the ratty water still laps the shore. Only when the water recedes will I be free. When will cockroach find him?

Chapter Thirty-Seven

KAORI

The forest floor rustles with the desperate scurrying of insects, rats, and snakes escaping smouldering leaves. They brush past my legs as I journey towards what they flee. The sharp crack of twigs has yet to reveal a stray Mayan, instead only wide-eyed deer.

Smoke stings my eyes and I struggle to scramble through the thorny bush. My robe sticks to my body as churning lava wilts the forest. I peer through the trees. The craggy lips of the volcano are illuminated with blood-red veins. A black plume of smoke bursts from the mouth and lightning scrawls elegant silver branches across the gloom.

I have to go back, but my feet have memory. They lead me along a known path rendered unfamiliar by the layers of ash and smoke. I am heading to Kairi's beach.

Finally I reach the tree where once a poison arrow struck and I stop as I see the frightful fruit now hanging from its branches instead of bunches of bright-yellow ganba.

And I scream.

With wrists, ankles, neck, and mouth wrapped tight in gobu, dangling from a long rope is Aito.

I vomit and the sound of my retching opens Aito's eyes a fraction.

He is still alive.

I cup his face gently in my hands and carefully unravel the gobu gag. A green bloodstone drops from his mouth. I pick it up and it burns my hand.

Breathe, you must breathe.

Overhead thunder rumbles. Whether mine or Kairi's, I do not know.

Keep control. I must keep control.

I put the bloodstone in my pocket. Aito moans.

"What have they done to you?" I kiss his mouth and his moans increase. "Don't worry, I'll get you down."

I begin unbandaging Aito's ankle but as the gobu loosens, blood drips onto my hand. The last strip falls and bloods gushes from Aito's severed tendon. I rewrap his foot.

Oh my ratty hell.

Thunder rumbles again and rain begins to fall. My rain. I fall to the floor and roll myself up into a coco. I*t is okay. It's okay.*

It isn't.

Kick.

Kick.

My robe pulses. Inside my stomach, life writhes.

I look to Aito. The wrist wraps must conceal severed veins. The neck a slit throat.

If I free him, he will die. If I leave him, he will die.

The sun is extinguished. The sky is black rain. The ash floor is oil but the volcano continues.

With a roar, the lava explodes, gurgling and oozing down the mountain to incinerate Mu.

"Aito, can you hear me?"

His eyelids flicker. I take his palm and place it on my belly.

"This is not the end. Do you understand?"

He moans.

Thunder rumbles overhead and lightning flashes between us.

"I'm so sorry."

I kiss his face until my lips are numb.

Kick.

I am so sorry.

I take my dagger from my robe and slice the gobu from Aito's neck.

Red liquid pours.

Chapter Thirty-Eight

KAIRI

"What is happening?" Kentaro whispers.

We have our ears pressed to the sealed opening of our pod. We took the thunder as the cue to seal it, but so far we can only hear the pounding of the rain, not the suction of a greedy wave.

"I can't hear anything, can you?" I say.

"No," Kentaro replies. "I knew Aito was not enough. I told you to use me."

I couldn't.

Takanori was right all along.

Kentaro is my weakness. I can't change my heart.

"It's too late now," I say.

"What are we going to do?"

I rest my forehead on the clammy pod wall. "I don't know."

Chapter Thirty-Nine

KAORI

I stagger back to Mu, past the skeleton huts abandoned by terrified Maymuans. When I reach the temple I see a swarm of bodies huddled together as protection from the downpour at the very top.

The sky is alight with the rattle of thunder and the crackle of lightning. I rest against the gold doors where Naho once warned me of a threat greater than I ever understood.

I can't enter.

I continue on and crouch on the grassy hill overlooking the beach where I was taught to master fear. If only I had learned the power to rip out my heart, to not love, and to live without consequence and fear. Then the waves would not be burning as they are now. I don't think I can keep my promise to Saki.

Rain hammers my shoulders, drowning the rumble of the volcano. Why did this have to happen? If only the prophecy had never been committed to the cave. Zealous Takanori had to go and make the ratty prophecy reality.

From our beginning, Kairi and I were divided, but we fought the expectations of others. Living with the rearers, we were drawn together like genmo to honeycomb. We were inseparable, Kairi's palm always soft and warm in mine. Even as unnameds in the temple we resisted the constant repetition of our differences.

What changed? Duty. Kairi's obsession with Takanori. Power. Takanori's obsession with Kairi. Naho and me. Me and Naho. Boar blood. Kentaro. In the creation hut. Him, before he was him. A May. Telling me what to do, who to be, when to carry life. How dare May dominate without the responsibility of Mu.

Breathe.

Slaughtered piglets. Headless unnamed. Poisoned carrier. Jellyfish-lashed face. Sacrificed Mayan. So much violence. Never knowing when to stop. Now it overwhelms me. May. The instinct to burn and consume.

Breathe.

I can't breathe. It's too much.

Let it go.

I can't.

Then *he* will win.

Let it go.

No.

I can't breathe.

I exhale.

And let go.

The tide gasps. No longer ebbing and flowing. Only ebbing.

With a tremendous rush the ocean recedes until there is only sand.

I sprint to the temple.

Chapter Forty

KAIRI

"Open it," I bark. Kentaro hesitates. I can't spend a single moment longer inside this wretched green womb waiting for Kaori. "Open it!"

Smoky air pours in when Kentaro unseals the pod. I splash into the water below and pace the shoreline.

Ratty Aito.

Has she seen him? Maybe she found a way to save him or, even worse, maybe I chose wrong and she never loved him at all.

Above, a cacophony of squawks pierces the ash sky. The buha of Mu are fleeing. Their bright feathers a peculiar rainbow across the tainted dusk.

I crouch as flocks of genmo, nullos, and even nabgars follow.

I watch the water.

Is it finally my time to take flight?

Chapter Forty-One

KAORI

Maymuan heads spin when I clamber over the top of the external staircase. Many hands tug on my robe, looking for reassurance I cannot give. I search for a flash of red.

Saki is with them.

"I am so glad you are okay." She looks closer. "*Are* you okay?"

The Experienced lean in and are afraid of what they see on my face. Lightning strikes the forest beside the temple and the Maymuans scream.

"Get as many of them as you can onto that green pod thing Ikki delivered," I say to Saki, but Takafumi squirms. "It is intended to survive a tsunami, isn't it? Isn't it?" I shout at him, but neither he nor the other Experienced respond. The rain falls heavily, stinging my shoulders. I lean into Takafumi and hiss, "Do you honestly still think you are going to sail away with my twin, without us?"

"No, no, of course not," the Experienced mumble, heads bowed.

"Get your Maymuans on the ratty thing. Now!"

The Experienced scatter and enter the Maymuan swarm. I make to follow but Saki grabs my arm. "You can't trust them."

Tell me something I don't know.

"These stupid Maymuans won't do anything without them. It is either save everyone with the Experienced or save no one at all."

"You can't stop the wave?" Saki asks, her lips trembling.

Tears sting my eyes. "No. In the forest... I found Aito."

Saki notices the patches of blood staining my robe. "Oh Kaori."

I rest my head on her shoulder and allow myself to sob for a moment,

"I..." It is terrible to admit what I am about to, but I need Saki to know. "I was glad it wasn't you."

Saki's eyebrows shoot up in surprise. "Don't say that."

I shake my head. "It's the truth. I do love Aito. I do. But I was glad it wasn't you. Turns out Kairi never knew my heart."

"But why is the wave coming?" Saki asks, in a final plea for the impossible. For me to stop the drowning of Mu.

"I couldn't control it... my rage... at the injustice of all that has happened."

Thunder claps above, shaking the sky.

～

Desperate fingernails claw the outside of the pod but we are full. I can't mourn those left behind. I have a duty to the souls within. An eerie silence falls. The Experienced, Saki, and I stand on the platform in the centre of the pod surrounded by kelp-comb cells stuffed full of overwhelmed Maymuans. Illuminated by the last of the sun's light penetrating the kelp, they wait for our guidance.

Experienced Takafumi raises his arms in the air and the Maymuans inhale. He gestures to the Experienced beside him. Together they raise their arms and hold hands in the air. At the end of the line, Experienced Takako extends her hand to me but I do not accept. Her eyes narrow.

They exhale, "Namu May Mu."

With a roar, the Maymuans reply, "Namu May Mu."

Experienced Takako smirks. Again the Experienced inhale. My legs tremble from more than the oncoming wave.

"Namu Experienced," they shout, but they're met with only silence.

Saki pushes me forwards.

"Namu Kaori," the Maymuans shout from their comb cells.

The Experienced retreat to the shadows at the back of the platform. I squint at the souls huddled in the comb. Water may be hurtling towards us but my throat is as dry as scorched grass. These Maymuans are mostly rurals. I have to trust them. They are of the land. If I speak with a mouth full of soil and all that is eternal they will hear.

"Do not be afraid. We shall go on. For those who are

willing, the wave brings hope. Passage to another time. A time of joy. And love. For this we must have courage because Mu is no more. There is only us. And a new land. Together we shall rise and create much more than we were allowed to imagine here. This time is ours. Do not be afraid."

I raise my left arm with my palm flat and facing my face and slam my other arm aligned with the horizon against my wrist to make the shape of an ankh. Disapproval rustles from the rejected Experienced cowed behind me. Defiance sweeps the pod. The Maymuans beat their fists against the kelp cells, enraged at our fate.

In their fists is the nunum of water. The violence and hysteria of a relentless wave. My wave. Irresistible. Frothing on the surface but churning with a rhythm as measurable and composed as the moon in its cycle. My moon blood cycle. *Kick*. My little one knows awe.

As before a hunt, I search for the space between. Where all that is pure resides. My foot pounds the rhythm of the between into the platform. I close my eyes. Louder. Until the beat bobs my head like sargassum. They respond. Feet join fists in thrashing the pod. *Pound*. Their fists punch my breast bone. I lean in. *Pound*. Their souls on my chest. *Pound*. Their heels kick the space between my shoulder blades. Raw body heat drips from the walls.

In the salty haze, we decide. We are united in leaving Mu. Disobedient. Uncontrolled by the Experienced. No longer disembowelled and patiently waiting for a sword through our necks. Fists become flat palms slapping the kelp. We sing, but not peacefully like the girnum. We squawk as disruptively and proudly as a barmuna. We unfurl our feathers, not for a mate, but in prayer for a new land.

Rushing water approaches. The pod shudders and bodies tumble from the cells. A wall of water annihilates the forest and screeches towards us.

I close my eyes. We must go on.

My wave slams into the pod, scoops us off Mu, and hurtles us towards the unknown.

Chapter Forty-Two

KAIRI

K entaro has joined me on the shore. We are searching
for answers outside the ratty pod. Since the buha
exodus there have been no more signs of Kaori.

"Maybe we should push them onto the water then
paddle with the oars," Kentaro says.

We have to otherwise we will soon be encased in lava I
can't stop.

"Wait." Kentaro frowns. "Listen."

I look around in confusion. "I can't hear anything."

"Neither can I. Not even the volcano."

The rumbling has stopped. The pod no longer quakes on
the sand either. What could snuff out a volcano as fast as a
lit torch dropped in water?

Oh bahm.

"She is coming! From the other side of the island." We
dive into the pod. "Quick, seal it!" I shout to Kentaro and

then race deeper into the pod and scream. "This is it. Get ready."

The Mayans in the pod and I crouch. A whisper of "Namu May Mu" escapes scared Mayan mouths but is quickly drowned by a deafening roar of churning water.

Kentaro kneels beside me. We lock eyes. I see my terror reflected in him. I claw my nails as far into the woven mat as I can.

The wave hits.

With an almighty snap, the benme roots are severed and I am no longer anchored to Mu.

Chapter Forty-Three

KAORI

Maymuans rattle around the pod. Water thrashes every wall and I fear the woven skin cannot endure the pressure. It will split and flood us all.

Maymuans scream and moan, water pounds, and still we roll.

A low rumble shivers the pod from within.

"Namu May Mu."

The chant is an incessant hum inescapable in the seamless pod.

Breathe.

I cradle my stomach and clutch Saki's hand until finally the pod bobs. The Maymuans crouched nearest to the Experienced rise and bow to them, but the majority of the Maymuans turn to me.

"What now?" Saki says. "They are waiting for you."

I don't know.

Experienced Takafumi fills my void. "We need the strong to go below and row us to safety."

A murmur ripples through the crowd. Words become distinguishable.

"To where?"

"What about Mu?"

Panic scuttles through the pod as the loss of the island becomes a stark reality.

I rise and clear my throat. "Mu has... gone."

"Gone? How?" they ask. Some sob. Most stare, unable to process my words. Hunger for subservience returns. Desperation growls through the rattled pod.

"Yes," Experienced Takafumi says, seizing his moment, "it was foretold. Mu has returned to the depths of the ocean. But do not worry, we have survived to find a new home."

The Maymuans stare at Experienced Takafumi.

He continues, "Now we must row."

Some of the stronger rurals surge forwards to help but there is no point.

"There are no oars," I say.

Experienced Takafumi frowns. "Of course there are."

After a moment of indignant feather-rustling, Experienced Takako goes below to confirm what I have told them.

"What will we do?" a Maymuan shrieks, and panic returns.

I don't share their panic. I don't care about their fears. I have my own unease. The walls of the pod are pulsating. I close my eyes but all I can see is Kairi laughing in his pod, surrounded by intoxicated Mayans. My hand becomes a fist in my pocket.

What's that?

I open my palm and see the bloodstone. Again it tumbles from Aito's slack mouth. I see him. Drained of blood. Scorched with lava. My blood boils over and with a lurch our pod begins to jerk in response.

"No! No, Kaori, please," Saki pleads. "Let's go."

"Go where? Should we follow behind Kairi and become ratty Mayans?"

The pod increases speed.

"No, of course not. We can do whatever we want. You can do whatever you want. Let. Him. Go."

Sorry, Saki.

He is not getting away.

Chapter Forty-Four

KAIRI

Dazed Mayans peel themselves from the body pyre in the centre of our pod. Kentaro pulls me to my feet. His nose is bleeding. Battered and bruised Mayans moan. My head aches but we have to move. Now.

"Get up!" I shout. "Where are the rowers? Get up now!"

The pyre collapses and Mayans stagger to their allocated roles. I grab Kentaro and as we reach the sealed opening, the pod lurches from the oars entering the water.

"Open it. Quick."

Kentaro scrambles to unseal the kelp and a welcome spray of salt water greets us from the outside platform. The water is still agitated. Froth covers the waves. A spluttering death rattle from drowned Mu.

I did it.

A hysterical squeal escapes my mouth.

I am free.

The ocean is littered with pods.

"Look." Kentaro points to the nearest one. A Mayan is waving a white strip of fabric from their platform. Kentaro hurries back inside and returns with my symbol of survival. He waves a red cloth. One by one the platform of each pod turns white as each opening is unsealed. My Mayans survived.

Kentaro and I squint into the sky. Above us, the last flock of fleeing nullos dictates our direction.

Inside the pod, Mayans without duties settle into their allocated comb. A hum of excited chatter swirls. I visit my comb to check on neighbouring Ayana. She is lying down with her little ones.

"We made it."

She smiles.

I nod, kneeling down so I can see if Kai has any bruises.

"Don't worry, he's fine," Ayana says. "Just a little shaken."

"Where are we going?" Hana asks, crawling out of the space to lean on my legs. Riku and Haru join her, peering at me, eager for an answer.

"Where do you want to go?" I say.

They glance at each other. Riku thinks for a moment. "Somewhere with a jungle."

"No, let's go underwater and live with the fish!" Haru says.

"How will you breathe, stupid?" Hana says, pushing Haru. "I think we should go wherever Kairi says we should go."

Ayana and I smile. "That's a very good idea," I say.

"When will we get there?" Hana asks.

"Enough of the questions. Kairi needs to rest and so do you." Ayana pinches each of their legs until they return to the comb and settle.

Ayana and I sit cross-legged whispering outside it.

"Is everything really okay?" she asks.

"Yes. I can't do a complete count of the other pods but from what I can see the majority made it. We will follow the nullos and no doubt we will soon find another island."

Ayana frowns. "What if we run out of food before we get there?"

"We won't." *I hope.* And if we do the weakest are going overboard with their legs and arms bound to conserve rations.

We sit in silence for a moment. I wonder if Ayana is thinking of Reo. My mind longs for Kaori. I see her swollen body floating face down in her beloved cove, nabgars brooding above.

"Do you feel that?" Ayana asks, breaking my grisly reverie.

I leap up in panic. The pod is no longer gliding forwards. With horror I realise Mu has woken from her watery grave and is slowly sucking us down to share her fate.

Chapter Forty-Five

KAORI

"Get off me!" My legs kick at red robes.

"You can't do this," they say. "You will kill us all!"

I don't care. He is not getting away. Not this time.

My fingers claw at the kelp until I tear through the opening. In the distance I can see the other pods.

"Stop. Please," they plead. "You don't have to do this."

"Get off!"

The Experienced are still trying to drag me back through the opening but I can see him. The pod with the red flag amongst all the white being sucked into my whirlpool.

"Talk to her. You must stop her before it's too late."

Saki is shoved through the opening.

We stare at each other. For a moment her mouth is ajar but no words come. Instead she kneels beside me and gazes into the eye of the whirlpool.

The Experienced groan in defeat.
We begin to swirl.

Chapter Forty-Six

KAIRI

N*o. no, no, no! This is not happening. Get out the way!*
I shove aside the bodies in front of me. Why are they just standing there?

Ratty hell. Move! Where the ratty hell is Kentaro?

"Kentaro! Kentaro!" I grab the throat of the nearest Mayan. She splutters in terror. "Find Kentaro."

I slip and slide towards the opening. Salt water pours into the pod. As I reach the rowers' hatch Kentaro appears, his face ashen.

"We can't stop sinking. We had to pull the oars in. The first set have snapped. I don't want to lose the replacements. What is happening?"

It is mem! I mean her. Ratty Kaori!

"Stay here," I say.

"Where are you going?" Kentaro panics. "Don't leave us."

"Stay here. When it stops, *row*."

A sharp jolt knocks us to our knees. I push Kentaro down the rowers' hatch and he lands with a crash below.

I crawl across the soaked platform to the opening. It is wild. The suction of the whirlpool roars from every direction. All I see is water.

And one other pod.

Kaori.

Deeper and deeper into the vortex we go. My fingers cling to the kelp, my legs flailing.

I will not go down like this. Before I join Mu on the seabed, she will see me.

I draw my dagger and bloodstone from my loincloth.

Chapter Forty-Seven

KAORI

Deep in the whirlpool below the cacophony of waves, I sail serenely. I could almost be with my turtles in the cove. I cup my belly.

You will never know this time. I pray for you to find a greater shell. A time and body worthy of your beauty. I love you. I know enough of you to remember and I will greet you in the next.

Kairi's pod is only a shadow cast on the wave wall at this depth. We will sink to the bottom of the ocean. Together. A black pearl returned.

Will Aito be there? Or Naho? She promised. In the snake.

～

"Am I dead?" I ask.

"No," Naho replies. "Would you like to be?"

It is warm here and I feel safe. "Not yet."

"Okay," Naho laughs. "Not yet."

I know it is warm. I recognise the sensation but I have no body. "What am I?"

"You are you," Naho says.

"But I can't see you."

"I am here."

"What now?" I ask.

Naho sighs. "There is much to discuss but first, my love, you must rest."

The glyph "love" squeezes me tight. Naho's love.

"I love you."

"I love you too, Kaori. I always have. And Kairi. Beyond the horizon there is a place. Without mu or may. Or he or she. I will meet you there where we will rest in love."

"But not yet?"

Naho sighs. "No, my love, not yet."

Red. Red? Fire? At this depth?

I rub my eyes but the sight remains.

Kairi's pod is a pearl no more. It burns.

Even here, at his end, he can't help himself. Chin up, defiant. Natural but abnormal. Ferocious but free.

Takanori was wrong. We are not the ending. We are the beginning.

Aset and Ra. Water and fire. Moon and sun.

A burning wave. It crashes inside me. It cleanses me. Of all the thoughts, expectations, and duties which were never my own. I am supposed to kill him. It was my destiny. Now I can choose.

Forsake him. Or save him.

Only one choice will free us all.

I make the sign of the ankh on my belly.

Chapter Forty-Eight

KAIRI

How does it feel to burn and drown?

Salt water sprays my face and floods my mouth. The scorching heat of the lit pod blisters my brow.

I close my eyes. I am going to die.

With Kaori, my twin. Kentaro, my true completing half. Ayana and Kai, my future. Because I couldn't change my past. I was afraid. I am always afraid. Takanori knew. He saw the fear. He recognised himself.

Will he be there, on the seabed, waiting for me?

I'm sorry. I am not May. It is a relief to drown with Mu.

But the little light that remained in the swirling dark ends as though it was never there. Extinguished. By what? By whom?

By her.

With an almighty roar the whirlpool collapses.

And we rise.

Chapter Forty-Nine

KAORI

Together we stand, Saki and I, leaning into the horizon. The water is still. Still and smooth as morgon petals as far as the eye can see. Pods bob under the twinkling stars. I cradle the life within me.

I love you. Please forgive my reckless rage. I will never abandon you. My every breath is yours.

I gaze across the scorched sea. Saki circles her arms around us. With a jolt we move. Into the future. Leaving Mu to rest.

Namu May Mu.

"Wait," Saki says. "We need them."

"No, we don't," I say, surveying the mass of white flags waving desperately for a sign of their leader.

"Not even if we chose a few?"

"They never chose me."

Saki gently squeezes our bump. "We need them."

The ocean returns to restlessness. The moon illuminates our path. We sail her light.

I squeeze the bloodstone in my pocket.

"Goodbye, Kairi."

Chapter Fifty

KAIRI

A warm mouth covers mine, sharing life. I roll over onto my hands and knees and vomit the ocean. I glance up and stars twinkle. The moon is full, casting her silver light. She winks down at me.

"Where am I?"

"With me on the pod... She's gone," Kentaro says. "She took most of the other pods. Well, at least half of them."

The moon blinks. I unfurl my fist and the bloodstone burns my palm. I bring it to my lips and cry.

"Thank you, Kaori."

Epilogue

KAORI

A trickle warms my legs. My centre trembles as life rolls violently within. My mouth moans unfamiliar sounds as a little body pushes hard on the base of my spine. Saki rushes to me and carefully removes my robe. I wrap my arms around her neck and hang naked as birth rattles my body.

Pop. Silky water soaks Saki's feet.

"I think we should get at least one rearer."

"No," I moan.

"But what if—"

"*No.*"

We have argued about using a rearer every rise since we reached this Redland, after a blur of moon cycles chasing the horizon. We sailed until finally we could sail no more. We had longed for land and that is exactly what we found. A place without water but an ocean of sand as far as the eye can see.

I don't need a rearer. This is not Mu. It will never be Mu.

This is the land of Aset.

In this moment, time itself seems to end.

I am you. You, my love, descend within me bringing rushes of exhilaration. I see you on a raft so close to the shore. We are here, little one, don't be afraid. You and I will do this together. Get ready. With each inhalation I draw you closer. I am careful to exhale gently and not set you further adrift.

I crawl like a jungle cat and Saki massages my lower back with oil from smashed seeds. We rub some between my legs as a curious forehead tears my skin. I rise into a squat and touch the skull between my legs. Saki gently pulls me to lie down on my back. The forehead retreats.

"No," I say again. This is *not* Mu.

"No?"

"Here." I return to my hands and knees and cling to the earth. "I need to see you."

Saki squats in front of me, stroking the loose curls from my face and with the next wave I push the raft as hard as I can. Shoulders.

"Help me." I climb up Saki into a deep squat. The final wave crashes. I roar and the body slithers from mine.

I cup the head and we stare into the scrunched face.

Silence.

Saki gulps.

Silence.

Drowned.

I cover the nose and mouth with my lips and suck until fluid fills my throat.

Blink.

Screams fill our hut. He screams. My he.

Ren.

~

Takafumi is pacing around my hut taking his time to get to the ratty point. I already know. The land our pods discovered is smothered in sand. For the past six moon cycles we have tried to settle, pinned between sea and dune.

The sun burns so relentlessly every rise we had to build huts at night and rest in the pods during the day. There are shrubs and trees so water is here somewhere, seeding the soil, but our throats are perpetually dry.

Kairi's rations are gone and I can only just about manage to churn enough fish from the sea to feed us all.

"We are restless."

We? I hate Takafumi so much.

"Who?"

Takafumi glares at me. "Your—what are we calling them now? Maymuans? Shells? Souls?"

"Okay, so everyone is frustrated, I know, but what did they expect?" I say. I know what they crave. Leadership. But I am exhausted. And afraid. Ren cries all day and I weep at night.

After delivering him with Saki I thought I would never know fear again, but tides wait for no one. Ebb and flow, my mind is weak, and already I forget the pure Mu power which flowed through my body during birth. And the vow I made to never abandon him.

"They need a leader," Takafumi says, a smirk flickering around his lips. "As we have already discussed, many resent being snatched from the protection of your twin."

"But—" I begin to defend myself but Takafumi raises his hand to my face for silence. He should be ratty grateful. I am so tired. I should snap his fingers off for disrespecting me like this.

"I know, I know," he drawls, "they are here now, they have to get on with it. I, of course, agree with you."

No, you don't, you rat.

"But I want you to be aware of how they are feeling. We only see you at the rise."

"Yes, feeding all you ungrateful boars," I snap. I can't help myself. I have to shut up. With every outburst Takafumi seems to grow in stature. From the blanket on the floor, Ren gurgles.

Takafumi smiles. "I understand. Being a carrier is not easy, Kaori. Now maybe you understand why we had to do the things we did on Mu. It truly was the best for all. I have offered many times, I will take Ren—"

"Get out."

"Excuse me?"

"Get out!" I scream.

Takafumi retreats but not without a sly, smug glance back at me.

Mymig. Ren wriggles and starts to cry.

"And I don't need you joining in now either!"

Where the ratty hell is Saki when I need her?

Ren's shrill, piercing cries rattle my mind.

Shut up. Please shut up.

I roll him off the blanket onto his belly and he screams into the floor. I curl up against the hut wall and stare at the tears running down his cheeks, his arms and legs flailing in the dirt.

Saki returns. She picks Ren up and cuddles him close. He splutters and gasps. She crouches down next to me, gently opens my robe, and places Ren on my breast. He suckles hungrily and we sit with only the sound of his slurps.

He finishes and begins to snore. Saki wraps him tight in the blanket.

"Not too tight," I say. She loosens the cloth.

When I unwrap him I see only Aito. I see his severed flesh. My eyes snap shut.

Saki gives me a gentle push. "Walk, Kaori. Walk where there is no sand and only sea."

I nod in greeting to those lingering around the pods. It is not returned. They all have mottled arms. My spine tingles as I realise the tall one has wounds that look fresh. I try and catch his eye but he avoids my stare.

Why are they so ratty ungrateful? Their huts are built. They are small and imperfect but they are complete. I even gave them doors so they don't have to feel like I am watching them all the time. But many still return to sleep in the pods because they are so unable to sever the cord to Mu. And to Kairi.

I finger the bloodstone in my pocket. I am ashamed to understand their attachment.

My mind constantly seeks my twin. In Ren's face I search not for Aito but for Kairi. Ren looks like neither he. Ren has my face and Saki's expressions. I miss how Kentaro would giggle as we roasted hunks of cracked coco over a Kairi fire smouldering on the sand. Kairi's eyeroll as I would bite off a piece far too hot for my mouth. Kentaro carefully wrapping charred leftovers in benme leaves for us to sneak back to our huts and enjoy later.

But that time no longer exists. It passed long before Mu drowned. We went beyond ripe. To a maggot infested rot. We got stuck in Takanori's putrid trap. And now I endure the stench of Takafumi.

I walk the shore until I am alone and unseen. I turn to greet the sea. Water crashes over my toes. I sink into the seabed as the current shifts the sand beneath my feet. Before the waves soak my hem, I unwrap and toss my robe on the beach. I swim a little and enjoy the chill of deep water against my bare skin.

Facing the sky, I let the water tug my unbraided hair until my curls bob. I float and drift out, straddling the horizon between an ocean below teeming with remnants of all that have ever breathed on land, and the vast sky above, abundant with hope, infinite energy, and all that will ever be. The violence of the freshly lashed arm disturbs my peace. How can I lead those drawn to such cruelty? I still shudder at the ankh scar on Saki's thigh. It is as raw to me now as it was then in my hut many moons ago. I could never demand such an initiation.

Maybe they would be better led by Takafumi. I know he whispers with those scarred by Kairi. They deserve him. But then, why did Takanori die? Not for Takafumi to take his place and revive the depravity of Mu in this land. Why spare Kairi? If not for another chance, a chance as rare as a white barmuna, to change. To live the same time in the same shell but choose to wade across an unknown pond and risk what lies beyond.

Splash. Something slithers over my throat. Black scales caress my body. I covet their embrace. Slender black bodies undulate and snare my limbs. They squeeze until remaining incapable becomes much more painful than the courage to break free.

And as sudden as rainfall, I know what must be done.

The tall he lazing against the pod glances up as I approach. His jaw falls, as does the fish bone he was picking his teeth with. The others follow his gaze then sprint off, kicking up clouds of sand. They scream warnings to all those idling around the row of beached pods, "She is coming!"

The tall he trips as he finally thinks to escape. I make sure to slither right over his trembling body.

Saki is not surprised to see who I have returned with. She grins. "Welcome back!"

The black snakes undulate in the air in greeting and I smile and peer around her.

"He just woke up," Saki says. "I'll go and get him."

Inside the hut I squeeze Ren tight and Saki binds us together with a long strip of gobu. She nods once in response to my murmured instructions. With Ren secure to my torso, I exit, blinking into the bright sunshine. Our hut is surrounded. Leading the islanders is Takafumi. I try not to laugh as I watch his eyes dart from snake to snake. The nest of snakes guarding my door parts as I enter the crowd. "Follow me." The snakes obey. As do Takafumi and the rest of the islanders.

I have returned with not only the snakes, I also bear the sea. My power is pure and full of joy like the glee of sea spray riding a crashing wave. The current in my bones flows to the mountains beyond the huts.

We ascend the low mountain that looms like a throne over our settlement, trampling through dense trees and undergrowth. The air is moist amongst the green. I am close.

Ren gurgles. I stroke his dark hair and peer into my own eyes. He looks at me expectantly. I run my fingers down the space between his eyes to the tip of his nose and whisper, "You wait and see what I am going to do!" He wriggles with excitement.

The summit is flat and narrow. The islanders have no choice but to stand with the snakes writhing around their feet. I search above. Raising my palms, I drag tufts of white clouds until there is no more blue sky. I inhale and they darken and crackle with lightning.

An anxious murmur rustles the islanders. They flinch at the first crack of lightning. I exhale and thunder rumbles. The mountain cowers but no rain falls. The islanders peer up, braced for a downpour. I take deep breaths and blow the black clouds until the sun can warm us again.

Takafumi frowns and looks frantically from the sky to my face. I smile and he glares, furious with fear of the unknown. I continue to smile because I know there is a sky he cannot see where purple clouds snap.

Time swirls the dust of the summit and an unease shivers the crowd. My snakes scrawl ankh glyphs in the dirt and I cuddle Ren and wait.

My body pulses with power. The eternal water of land, sky, and body ripples my soul. Finally, the trees rooted in the mountainside begin to tremble. The islanders chatter with excitement.

"Look!"

Takafumi's eyes widen in shock. Meandering across the vast desert is a wide blue snake. It slithers past the mountain to kiss the sea.

~

Ren and I leave the islanders enraptured on the peak to meet Saki at the water's edge.

With a splash, the snakes return home.

I unwrap Ren and we enter my new river.

I trace an ankh on his forehead then submerge him in the clear water. He emerges pure. The future the past tried to steal.

My future. Our future.

"Ren was the island's final treasure. The river is this land's first," I say.

"What will we call it?" Saki asks softly.

I close my eyes remembering one of the glyphs etched under the drawing of Aset in the temple, the one I didn't understand yet.

"The Nile."

The Mu Glossary

Mu | *he/she*
Mir | *his/her*
Mem | *him/her*
Mers | *his/hers*
Memself | *himself/herself*

~

Ankh | *symbol of life*

Barmuna | *peacock-type bird*
Bahm | *profanity*
Benme tree | *palm tree*
Bugir | *string instrument*
Buha | *toucan-type bird*

Carrier | *pregnant person*

The Mu Glossary

Cob | *corn*
Coco | *coconut*
Creating | *procreation*
Creation hut | *mountain hut for procreation*

Experienced | *island elder*

Gamgam | *bamboo*
Ganba | *citrus fruit*
Gebun | *medicinal plant*
Genmo | *honey bird*
Ghili | *chilli pepper*
Girnum | *songbird*
Glyphs | *words, written and spoken*
Gobu | *cotton*
Gubaga | *scavenger bird*
Guma leaf | *medicinal plant*

Hand | *group of rurals*
Habim | *jungle tree*
Hunmir wood | *fragrant wood*

May | *male*
Mayan | *pronounced [MAY–an]*
Maymu | *child up to five years old*
Maymuan | *island person*
Maymuans | *island people*
Mayu | *Mayan baby*
Megg plant | *hemp-type plant*

The Mu Glossary

Mignu berry | *poison berry*
Mimin | *sunflower-type flower*
Morgon | *lily-type flower*
Mu | *island name*
Mu | *female*
Mymig | *profanity*

Nabgar | *vulture-type bird*
Namu | *devotion to*
Namu Experienced | *devotion to the Experienced*
Namu May Mu | *devotion to the island of Mu and its people*
Nimi root | *contraceptive*
Nullos | *seagull-type bird*
Nunum | *drum*

Obi | *belt*
Orbit | *one year*

Pack | *group of hunters*
Preparer | *island person with food preparation role*

Ratty | *profanity*
Rearer | *island person with childcare role*
Rise | *morning or day*

Taka | *means honourable, also hawk*

Unnamed | *islander under twelve years old*

Acknowledgments

Thank you to my mentor, Daisaku Ikeda. Nam Myoho Renge Kyo. And to all the SGI UK members and SGI Japan members who have supported me in faith and helped me transform poison into medicine.

Thank you to my phenomenal editor, Bethan Morgan, for making my dream come true. Without compromise.

Thank you to the entire One More Chapter Team for all their sincere work on this book.

Thank you to Odera Igbokwe for their incredible artwork and for bringing Kaori and Kairi so vividly to life. Thank you to the One More Chapter design team for a stunning cover.

Thank you to all at Faber Academy, particularly my tutor, Tom Bromley, and my fellow speculative fiction writers, Dawn Brown and Gary Cockerill.

Thank you to the Society of Authors for their invaluable

advice. I was so grateful to receive a Taner Baybars Award for original fiction in the fields of science fiction, fantasy, and magic realism for this novel.

Thank you to Abigail Jackson and the Black Girl Writers free mentoring scheme for their phenomenal support and guidance navigating the overwhelming journey from submission to publication. Thank you to my wonderful mentors who gave their time and wisdom.

Thank you to Francesca Zampi for her guidance and generous insights into the publishing industry.

Thank you to the University of Liverpool Sydney Jones Library for a lovely place to edit my manuscript as an alum.

Thank you to my children, Midori and Airi, for their patience and to their father, Hiro, for our incredible decade in Japan, a country that has had a profound impact on my life and work.

Thank you to my Dad for a very early introduction to Afrofuturism through a childhood filled with George Clinton and Parliament/Funkadelic.

Thank you to my Mum for her love of travel, particularly crawling up the side of the pyramid at Chichen Itza in Mexico with me and my sister, Jo.

Thank you to Graham Moran for printing out my first draft, making a cover, binding it, and making me believe publication was possible. I love you.

Thank you to my friend, Taka Nakatomi, for sharing

paradise on Dainyu beach and always guiding me back to the embrace of water.

Thank you to Lisa Nevitt and Samantha Motion for being incredible women, friends, and for proving dream jobs are possible.

Thank you to Peter Banczyk for all of his love and care. I wouldn't be here without you.

And finally, thank you, my readers, for sailing to Mu. I can't wait to visit the new lands with you.

Weaving the World of Mu

The inspiration for *Beneath the Burning Wave* came from various documentaries I watched over the past decade. The first was a BBC documentary from 2011 called *Mixed Race Britain – Twincredibles* which explored the life experiences of five sets of black and white twins who were similar in many ways but who led different lives because of the colour of their skin. This made me think seriously about nature versus nurture.

I have my own experiences of being treated with kindness or cruelty by society because of the colour of my skin. I am mixed race and my skin is brown. In the predominantly white country in which I was born, the UK, I experienced traumatic racism and abuse as a child which I have struggled to recover from; but as an adult, when I visited South Africa, my brown European skin afforded me a respect and privilege from that society which was not shared by Black Africans. I began to think deeply about this wicked binary system of labelling and dividing people not only by skin colour but also in terms of gender. I thought about what it would take for a person to reject the illegitimate power they share with the dominant group or to rebel against being mislabelled inferior.

Another BBC documentary, *Japan: Earth's Enchanted Islands*, featured seventy-year-old Japanese women hunting one of the world's most venomous snakes on the island of Kudaka, and this inspired the opening scenes of *Beneath the Burning Wave*. The BBC documentary series *Human Planet* also inspired many of the rituals and hunting scenes on Mu.

All of these thoughts and ideas finally found a sense of place when I discovered the Yonaguni monument. The Yonaguni monument is a submerged rock formation off the coast of Yonaguni, one of Japan's southern Ryukyu islands. Many insist the rock formation is natural and a result of tectonic activity. However, there are those who believe the straight lines, symmetry, and sharp angles of the rock belong to a submerged pyramid from a Japanese Atlantis[1] or even from the lost continent of Mu…

I am a Black British author. In December 2020 the *Guardian* newspaper published a dialogue between Reni Eddo-Lodge and Bernardine Evaristo about their 'history making year'. They were the first Black British women to top the non-fiction and fiction paperback charts respectively. They discussed their hopes for black female writers in the future. In conclusion to a discussion about diversity in publishing they said:

RE-L: Absolutely. If publishers start publishing black writers' work in service of white self-help, it's a huge disservice to black [writers'] creativity.

BE: For me the most important thing is that black and Asian writers write across the board. Every genre, from literature to cookery to gardening books to thrillers.

RE-L: I keep coming back to what we discussed earlier: our works weren't commercial successes until they were. And for anyone coming up who is not white and is trying to write: listen to that! If we're in this time when things that weren't considered possible commercial successes in publishing *are* commercial successes, for any writer that has to be freeing. It's like: wow, I can write about anything I want.[2]

I believe my trilogy, The Mu Chronicles, is a significant change from the work being published by Black British authors. I believe the above discussion is alluding to the over-commissioning of novels or non-fiction books about racism from writers of colour. These works are all very important and I am eternally grateful to every Black British author who has forged the path on which I now walk. But which publishing doors do we still need to kick down?

My novel found a home at One More Chapter HarperCollins (OMC). I cautiously responded to their open submission in the summer of 2020 for black writers in solidarity with Black Lives Matter. George Floyd's murder was harrowing for the black community worldwide, therefore temporary, however well-meaning, allies are always a concern. I sent my manuscript to OMC despite hoping to eventually find a home with a more niche publisher, because my protagonists are not only characters of colour, they are also LGBTQ+, and my novel begins with neopronouns.

To my delight, I received a beautiful message from my now editor. My novel is heavily influenced by my decade living in Japan and my children were born in Japan. She understood my need to populate the lost ancient island with people who look like my beautiful children and she understood my reference to Naomi Osaka and Rui Hachimura for inspiration for the cover art.

We also discussed the importance of romantic queer relationships in fiction and the profound effect a novel like *Beneath the Burning Wave* would have had on me as a teenager, confused and ashamed about my feelings for girls as well as boys on my council estate in Knowsley. We discussed the importance of not only implying *special friends* or depicting an oddly asexual union, but instead celebrating kissing, cuddling, and fully fleshed-out same-sex people of colour relationships that are universal in their humanity and humane in finally being depicted in a story that is not entirely about race or sexuality nor centred on trauma.

As Evaristo implies in the aforementioned quote, it is long past the time for Black British authors to take up the space to write and publish whatever is in our hearts. I am excited to work with a digital-first publisher with an ethos of publishing page-turning fiction. I hope my trilogy achieves enough success with OMC to make it easy for more Black British writers to publish genre fiction, especially those from working-class backgrounds like myself. I hope my readers enjoy an unashamedly page-turning epic story with queer characters of colour. And my hope since starting my novel has always been that, if a reader can enjoy a tale told with neopronouns, then they will have no problem addressing a person by their chosen pronoun in the future.

Jennifer Hayashi Danns
August 2022

---

1. UMEWAKA, N. [11 March 2021]. *Japan's mysterious underwater 'city'* [online]. BBC. Available from: https://www.bbc.com/travel/article/20210311-japans-mysterious-underwater-city [Accessed December 2021]

2. KALE, S. [24 December 2020]. *'This has never happened before!' Bernardine Evaristo and Reni Eddo-Lodge on their history-making year* [online]. The Guardian. Available from: https://www.theguardian.com/lifeandstyle/2020/dec/24/this-has-never-happened-before-bernardine-evaristo-and-reni-eddo-lodge-on-their-history-making-year [Accessed December 2021]

Now read on for an exclusive preview of the second spellbinding instalment in The Mu Chronicles...

Across the Scorched Sea

Shadows prowl in the flicker of Takafumi's torch. Flashes of a banished red robe peek from beneath his dark cloak as he strides to the destiny denied him by cockroach Kaori.

Takafumi smiles thinking of her prone in her gilded chamber beside Ren, a restless reminder of her twin. He looks so much like Kairi, she probably sees herself in those blazing brown eyes but those who long for the island see Kairi.

He will return. He would never leave them there in Blackland. With her.

Takafumi searches for footsteps swept away by the tides of the desert. He squints into the night for any sign of others disturbing the sand. Wind swirls warm air across the vast open plain, whipping up sand to bend and contort in a futile flee from the stifling heat. Grains crumble beneath his feet, guiding him down a gentle slope towards a gaping black hole. His flame illuminates a low dark mouth with a craggy upper lip. Murmurs bubble and froth within. Takafumi enters.

Fangs protrude from the ceiling of the cave. Pockets of fire burn in the cavities on the floor. More teeth protrude from the sand ready to snatch those too willing to forget Mu.

"Namu Kai," Takafumi says.

"*Namu Kai*," roar the mottled-armed crowd panting with pleasure at the arrival of their leader.

Takafumi peels off his cloak and a thrill ripples through them. They eat the red robe and chew the soft fabric, savouring all that she has denied. Other Experienced join Takafumi, though not all. They aren't reckless, they will never replace her without patience. They also shed their skin and any pretence of civility is abandoned. The frenzied crowd tear strips, licking and sucking each piece, moaning, eyes squeezed tight, tongues licking the fanged roof in ecstasy. Saliva begins to drip from the ceiling fangs and the fire pits sizzle.

Experienced Takako and Taketo exchange a glance and nod at Takafumi. It is time.

Takafumi wipes sweat from his forehead, overwhelmed not only from the heat of the pit and the fever of the mob but the knowledge of what is to come. Takako approaches the altar eagerly clawed into the sand. The opposite of a grave, an elevated mound surrounded by a deep trench. Takafumi watches her enter the trench. She looks strange without her dreadlocks resting on her hips, as does he and Taketo without their silver nests perched on their head. She hacked them down, replaced with a short helmet of braids dyed black with the ink of crushed nettles. No grey in her Blackland, no respect for those who have lived longest. No honour. Only her and her followers adorned with gold. Takafumi had remembered to remove his gold before entering this fray.

Memories as sour as forgotten ganba cannot delay the ceremony any longer. Takafumi lays on the altar. Determined his trembling hand will not betray him, he whips open his robe and removes his creased arm from his sleeve. The altar shifts and crumbles a little. Takako gently raises his wrist above his head, exposing the soft underarm flesh. Fire blazes as the mob crowd the banks of the trench, shadows scuttle to peer from the ceiling. Water sloshes, life writhes in a sealed woven bag. The crowd part to allow Taketo entry.

"Children of Kairi," Takako bellows.

"Kai!" they shout.

"The Kai," Takako continues.

"Kai!" they reply.

Takafumi's exposed chest heaves. Sweat trickles down his wrinkled skin.

"Here in the Redland we gather where water cannot penetrate. Where she cannot flow."

"Kai!" they shout.

The prickly spines of the ceiling glisten, an angry sharp droplet formed long ago sneers at Takafumi. He closes his eyes.

"We honour him, we see him, we are *he*. Takafumi lead us to He. Lead us to He!" Takako screams.

"Kai," Takafumi murmurs, teeth bared and clenched.

Silence falls. Even the branches feeding the pits refuse to crackle.

Taketo draws the jellyfish from the bag, not quite the blue of Mu but as eager to maim.

The cave fills with Takafumi's screams.

The Kai scatter, careful to return to the Blackland before dawn. They will tell the others how Takafumi writhed and rolled into the trench. How they saved him, laid him on the altar, and held their spit-soaked palms on his wound until it no longer burned.

There is no more doubt.

The end of she has begun.

Don't forget to order your copy of *Across the Scorched Sea* to find out what happens next...

YOUR NUMBER ONE STOP

ONE MORE CHAPTER

FOR PAGETURNING BOOKS

One More Chapter is an
award-winning global
division of HarperCollins.

Sign up to our newsletter to get our
latest eBook deals and stay up to date
with our weekly Book Club!
<u>Subscribe here.</u>

Meet the team at
<u>www.onemorechapter.com</u>

Follow us!
@OneMoreChapter_
@OneMoreChapter
@onemorechapterhc

Do you write unputdownable fiction?
We love to hear from new voices.
Find out how to submit your novel at
<u>www.onemorechapter.com/submissions</u>